HOPELESSLY DEVOTED

Ben had never ever been able to make her feel so much—so very much.

Her fingers went up to stroke the back of his neck, and Sam growled in a manner that caused a shiver of electricity to skitter across every hair on her body. She was caught in a deep fog; a thick mist of pure feeling, that she couldn't—didn't want to—get out of.

"Sammy. . . ." His name drifted from her lips in a broken moan.

He bit the full flesh of her lower lip in a manner that was deeply satisfying and then gently stroked the same spot with the flat of his tongue.

"Rosy . . ."

His gritty voice pulled her back from the precipice, and slowly, reluctantly she opened her eyes. God, what was happening to her? This madness. This intense feeling that swept over her whenever he held her. It wasn't like this with Ben; it had never been like this.

Other books by Niqui Stanhope

Night To Remember
Made For Each Other
"Champagne Wishes" in Wedding Bells
Distant Memories
Sweet Temptation

Published by BET/Arabesque Books

HOPELESSLY DEVOTED

Niqui Stanhope

BET Publications, LLC
http://www.bet.com
http://www.arabesquebooks.com

ARABESQUE BOOKS are published by

BET Publications, LLC
c/o BET BOOKS
One BET Plaza
1900 W Place NE
Washington, DC 20018-1211

All Kensington Titles, Imprints, and Distributed Lines are available at special quantity discounts for bulk purchases for sales promotions, premiums, fund-raising, educational or institutional use. Special book excerpts or customized printings can also be created to fit specific needs. For details, write or phone the office of the Kensington special sales manager: Kensington Publishing Corp., 850 Third Avenue, New York, NY 10022, attn: Special Sales Department. Phone: 1-800-221-2647.

BET Books is a trademark of Black Entertainment Television, Inc. ARABESQUE, the ARABESQUE logo and the BET BOOKS logo are trademarks and registered trademarks.

First Printing: July 2002
10 9 8 7 6 5 4 3 2 1

Printed in the United States of America

For my family, friends, and all the enthusiastic readers out there! Thank you Reba Pollock for being such a great fan!

One

Rosalind Carmichael stared numbly at her brother. Her feet felt like solid blocks of ice, and a strange trembling was slowly making its way up the length of her spine.

"You did what?" she croaked.

Tony grabbed both of her hands and massaged them. "You've gotta help me, sis. There's no one else I can ask. And believe me, I've tried just about everyone."

Rosalind sank onto the sofa, and sat for a moment, her mind racing. "But—but what do you mean you borrowed two hundred thousand dollars? How . . . I mean, that's— You couldn't possibly have thought that you could put it back. You took that money without any intention of putting it back. You stole it."

Tony sank onto a knee before her, and Rosalind tried very hard not to see the little boy she had always gone to such great pains to protect. She closed her eyes to block the image, and then opened them after a moment spent massaging the tense spot between her eyes. Her gaze locked with wicked dark brown eyes. *Persuasive eyes.*

"Ros, I know what I did was wrong. But you've got to believe me. I really did intend to put it back before anyone noticed. But things just didn't work out the way I planned. And now—"

"What did you plan?" Rosalind interrupted with a tiny quiver in her voice. "Did you plan to win it back at the track? Was that the big plan?"

"I know you're mad. But what was I to do? I needed it."

Rosalind stood, took a turn about the neatly furnished sitting room, then returned to wag a finger at her brother.

"You . . . Anthony Carmichael, are a thief. A plain, honest-to-goodness thief. And sugarcoat it if you will, but that's what you are. And I—I will not be part of this. You've got to learn to stand on your own two feet. Maybe this will be good for you. I've bailed you out of trouble too many times. But this is it. Not this— not this time. You've never done anything like this before."

She stopped to draw breath, and then plunged on. "How could you? If Mom and Dad were alive . . ." She covered her face with a hand. "I can't even bear to think about it."

"They'll kill me, you know. Once they find out I'm the one who took it. You might as well start making funeral arrangements right now."

Rosalind put a trembling hand to her mouth. "You're just trying to scare me into helping you."

"You know I'm not. You've seen all of the reports on the news. This is a Jamaican posse . . . and they don't make idle threats."

"Then you should have known better," Rosalind said sharply, her eyes spitting fire. "How many times did I beg you to try and find legitimate work? How many times?"

She held up an imperious hand, neatly cutting off any possible response. "But would you listen? I could have predicted that sooner or later something like this would happen. And now you come running to me. And what do you expect me to do? Do you really think that I've got two hundred thousand dollars just lying around somewhere? How am I supposed to come up with all that money at such short notice?"

"You can ask . . . him. He'll listen to you. He'll give you the money.

Rosalind stared at her brother as though he had taken complete leave of his senses. "Him? Him who?"

Tony sighed. "Sam Winter, of course."

Rosalind gritted her teeth. *Sam Winter?* Not only was her brother stupid, he was also insane.

"I will not ask Sam Winter for anything."

"You've got to. Please, sis . . . you've got to. It's my only chance. My only chance. Don't you love me anymore?" He stared at her with large pleading eyes, and Rosalind turned away, trying her best to hold the tears at bay. He knew how to push her buttons, that much was certain.

"You know I haven't seen Sam Winter in almost six years. I haven't spoken to him . . . written to him . . . Nothing. Why in the name of heaven should you think he would first of all even remember me, let alone be willing to lend me such a sum of money?"

"Because he asked you to marry him. I know you couldn't have forgotten that."

Rosalind turned toward the window. How could she ever forget that particular incident? Never had she ever been quite so insulted in her life. Usually, a proposal of marriage was something to celebrate, but not when it was being offered by Samuel Winter.

She still remembered the first time she had met him. She had been working as a consultant in Los Angeles, happily designing business Web pages. Her consulting firm had sent her on assignment to Urban Gear Inc.

Everything had been fine until the day she was asked to deliver a portfolio of design sketches to the big boss, Sam Winter. She had been happy enough to comply. Even though she had by then heard many rumors about his generally unpleasant temperament, she had never been one to judge a person on the basis of hearsay. She had been perfectly willing to give him the benefit of the doubt. But all of the rumors had been proven true as she stood outside his office. He had been talking quite loudly on the phone. So loudly that she had heard every word he said in crisp detail: *"When I choose a woman to marry, it certainly won't be for her intellect. She has to be a big-boned gal. A strong horse of a woman . . . with wide hips and a big behind. Good for childbearing, cooking, cleaning, and looking after me. I don't really care that much what she looks like. As long as she doesn't have a face like the underbelly of a squid, she'll suit me fine. Of course, she has to exhibit some signs of intelligence. I have to consider the children, after all. I don't want a brood of idiots walking around. . . ."*

She had knocked sharply on the door then, and entered to his irritable, "Come on in, for God's sake."

Whereupon she had almost broken into gales of laughter at the stunned, fish-eyed look on his face. No doubt he had been expecting a male Web designer, since most of the designers in the company were male. She knew he was wondering, too, if she had overheard him. But she hadn't given him the satisfaction of that knowledge. Instead, she had smiled at him in a bright knowing manner and not said a word about his ridiculous comments.

From then on, he had made her life absolutely miserable. Nothing she did was ever good enough for him. He made her work late almost every night of the week, redoing this or that. Totally trivial things any normal person would have easily overlooked. She had come to despise him in a very short period of time. Then one evening, when she was close to genuine exhaustion, he had made a surprise visit to her tiny cubicle. She had been reading a passage of scripture right then, searching for the strength to continue. He had perched his unusually large frame on the edge of her desk and let loose a diatribe she would not soon forget. *"You know God doesn't exist, don't you? Or are you one of these bleeding-heart Christians? A Bible-thumping hypocrite?"* And when she had just stared at him in dumb amazement, he had thrust the knife home with vicious intent. *"There are only two kinds of people who believe all that trash. Fools, and dreamers. And based on your work here so far, you don't need to tell me which group you fit into."*

And after insulting her and a good percentage of the world's population in such an uncalled-for manner, two months hence, he had had the unmitigated gall to present her with a battered ring she was certain he had just extracted from a box of Cracker Jacks, and in a decidedly unpleasant manner, say, *"Well, this must be your lucky day, Rosalind Carmichael. Against my better judgment, I have decided to ask you to be my wife."*

She had almost lost her head. It was all she could do not to knee him solidly in the groin right then and there. But she had been a lady about things. She had held on to her dignity with difficulty, and told him in a voice that shook only once, exactly what she thought of his proposal. She would also have added that since she was not a "strong horse of a woman," she very much doubted that she would suit him. But at the last minute her courage had failed her.

Just thinking about him now caused her blood pressure to rise by several notches. She hated him. Really hated the man.

She turned to Tony with glittering eyes. "There is nothing on this green earth that would make me ever—ever speak to Sam Winter again. Not to mention ask him—"

A loud report interrupted her before she could finish, and Tony, in a burst of unbelievable speed, grabbed her and flung himself to the floor, knocking several vases from their perch.

"I told you. They're coming to get me. They're coming to get me."

And, for a panicked few minutes, as they lay huddled together on the shiny floor of her apartment, Rosalind was actually convinced that someone was coming. She waited, with pounding heart and sweating palms, for the telltale sounds of heavy footsteps on the stairs, the hairs on the back of her neck standing at rigid attention as she waited for the door to be kicked open. And beside her, her big, brave brother, Tony, mumbled incoherently through chattering teeth.

Several minutes and a couple of bruised shins later, Rosalind realized that the sound that had sent them both diving for the floor was not a gunshot. It had been nothing more than the sound of a car backfiring.

She dragged herself from Tony's viselike grip, brushed herself off, and said with grim determination, "Tony, go and change your pants. I'll ask him."

Two

Rosalind stood now, on the front stairs of a large ultramodern mansion in the exclusive neighborhood of Mendham, working up the courage to press the buzzer. She'd had no idea at all where Sam Winter was in the six years since she had left Los Angeles for Madison, New Jersey. She had, in fact, not given him a second thought. But she would never have guessed that he was also living in New Jersey, not two towns away from her.

She ran a restless hand through her shoulder-length sweep of wavy raven hair, straightened the sleek navy suit she was wearing, then gave the buzzer a sharp ring. If fate were kind, he would probably not even remember her. No doubt he went about the place scattering his proposals of marriage to any big-boned woman who would allow him within shouting distance.

She waited for a few seconds and then leaned heavily on the bell again. In a house this size, he would quite probably have an entire bevy of housekeepers and maids at his beck and call she suspected.

The sounds of unhurried footsteps had her taking a preparatory step back from the smooth, lemon-polished oak doors. Her fingers curled into tight fists as she waited for what seemed an inordinate amount of time. Unconsciously her chin tilted up as the beautiful double doors swung open. It would be the housekeeper, she knew. And a soft smile fluttered about the corners of her lips. But the beginnings of the bright radiance spreading across her face froze at the sight of him. The years hadn't changed him at all. He was still as tall as she remembered. A red-boned hulk of a man with dark brown hair and demon-black eyes. Eyes that were looking at her now with cold dislike.

Rosalind drew a sharp, filling breath, and prepared to be as pleasant as she could manage. *This is for Tony. For Tony,* she reminded herself.

She cleared her throat. "Mr. Winter . . ."

"Yes? What is it? Come on. Come on. Spit it out. I don't have time to waste."

Rosalind blinked at him. It would seem that the years had not improved him a bit. He was definitely still one of the rudest men she had ever had the misfortune to meet.

"Do you remember me?"

His eyes flickered over her in a manner that made her cringe inside. "I remember you."

Rosalind swallowed the desire to turn and beat a hasty retreat back to the safety of the little car parked just behind her.

"Can I come in?"

He stepped aside and motioned her in with an abrupt, "I guess since you're here, you might as well come in. But I can only spare you a few moments. I have a very busy schedule today."

He led her to his office, and along the way, Rosalind couldn't help but notice the hollow emptiness of the house. It was almost as though no one lived there. The walls were bare, the furniture, sparse at best, and the warmth, totally nonexistent. The house should have been a beautiful one, but it was as cold and emotionless as the man who inhabited it.

Once in his wood-paneled office, which was situated on the first floor of the sprawling house, he closed the door and pointed to a burnished leather seat.

"Sit. Sit, for God's sake."

Rosalind perched herself on the edge of the chair, and with tightly compressed lips said, "Please, if you can manage to restrain yourself while I'm here . . . Do not take the Lord's name in vain."

He sat behind the massive desk, and for an instant a flicker of something very like amusement glittered in his eyes.

"That's right. You are a Christian, aren't you?"

"Yes, I am." *And you are the devil incarnate.*

When Rosalind made no further attempt at conversation, he leaned forward and said, "As much as I enjoy this staring match that we're having, I have to assume that you came here with a definite purpose in mind?"

"I did." She was just as crisp. Just as emotionless.

"Well?"

"I—I have an unusual request."

He steepled his fingers beneath his chin. "I'm listening."

"It's—it's my brother, you see." And she rushed on, not even pausing once for breath. "You probably don't remember him. He used to live with me when I was in L.A. He's my baby brother and—and he's a really nice kid, a little mixed-up but basically good—"

"Believe me," he interrupted. "I'd love to sit here and listen to your brother's long list of wonderful qualities . . . but I just don't have the time. So if you can cut to the chase, I would very much appreciate it."

Rosalind bit back the hot retort that sprang to her lips. It wouldn't do at all to lose her temper with him. He was her only hope. Tony's only hope.

"I need two hundred thousand dollars." There. She had said it.

He sat back in his chair, and the face that had been so expressionless, was even more so now.

"Two hundred thousand dollars," he repeated in a way that caused the hackles on Rosalind's neck to rise.

"It's for Tony," she said quickly. "Not for me. I know it's a lot to ask . . . given the fact that—that we didn't part on very good terms six years ago. But it's a desperate situation. Tony absolutely has to have this money. If he doesn't get it by the end of the week . . . the consequences could be very serious."

"Really." His tone indicated that he couldn't have cared less. "And why should this concern me?"

Rosalind looked down at her clenched hands. What could she say? How could she convince him to help her? There was no valid reason on Earth why he should. She was nothing to him. He was nothing to her. They disliked each other intensely.

"I'll—I'll work for you for free. Design Web pages . . . In the last several years I've gone into development. So I—I can actually develop the technology behind your user interfaces now. All that costs a lot of money, as you know. I'll do it for you for free. For as long as it takes to repay you."

He leaned forward again, eyes gleaming like Beelzebub himself. "An interesting offer. But not good enough, I'm afraid."

A chord of perspiration trickled down the middle of Rosalind's back. He was going to make her grovel. He wanted her to completely humble herself before him. Well, she wouldn't do it. She just would not do it. She would find another way. Maybe she could get a loan from the bank. Or maybe Ben would help her. He was a struggling medical resident, but his parents had established a trust fund for him. Since she and

Ben were going to get married anyway, surely he would lend her fifty, maybe a hundred thousand dollars?

Rosalind gathered her purse and stood. "I'm sorry I bothered you with this. Forget everything I just said."

"Sit," he bellowed. "I didn't say I wouldn't help you."

He spun in his seat, turned the computer on, and commenced typing away at a breakneck pace.

Rosalind sat again, watching him with a frown of puzzlement creasing the smooth skin between her eyes. In less than a minute he was through, and printing whatever it was he had just typed. He whipped the paper from the printer, studied it for a moment, and then turned in his seat to face her.

"There isn't anything you wouldn't do for that brother of yours, is there?"

"I love my brother, if that's what you're asking," she said.

He shoved the square of white paper toward her across the flat of the desk, and said with a gritty note in his voice, "Well, isn't that lucky for him?"

Rosalind crossed her long smooth brown legs before her and noticed in an academic manner that his eyes followed the movement before refocusing on her face. She picked up the single sheet of paper.

"What is this?"

"My terms." He sat back to regard her with what she could only describe as a completely demonic expression on his face.

Her eyes darted quickly over the document, and when she looked up again, it was to find him watching her still.

"You can't be serious," she said through tight lips.

"I'm very serious. If you want the kind of money you say you do, then you have to be willing to pay the price."

Rosalind swallowed at the sudden dryness in her throat. She tapped the paper with a neatly manicured nail.

"What you're suggesting here is—is . . ."

"Yes?"

"Ridiculous."

He shrugged massive shoulders. "Take it or leave it. It's up to you."

She met his eyes directly and realized that he meant it. She looked at the paper again, her eyes darting over the face of it, skipping words here and there, but absorbing the absolute enormity of what he was requiring of her. *"In return for the sum of two hundred thousand dollars, Rosalind Patricia Carmichael . . ."*

How did he know her middle name?

Her eyes darted back to the sheet.

". . . will live and work at 129 Beaumont Road, Mendham, NJ, for a period of no less than one year. She agrees to perform the following domestic services: cooking, cleaning, general housekeeping."

Her eyes skipped down to the belly of the first paragraph. *She also agrees to design and develop an unlimited number of Web sites on an as-needed basis, and will work as personal assistant to Samuel Robert Winter in a general administrative capacity and will be at said employer's beck and call seven days a week, twenty-four hours a day."*

The breath paused in her lungs as she read bits and pieces of the final paragraph. *"She also agrees to perform other necessary duties, including, but not limited to: therapeutic back massages, leg massages, and daily kisses. . . ."*

She rested the paper again on the face of the desk. That was the long and short of it. This was what he demanded in return for the two hundred thousand dollars, which would quite likely save her brother's life.

There was no doubt about it. Sam Winter was crazy. Why would he do this? He wanted to punish her. That was obviously what he had in mind. His fragile male ego had never gotten over the fact that she had turned him down years before. It probably still rankled that she, a tall, big-boned woman, had no particular use for him. Obviously he had thought that she would've been grateful that he had noticed her. She pitied him. Pitied the cruel vindictive spirit that had made him even think that he could insist on such humiliating terms of repayment.

She looked up at him with glittering coal-black eyes. Hot blood had given her oval face a strange pulling beauty.

"I won't agree to this," she said, enunciating each word with distinct clarity so that there could be no chance of his misunderstanding her.

He came to his feet and stood looking down at her with hard unreadable eyes. "You know there's no other way for you to get this sum of money. And what I've asked of you isn't so terrible . . . in exchange for what you will get."

"You're a—you're a . . ." She struggled to think of a word that would properly describe what it was she thought of him.

He helped her, in a matter-of-fact manner. "I'm a what? A bastard? A devil in human form?" He stuck both hands into his pants pockets. "I've been called all that and much more. So I don't think you'll be able to come up with anything more original."

Rosalind came to her feet. Almost five foot ten, she was still much shorter that he.

If she never saw him again, she fumed silently, she would be one of the happiest people on Earth.

"I will get the money elsewhere. I want to thank you for being so understanding."

His eyebrows raised a fraction. "And how do you intend to pull off this miracle?"

"You may not know it," she sniffed, "but I am engaged to be married." She raised her left hand so that he might see the ring. He ignored it.

"To Ben Mitchell . . . a struggling medical student who doesn't have two dimes to call his own."

"He's a medical resident, not a student. And he does have some money put aside for a rainy day."

"And you figure this is that rainy day. You really think he'll give you two hundred grand . . . even if he has it to spare?"

"He loves me," she said. "Something you know nothing of. Something you may never know anything of."

Silence greeted her last remark, and something dark and turbulent flashed in his eyes. *Hatred,* she hazarded.

"You love him . . . maybe. But, you need me. And you will come back to me, because you know that I'm the only one who can—or will—help you."

"I feel really sorry for you, living alone here in this huge mansion with nothing and no one for company but your millions. It must be a great comfort for you, especially at night. God knows there's probably no one who would put up with you for even a second."

He actually smiled at that. "Well, I'll soon have you for company," he said.

And Rosalind's already-simmering temper boiled over. "Don't count on it."

She marched to the office door, yanked it open, and walked briskly toward the front door of the house. She could feel him watching her all the way. And it was only when she was seated behind the wheel of her car that she realized that she hadn't drawn a single breath the entire way.

Three

Later that night, as Rosalind put the finishing touches on a sumptuous dinner of barbecued steak, chilled potato salad, collard greens and corn bread, her mind drifted back to her meeting earlier in the day.

The nerve of the man. The absolute nerve. To think that he had actually thought that she would agree to become a virtual prisoner in his house, cooking, cleaning, scrubbing, and *kissing* him everyday? The years of solitude had unhinged his mind.

After leaving his house, she had gone straight to her bank. She had had a long and very enlightening talk with one of the senior officers there. She had twenty thousand dollars in a money-market account. She also had a weak portfolio of various stocks and bonds that, even if cashed, would not net her anything appreciable. She had five thousand dollars in a joint checking and savings account, and she would probably be approved for a loan of up to fifty-thousand dollars, but definitely no more than that. So the most she could hope to raise on her own was about seventy-five thousand dollars. Not nearly enough to save Tony's skin. She had thanked the financial adviser for explaining things in such great detail, and had left the bank in a haze of near despair.

She then realized that her only hope was that Ben would lend her the rest of the money. On her way home, she had decided to cook her fiancé an especially nice dinner, get him into a really receptive mood, and then bring up the subject of the money. It was the only way out of the mess, which Tony had created for himself.

She sliced several large lemons, and juiced them with unnecessary viciousness, adding large quantities of water, stirring in sugar and then a dash of essence of vanilla.

Sam Winter thought too much of himself. That was a large part of his problem. It did surprise her though, that no one had agreed to marry him in the years since she had seen him. For even though he was the most unpleasant human being she had ever run into, as a physical specimen he was not unattractive. He wasn't her type, of course. She didn't like large men. She preferred men who were around her height, men who didn't tower over her in the manner in which Sam Winter did. Men who were sweet and kind. Tender. Generous. God-fearing men. Definitely not unrepentant atheists. She could never have anything to do with a man who didn't have a healthy respect for the Almighty. Even if he didn't have a formal understanding of God and religion, he should at the very least believe in the existence of a Supreme Being. She didn't ask much when it came to men. She didn't much care if they were rich or not. But she did care very much about their spiritual understanding. That was important to her. Very important.

She was sure that it was Sam Winter's strange mixture of peculiar problems that had prevented him from getting married. He had seemed in a tearing hurry to tie the knot when he had approached her with his preposterous proposal. Obviously he had been

in need of a servant of some type. Someone to wash,
cook, and clean for him, and at night warm his bed.
She could find no other reason to justify his behavior.
And since one woman was just as good as any other
to him, she was certain that he would have gone on
his merry way and made similar proposals to any number of other women. Big-boned gals, all of them, she
guessed, since he did have a particular preference for
horse-faced women with big behinds. No doubt, too,
they all had turned him down, hence his current un-
married state.

She ladled a heaping quantity of potato salad into
a nicely cut glass bowl, sliced several circles of red
onion atop, and then covered everything with a tight
rectangle of plastic wrap.

It took several trips back and forth to the neat little
dining room, with its long, highly polished, brown lac-
quer table to arrange everything. When she was
through setting the table, she added two long, tapered
candles she had been keeping for a special occasion.
She set the oven to warm so that the hearty slabs of
meat would be tender and succulent when she was
ready for them, then she hurried off to her bedroom.
Ben was almost always on time, and she wanted to
make certain that she had a chance to check her face
and dress before he arrived.

She already knew what she was going to wear: her
burgundy dress, which hit her at midthigh. Ben loved
it. Whenever she wore it, he was forever running his
hands up and down the long, smooth length of her
legs, and saying with something very like wonderment
in his voice, "I see legs all day at work, but how do
you manage to make me forget all that? You have the
best legs of any woman I have ever seen."

She pulled the dress from a garment bag and slid
into it quickly, wiggling a little to get it up over her

hips. She ran a hand down her hard, flat stomach to smooth the velvety fabric, then looked at herself in the mirror. No matter what Sam Winter thought, she did not have big bones and a big butt.

She went to her dressing table, gave her face a quick dusting with gold highlighted face powder, then ran a shimmering orange-gold lipstick across her lips. She sat on the padded pink stool to apply a soft black eyeliner and a smattering of rouge. When she was through, she brushed her sleek shoulder-length hair into soft ebony waves, then spent a moment curling the ends of her hair. Her favorite fragrance was applied to the pulse points at her throat, wrists, and behind her ears.

By the time she was through, the front door buzzer was going. She gave the elegant gold watch on her wrist a quick glance. Ben was right on time. Just as always. The only time he was ever late was when he was detained at the hospital on an emergency case.

She walked to the door and pulled it open, a smile of welcome on her lips. "Come on in, darling. You must be really tired."

"Well, thank you. I didn't expect such a cordial welcome."

The breath in Rosalind's lungs came to a startled halt. Sam Winter. *What is he doing here?* She hadn't even thought that he knew where it was she lived. She certainly hadn't told him.

"What do you want?" The smile of just seconds ago had frozen on her lips.

He stood nonchalantly in the doorway dressed in exactly the same clothes she had seen him in earlier.

"Well, now that we've got the pleasantries out of the way, can I come in?"

Rosalind gritted her teeth. No doubt he was here

to add a few additional conditions to the list he had typed and shown her earlier.

"As a matter of fact, you can't. I'm expecting my fiancé at any moment."

"This won't take long." And he stepped forward without waiting for further invitation to do so.

Rosalind was forced to step backward and out of his way or run the risk of him walking into her.

Once he was inside, he looked around her apartment with a critical eye.

"I didn't know you liked African art," he said, gesturing to several Ashanti and Yoruba pieces on the walls.

"Look," Rosalind said, "I don't want to be rude, but this really isn't a good time. What was it you wanted?"

He gave the kitchen a flickering glance. "Dinner would be good. I haven't eaten a thing all day." He wasn't going to guilt her into offering him a plate of food. She'd cooked just enough for herself and Ben.

"There's a nice Ethiopian restaurant about two blocks from here. But you didn't come here to talk about food."

"No. I wanted to know how you were progressing raising that sum of money."

Rosalind stared at him with open dislike. He had come to gloat. "I'm doing just fine, thank you. I won't be in need of any assistance from you."

"So, your . . . fiancé has agreed to advance you the money?"

"He will."

"And that's what the dinner . . . and this vulgar dress are in aid of?"

Vulgar dress? There was nothing even remotely indecent about the outfit she was wearing.

She walked pointedly to the door and opened it. "I

didn't invite you here, so you don't have to like my dress."

He didn't take her not-too-subtle hint, and she was forced to close the door again.

"I didn't think a *Christian* would wear a dress like that."

"Look," Rosalind said. "Before today, we hadn't seen each other in years. I apologize for coming to you in the manner in which I did. I shouldn't have done it, but I was desperate. But that does not now give you the right to intrude in my life in any way."

His eyes bored into hers for a long moment of silence before he grated, "Yes, only Ben and Tony have that right."

Rosalind said nothing in response. She just wished he would go. She wasn't sure how she was going to explain his presence if Ben showed up right then.

"Well," he said after a moment, "my offer still stands. But you have until tomorrow to make up your mind if you want my help or not. I have a business transaction that I'm currently considering. If you have no use for the funds you requested, I will earmark them for this new project."

Rosalind opened the door again, and this time he walked toward it. "I told you that I wouldn't need the money after all."

He paused in the arch of the doorway, looking down at her. "Well, you have until tomorrow to decide." His eyes flickered over her. "And at this dinner tonight, don't be too easy with your virtue . . . or have you already given him all that you have to offer?"

Rosalind's mouth opened and closed soundlessly. How dare he say that to her? He knew nothing about her. Nothing about how she lived. And he had no right to judge her. No right at all. It was her life to live as she pleased.

She slammed the door behind him without uttering one single word in reply. He had completely ruined the evening for her. Completely. Any joy she'd been feeling until then, he had sucked right out of her.

When Ben showed up half an hour later, she tried to recapture her earlier mood, but it was no good. Sam Winter had ruined everything.

Four

After dinner, Rosalind had curled into Ben's arms, given him a moment to get really comfortable in the ultrasoft settee, and then launched right into the heart of the matter. Ben had listened in stony silence, then without further discussion, said. "No, Rosalind. I told you that I couldn't touch that money. That's our nest egg. And I won't touch that for anyone. Not even for you . . . especially not for Tony. That young man is a wastrel. And he'll never be anything more than that. Babying him like you've been doing all his life has just helped him faster along the path to absolutely nowhere."

Rosalind had begged, pleaded, and then finally resorted to tears. But it had all been to no avail. Halfway through her grand finale, Ben had actually fallen asleep and was therefore largely unaware when she turned on the waterworks.

Rosalind had left him asleep on the chair, and had gone to stand at one of the large plate-glass windows, her brain numb and throbbing. *Where else can I turn? Where else?* All of her relatives were largely poverty-stricken. There was no one else to ask. *No one except the hound from the pits of hell—Sam Winter.* Could she possibly live in his home for an entire year without losing her mind entirely? Could she really stand interacting with him on a daily basis, listening to his non-sensical views on everything from women to religion? And what about his other ridiculous requirements? The massaging and kissing? How would she make it through that?

Ben left around midnight. He hardly ever spent the night with her. He never had the time. A resident was always on call, he would always say. So she never argued. She knew that one day he was going to be a brilliant surgeon. And she didn't want to stand in the way of that.

Rosalind didn't make it to bed before two A.M., since Ben had been too tired to help her with the clearing and the washing of the mountain of accumulated dishes, pots, and plates. Her sleep had been fitful, filled with desperate sweaty dreams.

In the morning she awoke with deep dark circles beneath her eyes. She stared at her face in the bathroom mirror after taking a long and steamy shower. It seemed thinner, her cheekbones more prominent. If anything, she probably did resemble one of Sam Winter's horse-faced women right then, she thought ruefully. She dressed without her usual care, quickly choosing a short white T-shirt and a pair of faded blue jeans, which clung to her long legs and flared into ragged bell-bottoms. Her hair, still damp from the shower, was quickly blown dry and given only the most cursory of curling.

Rosalind tried her best not to think too much about the ordeal ahead. Overnight she had decided that she probably had very little choice now. To save Tony's skin, she would have to become Sam Winter's prisoner. He would probably torture her in little ways each day of the agreed-upon year. But she would try her best to ignore him, no matter what he said or did. If possible, she would get him to reconsider certain aspects of the agreement. Massaging his bad back, yes. But kissing him, no. She would not agree to that. There was a limit to what she could stand, and that was way past the acceptable threshold.

Before leaving home, she called her brother and left a message for him on his answering machine. She let him know that she had found a way to get the two hundred thousand dollars, and that she would explain everything to him later that evening.

With that taken care of, she set off in her temperamental old Toyota hatchback. Less than ten minutes later, she was pulling into the winding tree-lined lane leading to 129 Beaumont Road. She parked next to a sleek-looking Mercedes-Benz convertible, and climbed tiredly from her car. It would seem that Sam Winter had a visitor or visitors. Or maybe the car was his. Either way, she didn't care. She just wanted to get the whole matter over and done with as soon as possible.

Her brow furrowed a bit as she approached the front doors. Maybe Ben had been right about a few things. Maybe she did baby Tony too much. He was, after all, a grown man now. Not a child. He was almost twenty-five years old. And he had managed to do absolutely nothing with his life. He had decided against going to college, and as far as she could tell, had done nothing at all to improve himself. He seemed perfectly content to play at life, creating nothing but carnage as he went along his merry way. Maybe, in her attempt to protect him from life, she had somehow managed to encourage him in his totally irresponsible behavior.

The front doors opened before Rosalind had a chance to ring, and a balding middle-aged man she didn't recognize invited her in with a large smile.

"You must be Rosalind," he said, and stretched a hand to envelop hers.

She accepted the outstretched hand and assured the man that she was indeed Rosalind.

"We've been waiting for you."

Rosalind frowned. "Pardon?"

The man beamed at her. "I'm Steve Jenkins, Sam's lawyer." He motioned for her to follow him, and Rosalind did so on slightly shaky legs. What had she gotten herself into? Should she also have had the presence of mind to show up with her own lawyer? And what presumption on the part of Sam Winter. To actually expect that her acceptance of his offer was a foregone conclusion.

The man in question suddenly appeared in the doorway of his office. Rosalind gave him a tight "Hello," and continued into the room without saying anything further.

Sam said to his lawyer, "Give us a minute, Steve?" and then closed the door behind Rosalind, locking the lawyer out.

Rosalind swallowed the dryness from her throat and prepared herself for whatever onslaught was in the offing.

"You look tired," he said almost immediately.

Rosalind rubbed a self-conscious hand down one cheek and said, "I didn't sleep well last night."

"Mmm," he said, "you look about ready to keel over. Have you had breakfast?"

Rosalind tightened her grip on her purse. "No, but that can wait. I wanted to discuss your offer with you."

Sam went to the phone. "That can wait. I'll get you something."

And before she could properly protest, he was already dialing. "I sometimes use a chef," he said, looking at her again. "I brought him from L.A. Found him at one of my favorite restaurants off Wilshire. What would you like? French toast? Eggs? Pancakes?"

Rosalind sat in the chair before his desk. She didn't want to weaken her stance with him by caving in to the first considerate thing he had ever done for her.

"Coffee," she said. "Black, please."

"That's it? Nothing to eat? You're so thin. Much thinner than you were in L.A." Rosalind crossed her jeans-clad legs. She had lost some weight of late, but she didn't think she was particularly thin. At least not unattractively so.

"A bagel and some cream cheese if you have it, then."

He spoke rapidly into the phone, asking for what she had requested, as well as a varied selection of jams, jellies, and croissants. When he was through, he replaced the phone and sat looking at her.

"So," he said after a moment of silence, "Ben didn't come through?"

Rosalind frowned. She had been expecting the question but had hoped that he might have had enough tact not to bring up the matter.

"No. He couldn't spare it right now."

"Not even for his beloved fiancé?"

A frown marred her brow for a moment. "I know you find this situation amusing on some level. But let me tell you, I don't find it at all funny."

He stood and came to lean on the desk right beside her. "You know," he said, and his hand went out to stroke a thick curl of hair away from her face, "you're too sensitive. You've always been too sensitive."

She looked up at him, meeting his blacker-than-night eyes. She sensed that somehow his attitude toward her had softened, and she looked up at him, her eyes unconsciously pleading.

"Couldn't you lend me the money on normal repayment terms?"

"No." The familiar hardness was back in his voice. "Either you accept the terms I outlined yesterday, or it's no deal."

"I won't agree to any of the more familiar duties you stipulated."

"Like which ones specifically?"

Rosalind took a sharp breath. He was going to make this as difficult as possible for her—that was abundantly clear.

"You know exactly what I mean. The—the . . . massaging . . . and . . ."

He folded his arms across his chest. "I am not open to negotiation on any of the items outlined. If you love your brother as you say you do, then you won't quibble about my minor eccentricities. . . . And I haven't asked that you do these things forever. The repayment term is just a year. After that, you can go back to your dull little life . . . if you so choose."

Rosalind half rose from her seat, and then rethought the ramifications of telling him what exactly he could do with his money. He had her back to the wall, and he knew it. She had no bargaining chip. Nothing. He was holding all the cards and was doing a very good job at calling all the shots.

"When would I get the money if I agreed to what you say?"

He propped long fingers beneath his chin and his eyes gleamed with deep dark lights.

"Right away." He pulled open a desk drawer and removed a long flat leather-bound checkbook. "As soon as we formalize things with a legal contract. I don't want you going back on your word."

"I'm not likely to do that," Rosalind said, a huffy note in her voice. "I'm completely trustworthy."

He smiled at her in an unpleasant manner. "No one is completely trustworthy. Many years in business have taught me that."

"Well, if you think that about me, I don't see why you trust me in your house at all. Aren't you afraid I might steal the silver or walk off with a stereo or TV or something?"

He shrugged. "Those are just things. Things can be replaced. I'm more concerned about you keeping your word to me and not deciding to disappear in the middle of the night once you bail Tony out of his current predicament."

"There's one thing you'd better learn about me, Sam Winter. I am a woman of my word. If I agree to something, I agree to it. You don't need a written document to keep me honest. . . ."

He picked up a thick, expensive-looking pen, examined the tip then handed it to her.

"That's good to know. But, if it's okay with you, I'd just as soon have your John Hancock on this piece of paper. Steve has prepared the document and will also witness the signing of it. If there's anything you don't understand, feel free to have him explain."

Rosalind accepted the pen, and looked down at the off-white sheet of paper. Her heart was beating like a trip-hammer in her chest. What was she doing? Was she crazy? She couldn't sign it. She couldn't agree to such an arrangement. It was just not to be believed.

"Are you ready?" His voice brought her out of the pit of trepidation she'd been sinking into.

Her brain screamed *No*. But somehow she managed a scratchy "Yes."

Sam went to open the office door, and he bellowed into the bowels of the house. Steve Jenkins appeared moments later with a cream-filled croissant in hand.

"Everything all set?" he asked while taking a huge bite from the corner of the pastry.

Rosalind took a breath. She felt as though she were signing her entire life away. "Is there any way of breaking this contract, Mr. Jenkins . . . if—if . . . ?"

"Call me Steve. And yes, the contract can be broken, but not without substantial financial penalty."

"Meaning what?" Rosalind's brow furrowed.

"Meaning," Sam interrupted, "should you renege on your side of the deal, or attempt to sever this arrangement, you will be required to pay me a prorated sum plus interest."

Rosalind stared at him. *Interest? A prorated sum plus interest?* He really was a money-hungry coldhearted bastard.

She read the document again, carefully, her eyes hunting for any additional stipulations.

"Everything satisfactory?" Sam asked. Rosalind's eyes flashed.

No. Everything is not satisfactory. Things will probably never be satisfactory ever again. She signed the bottom of the document with a steady hand.

"My turn," Sam said. Rosalind handed him the pen and the sheet of paper. He signed quickly and then handed the paper and pen to Steve Jenkins, who put down his half-eaten croissant, wiped his hands on a square white napkin, and then signed in the area that said: "Witnessed by."

The entire thing had taken less than two minutes to accomplish. Two minutes to sign her life away. Rosalind looked across at the man who would now control her movements for the next year. There was a slight red flush across both of his cheekbones and a strangely triumphant expression on his face.

"Now for the check," he said. And he opened the leather folder and removed a machine-printed check.

"Two hundred thousand dollars," he said, and handed it to her.

She accepted the check with a mumbled "Thank you."

Steve Jenkins closed his briefcase with a snap. "Well, I think I'm done here." He looked at Rosalind, and for a brief minute his eyes seemed to reflect a certain amount of pity. "Don't worry so much," he said. "Everything will be fine."

"See yourself out, Steve. Rosalind and I still have additional business to discuss."

The sound of the front door closing behind the lawyer made Rosalind's heart pound with dread.

"I'll tell Phillip to bring in the food now."

"I'd just as soon just go and get this—"

"You work for me now," he interrupted. "And I say you eat."

Rosalind gritted her teeth. So, this was how it was going to be. He was going to boss her around and force-feed her monstrous quantities of food. Well, she would go along with things right then, but he would soon learn that she was not the kind of person that he could bully.

Minutes later, Rosalind was nibbling halfheartedly on a warm bagel and listening to him rap out various instructions.

"I want you here first thing tomorrow. You can bring whatever things you like. I'll make arrangements for your apartment to be closed and the stuff you have there stored."

Rosalind choked on a mouthful of bagel and went into a coughing fit before she could ask, "Stored? What do you mean 'stored?'"

"You'll be living here. You'll have no need to go to your apartment. You should have bought yourself a condo anyway. Renting is a waste of good money."

Things were moving just a little too fast for Rosalind, and she held up a hand and said as firmly as she could manage, "I'll decide whether or not my apartment is to be closed. Not you."

He shrugged. "If you want to waste your money in that way, then go ahead. I'll be paying you a small salary—enough for your necessary items but not enough for you to afford to keep a separate dwelling."

Rosalind took a deep sip of black coffee, and the soothing bitter warmed her throat and stomach and gave her time to think. He did have a point, as much as she hated to admit it.

"I'll arrange things myself," she said with an obstinate note in her voice.

"Have it your way. But you're my property now, Rosalind Carmichael, and I get to say what you do and how you do it."

Rosalind gave him a sour smile. *His property? Well, he'll soon learn differently.*

Five

Ben was livid, and Rosalind watched him with a mounting sense of desperation as he paced back and forth in her apartment. He paused to give her a very unloving glare and said through clenched jaws, "Let me get this straight. You're going to be doing what, again?"

Rosalind nibbled unconsciously at the corner of a nail. "It's just for a year. I told you that. And it wasn't my idea. It was the only way of—of getting the money Tony needed. He's in trouble. Big trouble."

"Tony, Tony, Tony," Ben bellowed. "That's all I ever hear from you. It's Tony needs this . . . Tony wants that. Do you ever think about what I need? What I want?"

"Yes, I—"

He interrupted her with a biting "And now you tell me that you're going to live in some man's house for a year, just so your darling boy, Tony, can get his greedy little hands on two hundred thousand dollars. Do you know what you've done? Do you know what that makes you?"

"It's a perfectly legitimate job." She couldn't tell him about the kissing and massaging requirements.

"And if you believe that, I've got a nice little bridge

in Brooklyn I'd like to sell to you. Wake up, lady. This—this . . . what's his name?"

"Samuel Winter."

"This Samuel Winter person has bought you. Lock, stock, and barrel. Use your brain, for God's sake. You do have one, don't you?"

Rosalind breathed deeply. She didn't want to lose her temper. He had a right to be upset, she knew that. It wasn't every day your fiancée let you know that she was moving into another man's house. But she wouldn't take very much more of his shouting. He had never shouted at her before, and she didn't like it. Didn't like it at all.

"You've got it all wrong. Sam Winter and I despise each other. He has some very twisted views about women—trust me. He has no interest in me whatsoever. Or I in him. He's cold, heartless, and . . . and totally uninterested in women in that way." She could also have said right then what some of those twisted views were, that she had actually heard the man say, *"Getting women is easy, if you understand what they want from you. All you have to do is mention the word* love, *and they all turn into a pack of simpering buffoons. My feeling is this . . . give them what they want, and they'll give you what you need. . . ."*

But Ben in his current mood was likely to misinterpret even so obvious an indication of Sam Winter's disdain for the entire female gender.

Rosalind forced her thoughts back to the matter at hand. Ben was staring at her with gleaming eyes. "What do you mean . . . 'in that way'? Are you saying that he doesn't like women?"

She nodded, hasty to agree and appease him. "More than that. Not only does he not like women, but he really can't stand me."

"So why, tell me, did he agree so readily to lend you not twenty, or twenty thousand, but two hundred thousand dollars? Is there something else you're not telling me?"

She shrugged. "I told you he's a bit odd. He's not like normal men. For one, he's an atheist, and he—"

"Odd? You're telling me the man is odd, and in the next breath you say that you're going off to live with him. Have you thought about the possibility of being murdered in your bed by this person? What if he breaks into your room in the middle of the night and cuts your throat? Or worse?"

Rosalind swallowed. For some reason, she had never thought of these possibilities. Sam Winter had many faults, but somehow she had never felt threatened by him. She seemed to know instinctively that he would never hurt her. Not physically anyway. But how could she explain this to Ben? He would never understand. He would call it foolish women's intuition.

"I don't think he's violent." *Demonic perhaps, but not violent.*

Ben sank into a chair. "And who's going to cook me dinner and take care of my laundry and other stuff?"

Rosalind came to sit beside him and placed a hand lightly on his back. She was thankful that he was slowly beginning to accept things.

"Don't worry about that. You can still drop your clothes off. And I'm sure I'll be able to cook and do the things I'd usually do for you. I'm just going to be working for Sam Winter, you know," she said with a little laugh. "Nothing will really change. I promise you."

"So when do you move in?"

Rosalind curved a slender arm about Ben's waist and rested her head against his shoulder. "He said he wants me there tomorrow."

Ben shifted her away from him. "Don't lean on that

arm, sweetheart. You know I have a problem with blood flow in that one."

Rosalind straightened. "Sorry." She had forgotten for a moment that he was a surgeon in training and that his arms and hands were of supreme importance and could not be traumatized in any way.

"Go and get me something to eat, darling? I'm on call again tonight and I'm really going to need my strength. . . . All those sick people. Sometimes you wonder if it will all be worth it. General surgeons don't make as much money as those who go into some of the more interesting specialty areas." He shrugged. "But . . . we'll see. . . . If necessary, I can always change course."

Rosalind smiled at him. He was back to his calm and easygoing self. Things were going to be okay.

Later, it was with a sense of near contentment that she drifted off to sleep. It was just a year. Just a year. And when it was over with, she would be able to go back to her life. She'd be able to start planning her wedding. Although she and Ben hadn't set a date yet, it was only a matter of time. As soon as he finished his residency, they would get married.

Rosalind slept curled into a tight little ball, her hair spread out around her like a silken cloud, a mysterious smile on her lips.

Not ten minutes away, Sam Winter passed the night in an entirely different manner. After Rosalind Carmichael had left him, he had gone back to work and had stayed at his desk for the duration of the day, handling business in Los Angeles and Paris. He worked until midnight, hoping that somehow the insomnia that had plagued him for years would be overwhelmed by physical exhaustion. But at two A.M. he was still wide-awake, lying on his back, shirtless, staring at the white spackled ceiling, his mind still churning. He had fought against the weakness in him for years, but it was too strong, and he had abandoned the fight. It made no sense any longer. Maybe it had never made any sense. Maybe all he needed was to lie with her. Hold her. Feel her heart beat strongly against his. Maybe these things would be enough. Maybe.

At six A.M., he drifted into a troubled sleep filled with dreams of loss. It was the same dream he'd been having for most of his adult life. He was alone. Abandoned. No one wanted him. No one would ever want him.

He awoke with a hollow feeling and a buzzing in his ear. He turned slowly, his hands searching for the alarm clock on the bedside table. He grabbed it and stared at the face. Eight o'clock. He was out of bed in an instant. The sound that had pulled him from slumber was the front doorbell.

He dragged on a T-shirt and a pair of jeans, then went into the attached bathroom to throw some water on his face.

Outside, Rosalind leaned on the bell again. Where in the world was he? She'd been ringing for more than ten minutes now. Had he forgotten that she was coming? Had he gone somewhere?

The door was pulled open before she could find an answer to that.

"Are you going to break the bell?"

Rosalind removed her finger from the button. He looked particularly disagreeable this morning. Stubbled chin. Wild hair. Crumpled clothing.

"You did ask me to be here first thing this morning."

"A woman of her word," he said with a nasty tone in his voice.

Rosalind ignored him. She had decided on her way over that that would probably be the best approach to take with him. No matter what he had to say, she would just not pay any attention to him. When he realized that he couldn't get a rise out of her, he would soon abandon her for other more interesting prey.

"I brought some of my things. I'll have to make several more trips later on for other stuff."

He looked at her with unsmiling black eyes. "Well, come in, then. There's no need to stand there looking like a scared little rabbit."

Rosalind gritted her teeth and bent to retrieve the huge duffel bag at her feet. If she managed to make it through the day without bashing him about the head with a vase or some such object, she'd probably be able to survive living in the same house with him for an entire year.

"Leave that," he said. "I'll carry it."

Rosalind heaved the bag onto her shoulder. "That's okay. I can manage."

"I'm sure you can. But I'll still take it." And he whipped the bag from her, slammed the door and then walked off without another word.

Rosalind hurried after him, fuming silently. He really was an extremely unpleasant man, not to mention rude. He walked rapidly down the polished hallway and stopped before a little door.

"You're going to be on the second floor," he said, reaching out to press a button. Rosalind stared. An elevator? She had heard of such things in private residences, but she had never actually been in a house that had one.

She followed him in and stood at the opposite end

of the small lift, keeping her eyes resolutely on the floor. In hardly more than a few seconds, the doors were opening onto a long corridor. And again he started off without her, and she was forced to follow him. He stopped a short distance away before two white double doors, inserted a key, and pushed the doors open.

"You should be fine here," he said. "And you'll be close enough to come to me during the night should I need you."

The hairs on the back of Rosalind's neck were suddenly at rigid attention. *Come to him in the middle of the night?*

"W-what?" she stammered.

He looked down at her with raised eyebrows. "Don't get any ideas into your head. I don't have any designs on your virtue. You're definitely not the kind of woman I go for." And he looked her over with disdainful eyes. "You're way too skinny . . . right now."

Rosalind's chin tilted a little, and her satin-black eyes glittered with ire. "Yes, and we can definitely thank God for that."

She brushed by him, entered the room, and came to a dead stop. The rest of the house had been almost monastic in its décor, but this room—this room was nothing short of opulent. The walls were done in a soft white with hidden silver flecks. At the windows were delicate mauve curtains. Thick-pile white carpeting ran from wall to wall, and a canopied four-poster bed stood in the middle of all of this, sporting one of the largest white teddy bears she had ever seen.

"The room's self-contained," he said from somewhere behind her. "The bathroom's around that corner."

"Oh," she said, because she could think of little else to say. She had expected a bare little room in the cellar or the attic. Something full of cobwebs, dust bunnies, and vermin. She had definitely not been expecting him to give her a room that would rival the splendor of any palace.

"Well, don't stand there all day. We've got work to do." His grating voice shook her from the temporary malaise that had seized her. "Get changed and then meet me downstairs in the office in fifteen minutes. I expect you to be in professional dress . . . today, and whenever the occasion calls for it." His eyes flickered over her. "Do you understand me?"

"Yes, sir," Rosalind said, a hard undertone in her voice.

He nodded briefly at her, and with that disappeared down the corridor.

Exactly fifteen minutes later, Rosalind was dressed in a snappy pin-striped navy blue pantsuit with matching blue pumps, her wavy locks secured in a tight bun. She paused before his office door, drew a tight breath, and then knocked.

"Come, come," he called out in the most irritating manner. Rosalind counted to ten before entering, and whispered a heated prayer that she'd be able to hold her tongue.

"So," he said as soon as she was seated, "did you take care of young Tony?"

"Yes," she said without volunteering further information.

He leaned forward. "You know," he said, "in addition to losing more weight than I'm sure is healthy, you appear to have lost your tongue, too. Is this what I'm to expect for the next year? 'Yes, sir. No, sir?' Has that worthless fiancé of yours knocked all of the spunk out of you?"

Rosalind's fingers bit into the soft palms of her hands. She didn't think she was going to be able to do it. He wanted her to lose her temper, and he was most likely going to get his wish before the end of the hour.

"I don't want to be rude to you," she began in a slow and labored manner, "but I have to warn you that if you continue to attack me in this way, I won't take any responsibility whatsoever for the outcome."

His eyes glinted at her, and she tried her best not to notice how much like a particularly sleek cobra he looked.

"So, you think I'm attacking you . . . do you?"

"I think you get some sort of perverse enjoyment out of making me miserable."

He smiled at her in a manner that for some reason made her nervous, and then opened a desk drawer and extracted a flat white package. He handed it to her.

"Sign everything," he said.

"Look," Rosalind objected immediately, "if you've added additional stipulations—"

"You've three cards," he interrupted. "Platinum MasterCard, American Express, and Diners Club."

Rosalind ripped open the envelope, then looked up at him. "I don't understand."

"Never used a credit card, either, I suppose?"

"Of course I've used—" And then she stopped herself. He was bating her again.

"As I told you yesterday," he said, "you're going to be responsible for the upkeep of this house as well as a lot of other things. You will also have to travel with me whenever I go on business trips. You'll use those cards to take care of expenses. You have a monthly spending limit of ten thousand. The bills, of course, come to me, so if you're ever tempted to go crazy and buy a condo in Hawaii, I'll know about it."

Rosalind looked down at the cards, and then up at

him. *A monthly spending limit of ten thousand dollars? Was he out of his mind?* "Are you pulling my leg?"

"And why would I do that?"

She looked at him with huge unblinking eyes. "It's . . . just that . . ."

He gave her a hard look. "Yes? What's the problem?"

What was the problem? It was just inconceivable that first of all he would trust her with such huge sums of money. But that aside, why in the world would he think that she would require a monthly budget of ten thousand dollars?

"Forget I said anything," she said, and bent to fill out the paperwork. She very dutifully signed the back of each of the three credit cards and then handed the sheaf of papers back to him. He accepted them with a brisk, "Right. Next thing is your hair."

Rosalind's hand flew self-consciously to her tightly secured mane. "What's wrong with my hair?"

He gave her a slitted-eye look. "I don't like it like that."

She was severely tempted to say, "That's just too bad." But instead she said in a sweet voice, "Really? Well, I can't please everyone, it seems."

He rose from behind his desk and before she knew what it was he intended, he was standing before her. She barely managed a startled, "What are you . . . ?" before her hair was tumbling to her shoulders. His big fingers dug into her hair, and instinctively she struggled to free herself.

"You had no right to do that," she bellowed at him, all the while pushing thick curling locks away from her face.

"I have every right to for the next year."

And he stroked a large gritty thumb down the curve

of her ear and then settled on the fat of her lobe to gently massage.

A rough sweetness filled her blood at the raw feel of him, and Rosalind pulled away from him, her heart thrashing wildly at her ribs.

"Don't ever do that again," she said a trifle breathlessly. "I'm not here to be mauled by you at every possible turn."

He folded his arms across his chest, and endeavored to look even more imposing than he usually would. "That's Ben's province, right?"

Rosalind swallowed in an awkward clenching manner. "I know you have no regard for women. But . . . at least Ben does," she finished lamely.

"Ben doesn't love you, and you know it. He doesn't know a thing about you. Doesn't understand or even care to understand what it is you really need. To him, you're just a nice piece of . . ." And he let the rest of his sentence trail off.

Rosalind gaped at him. *He's crazy.* Maybe Ben had been right all along. She had moved into the home of a lunatic. She took a cautious step away from him. It would be best not to get him too excited. She didn't know what she would do if the madness he was obviously battling suddenly overwhelmed him. They were so isolated on the sprawling property.

"Well, thank you for the insight on Ben and my relationship. But I—"

"If I loved you," he interrupted, "I would always have time for you. I'd make the time. You'd be more important to me than anything else I was doing. More precious to me than any little material thing I possessed."

Despite her every effort to prevent it, a tidal wave of hot blood rushed to her face. It had suddenly dawned on her what it was he was doing. His words returned to beat frantically in her mind. *"Getting women is easy, if you understand what they want from you. All you have to do is mention the word* love, *and they all turn into a pack of simpering buffoons."*

He was attempting to humiliate her by proving his hypothesis. She knew that he felt that women in general were simple-minded, and easily manipulated. But six years before she had proven that his ridiculous views about women were just that. Ridiculous.

But now he was back with a vengeance because he hated to be wrong about anything. As he himself had told her once. He was perfectly willing to go the distance to get what it was he wanted. And she realized now that what he wanted was her groveling, humiliated defeat. What a joke it would be if she actually began to feel tender emotions for him. How he would laugh at that in his private psychotic moments.

Rosalind seated herself again in the chair and said in a very firm manner, "Listen to me, Mr. Winter. . . ."

"Sam," he said. "It seems kind of silly to observe this kind of formality when we were almost married once."

Rosalind ignored that. There had never ever been a chance that she would have accepted him.

"Listen to me . . . Sam. If this working and living relationship is going to work out over the next year, we're going to have to establish some ground rules."

"Go on, I'm listening." And he rested on the desk, entirely too close to her as far as she was concerned.

"I think we need to understand that any physical contact between us should be kept to the absolute minimum. And . . ." She continued as he got ready to speak again. "And there's no need whatsoever to think that we need to talk to each other about any of our private affairs."

He straightened from his slouch against the desk.

"Fair enough. I think you should consider what I said about Ben, though. He's not the right man for you."

"I don't want to discuss that."

He shrugged. "Let's go take a tour of the house. I want you to fix the place up completely. Buy the furnishings, whatever else you think might be appropriate. I haven't had the time. . . ."

Several hours later, Rosalind was dressed in a soft pair of cotton shorts and standing before the massive floor-to-ceiling mirrors in the bathroom. She had spent the better part of the day following Sam Winter around, making frantic notes as he rapped out long lists of autocratic demands. He wanted her to order furnishings, a piano, paintings, carpeting, and more.

They had also taken a look at the grounds. There was a huge kidney-shaped pool with attached Jacuzzi, but it required cleaning. There were also tennis courts, a small fruit orchard, and a cabana. It was an absolutely huge property that she was certain must have cost the world to acquire. It was really the kind of estate designed for a family with lots of kids, and she found it interesting that Sam Winter had thought to buy it at all. It was far too large a place for just one person.

She brushed her hair vigorously and in an act of defiance, swept it again into the tight bun of earlier in the day. It was obvious that she would never understand the man who was now her employer, and she refused to even waste the time trying to figure out why it was he did the things he did.

She put the brush down, and went to collect the huge multicolored beach towel neatly folded on her bed. For some inexplicable reason, she suddenly felt nervous. Her heart was beating at an abnormal rate in her chest and a light flush of perspiration peppered her face.

As she walked in the direction of his suite, she tried to remain composed. It was just a massage, for heaven's sake. She wasn't about to be drawn and quartered. How bad could the experience really be?

His suite was on the same floor, but even so, it was quite a distance down the wide polished hallway. She paused now just outside the large double doors, unconsciously chewing on the corner of her lip. She had just about marshaled the strength that would be needed to endure the ordeal ahead when one of the doors was yanked back and there he stood, stripped to the waist with a thick white towel wound about his hips. His eyes flickered over her upswept hair, and then he stepped aside without a word and motioned for her to enter. Rosalind hesitated for just a moment in the doorway. She felt suddenly like a small animal caught in the jaws of a large metal trap.

"Are you thinking of coming in anytime soon?"

His biting question propelled Rosalind into motion. She was trying so hard to get along with him; why was he making it so difficult for her?

She stepped into the room, closed the door, and did her level best to ignore the fact that he was quite probably naked beneath the towel. Her eyes darted about the suite. It was almost as bare as a monk's bedchamber.

"Get onto the bed please," she said in a brisk professional voice. Then, as though on an afterthought, she asked, "Do you have anything on under that towel?"

He gave her a sardonic look. "Were you hoping I didn't?"

Rosalind met his hard black eyes and thought for the umpteenth time how very much she disliked them.

She moved quickly to the bed, spread the thick towel under her arm, and said, "Lie on your stomach."

The quicker she rubbed his back, the sooner she would be able to get back to her room so that she might give Ben a call.

He lay flat on his stomach with his arms pillowing his head. "You'll find some oils in the drawer," he said, pointing at the bedside table.

Rosalind gave him a startled look. Oils? Did he think he was in a professional massage parlor?

She pulled the drawer open and grabbed the very first bottle her fingers settled on. The label said Passion Ruby, but strangely it had no scent at all. She poured a good quantity into the palm of her hand. He turned his head to look at her, and Rosalind experienced a confusing rush of heat at the odd look in his eyes.

"Where is the problem spot?" she asked in a voice that was scratchy and thick.

He gestured with an arm. "Low down. Near the base of my spine mostly . . . but it's really my entire back."

Rosalind nodded. "Right," she said, and bent to her task. She let the oil drip slowly along the length of his spine, from the nape of his neck all the way down to the painful spot. Then her long fingers went briskly to work, kneading muscles that were suddenly hard beneath her fingers.

"Sam," she said after a minute of intense rubbing, "You're tensing up on me."

He turned again to look at her, and this time his eyes were angry and strangely tortured.

"How many times have you done this?"

Her fingers paused. "What?"

"You seem to be abnormally good at it."

"Well, since you pay me to do this . . . if I am abnormally good at it, as you say, you should be happy about it."

Her fingers resumed their journey, dipping now to the spot just above his tailbone, all ten digits slowly massaging the area.

His right hand balled into a fist, and a groan that sounded to Rosalind like pure agony, had her pulling back from him hastily.

"I'm sorry," she said. "I didn't realize it was so painful."

He turned over slowly, and Rosalind caught her breath. Instead of agony, it was wild desire she saw in his eyes. There was no mistaking it. Somehow, unwittingly, she had hit upon some chord of intense feeling in him because . . . He wanted her. Good God Almighty. . . .

He pulled her toward him in a sudden quick movement, and Rosalind was taken so completely by surprise, that she very nearly fell atop him.

Sam smiled at her in a manner that struck pure terror in her soul, and in a gritty voice said, "I would like my kiss now."

Six

Sam held her face between his hands, and his lips moved over hers in a manner that demanded a similar response. For just a moment, Rosalind's lips softened to him, and then she remembered that she was not free to kiss any man in this manner other than Ben. She was engaged to marry the man of her dreams, for heaven's sake. A surgeon. She loved him. He loved her. She couldn't do this. She couldn't.

She struggled against the immensity of Sam's chest. But he held her firmer still. His teeth closed on her upper lip and bit softly. And through the haze of heat that flooded her blood, she heard him whisper, "Please, Rosy."

Rosalind's lips parted, and he deepened the kiss in an instant, his tongue moving to stroke the sensitive roof of her mouth. A hair-fine shudder rippled through her, and again she made an attempt to free herself.

"No . . ." she muttered.

"Yes," he said on a husky rumble, and shifted her mouth back to him. He muttered fiercely against her lips, "He doesn't know what you like, but I do. Give me a chance. Please, my love."

And it was the word *love* that brought her back from whatever madness had her in its grip. In an instant,

she remembered whom it was that she was kissing—
the man who used the word *love* skillfully, calculatingly,
and completely for his own purpose. She knew without
question that his primary purpose was to prove that
she was no different from all of the other women who
became simpering buffoons at the mere mention of
it.

She pulled herself roughly from his arms and
looked down at him with blazing eyes. "If you kiss me
like that again . . . I will leave this house, contract or
no contract."

He stared up at her in silence, his face expressionless, black eyes unreadable. He swung his long legs to
the ground and stood, towering over her again.

"Don't forget you still have my dinner to prepare,"
he said. "Over this next year, I intend to get my
money's worth out of you, whether or not you have
the integrity to honor our agreement."

With fingers that trembled slightly, Rosalind folded
the large towel still spread on the bed. This was what
she had feared. A year of fights and turmoil. Their
personalities were so much in conflict that there was
no way that they were ever going to get along. And
the fact that he didn't appear to regard her engagement as anything serious, annoyed her even more.

With towel neatly folded beneath her arm, she
asked in a tight voice, "I thought you'd brought a
chef in from L.A.?"

"I've given him some time off. And as you'll remember, part of your contract with me stipulates that you
cook dinner every evening."

Rosalind suppressed a sigh. "What do you feel like
eating?"

He looked at her with glinting eyes, and she felt
the blood slowly creep toward her head. *Trust him to
turn a perfectly innocent question into something sexual.*

"Anything you come up with is okay by me. I'm easy to please."

The ringing of the front doorbell saved her from having to respond. Her eyes lit up. *Ben.* He had promised to stop by that evening to see how she was doing.

"I'll get that," she said, and hurried off in the direction of the sound. She was vaguely aware that Sam had followed her, but she was too anxious to answer the bell to worry substantially about him. She flung the doors open and almost hurled herself into her fiancé's arms.

"Ben," she said happily, and peppered his face with a succession of completely unrestrained kisses.

Ben grinned down at her. "Well, now that's the way a man should be greeted." He gave her a tight hug. "Feel like dinner and a movie?"

"She can't go," a gravelly voice just behind said.

Rosalind pulled Ben into the house and closed the door before saying, "Ben, this is Sam Winter, my boss. And yes, I'd love to go to the movies." It was open defiance, but she didn't care. After she was through making his dinner, she was on her own time and could spend it as she pleased.

Ben shook hands with Sam, casting a dubious glance at the towel he still had wrapped about his waist.

"As I was saying," Sam grated, "I need Rosalind tonight. And will every night this week and next. We're going to Las Vegas tomorrow."

Rosalind turned incredulous eyes in his direction. *Las Vegas?* This was the first time he had mentioned any such thing. They had spent the entire day making extensive lists about furniture, carpeting, plants, and other household items. And now here he was talking about going off to Vegas. He was just being deliberately obtuse, and she would have it out with him before things proceeded any further. He couldn't be allowed to think that he had the right to control every second of her time.

"Ben," Rosalind said in deceptively soft tones, "will you wait in the sitting room? I'll be out in a little while."

Ben looked at her in an inquiring manner, and she added, "It's a scheduling matter." And she turned to Sam with a little smile curling the corners of her lips. "I'd like a word with you, if you don't mind."

She walked briskly back toward the office and waited for him with burning eyes. She was even more irritated to note that he had followed her at his own leisurely pace. He closed the door and leaned on it.

She didn't waste a single moment. "Let's get one thing completely straight," she said. "You don't own every second of my time. Between normal working hours, you have the right to say what I do, how I do it, and with whom. But once the clock is off, I get to choose how I spend my time."

Sam walked across to his desk and pulled open the middle drawer. He removed the contract. "I'm afraid that's not what you agreed to here."

"What?" Rosalind almost bellowed.

His eyes were mocking, and it was all she could do not to slap the smug look from his face.

"Didn't you read the fine print?"

No. She hadn't bothered to read that. What an absolutely underhanded trick.

"Can I see that?" And she almost snatched the document from him. Her eyes skimmed the clauses, and then dipped to the tiny print at the bottom of the page. Her jaw was tightly clenched by the time she was through. He was an unscrupulous devil. He did control every second of her time. She handed back the contract. Maybe if she tried a different approach with him, she might be more successful. She had tried fighting him thus far and it had gotten her absolutely nowhere. Maybe if she was sweeter to him, things might improve.

"Sam," she began again, "I need to get out. . . . I've been cooped up all day. Please, I need to."

His expression was not encouraging, and she stretched out a soft hand and gripped his arm. She felt the muscles flex beneath her fingers.

"If you need to go out, I'll take you," he said, and his black eyes were as hard as stones.

"I have to be allowed to spend time with my fiancé. Why would you deny me that?"

He yanked the desk drawer open again and began pushing things around inside. After a minute, he looked up to say, "I told you. That man out there is not the right one for you. I've always thought you to be an intelligent woman. Why it is you're incapable of seeing what's right beneath your nose, is beyond me."

Rosalind felt the anger beginning to rise in her again. What gave him the right to say who was or was not the one for her? How dare he be so presumptuous?

"It's not up to you to decide who I choose. I've never once tried to tell you who to see."

He chuckled in a hoarse way. "That would certainly be a pleasant surprise if you did."

"I'm going to marry Ben," she said in a firm voice. "Whether you approve of it or not."

"If you marry him," he said, in a voice that was equally soft, "I will destroy your little surgeon. That much I promise you."

Rosalind stared at him. He *was* crazy. Stark raving mad.

"You're mental," she said. "Maybe you spend too much time all alone. Maybe you—"

"Maybe I need a woman," he interrupted.

"Well, find one of the horse-boned ones you like so much," she bellowed, "and stop taking out your frustrations on me."

They stood staring at each other, chests heaving. He turned toward one of the giant plate-glass windows, presenting her with the wide expanse of his back.

"Go this once. But be back before midnight."

Seven

"You know there isn't anything Sam Winter wouldn't do for you. And it's always been so," Tony said. He stretched lazily on the large double bed, a hand propped beneath his head. "Why don't you like him, sis? As men go, I don't think he's so bad."

Rosalind emerged from the bathroom with a stack of clothes in her hands. "You don't know him as I do. Trust me."

Tony turned onto his side. "Sometimes I wonder if you know him as well as you think."

Rosalind folded the clothing in her hands, and plunked them into her rollaway suitcase. "He's an atheist. Did you know that?"

Tony shrugged. "Have you ever spoken to him about that? Or tried to help him in any way? You are a Christian. But you haven't been behaving in such a Christianly way toward him. He did help us out, after all. Maybe he needs your help."

Rosalind busied herself with stuffing additional items into the suitcase. She didn't want to think about what Tony had just said. There was an element of truth to it. Maybe Sam Winter did need help. But why did she have to be the one to provide it?

"You're just feeling more charitable toward him because he was responsible for saving your skin, Tony.

By the way . . . is everything settled with that little situation? I mean . . . you did put the money back?"

Tony sat up. "I may be irresponsible from time to time, but trust me, sis, I'm not crazy. I value my safety. The money is back where it belongs. And . . ."

Rosalind looked sharply at her brother. "And?"

"I've enrolled in a program."

"You . . . what? Tony, please tell me you haven't gone off on another of your wild schemes. Look at the mess this last one has gotten me into."

Tony chuckled. "Come on. You know it's not as bad as all that." He spread his arms. "Look at you. You're living here in a mansion in Mendham in a beautiful suite—"

"As a virtual prisoner," Rosalind interrupted. "With a psychotic atheist for company . . . who might very well decide to do away with me in the middle of the night."

"Well, that's one thing I know you don't have to worry about. Sam Winter would never hurt you. If there's any hurting being done, my guess is it's all one-sided."

Rosalind dropped her bag of toiletries into the suitcase and zipped the luggage closed. Tony was talking a lot of nonsense as usual. Maybe it was possible to hurt Sam Winter, but she certainly did not possess what it took to bring that about.

"Why should anything I say or do have any effect on Sam Winter . . . not to mention cause him grief?"

Tony lifted a large red apple from the fruit basket on the bedside table and bit into it. He chewed thoughtfully before saying, "I think you're letting this ridiculous dislike of your employer blind you to what's really obvious to me . . . and to everyone who has ever observed him whenever you're around."

Rosalind threw back her head and laughed heartily.

"Tony, I don't believe it. You're getting soft in your old age."

"I mean it," Tony said. "I think if you slept with him, he'd be the sweetest-tempered man around. Haven't you noticed how he looks at you? He wants to bed you in the worst way."

Rosalind slid into a pair of black suede pumps and gave herself a critical once-over in the mirror. When she was satisfied with her reflection, she turned back to her brother.

"Sam Winter doesn't even find me vaguely attractive. He's just a very, very strange man. And believe me, there's nothing I would like less than going to bed with him. He is most definitely not my type."

Tony raised both eyebrows. "Such strong words. I'm beginning to think that you've been hiding some really hot and passionate feelings from him."

"What?" Rosalind sputtered. "Don't be—" But her words were cut short by a knock at the door. "That'll be him now," she whispered. "I hope he didn't overhear any of the ridiculous nonsense you've been saying."

Rosalind went across to pull open the door. "I'm not behind schedule," she said immediately, not at all sure how to interpret the thunderous expression on his face.

"Didn't I tell you that I didn't want you entertaining anyone in your room?" he almost bellowed.

Rosalind's lips tightened. "Listen to me, Sam Winter. I'm a grown woman, okay? And I'm getting a little sick and tired of your ridiculous rules and regulations. If I feel like entertaining someone . . . in my room, I most certainly will. And"—she raised a finger to wag it at him—"if you don't like it, you can just fire me."

Tony came to stand behind his sister. "Sam," he

said, "I'm guessing you don't remember me. I'm Rose's brother."

Sam's brows snapped together. "Tony?"

Tony smiled and extended a hand. "That's right. I just dropped by for a quick visit. Rosalind told me that she's leaving for Las Vegas today . . . for a week, maybe two."

Rosalind left them both at the door, and went about the room gathering up a few last-minute things. She folded two very businesslike power suits onto padded hangers, and tried not to strain to hear what was being discussed at the door. She had never had the impression that her brother and Sam Winter cared very much for each other, but strangely they seemed to be getting along like a house on fire.

Rosalind closed the suit bags, then went into the bathroom to linger over the sink. She checked the soft matte makeup on her face, freshened her lipstick, and ran a quick comb through her hair. Their flight was in three hours and she was already all set to leave.

She gave her watch another look, and then picked up the wall phone in the bathroom. Ben would be between rounds now. He should have just enough time to say a quick goodbye.

"Ben?" she said after a brief moment of hearing ringing on the other end of the line. "Hi, sweetheart."

"Rosalind," came the slightly irritable response, "what is it? I told you not to call me on my cell unless it was a clear-cut emergency."

Rosalind nibbled on the corner of her bottom lip. "Sorry. But you remember I'm going to Vegas today?"

"Right."

"I don't want to go," she said softly. "It's my job to go."

"I've heard it all before. What Sam Winter wants, Sam Winter gets. Am I right?"

Rosalind suppressed a sigh. Lately she and Ben were almost always on the edge of a fight. He just didn't seem to understand what an absolutely difficult situation she was in. Sometimes she even thought that he didn't care.

"For the next year, I'll have to do as he says. But a year's not a very long time."

There was a brief pause and then Ben said, "Rosalind, I really don't have the time for this okay? I need to have a bite to eat, and then get back to the E.R."

A flush of hot tears rushed to the backs of her eyes. "I just wanted to say bye to you before I left."

For an instant, in the background she could hear him being paged. She swallowed away the salty tears and said very solidly, "Ben?"

"I've gotta go," he said. And Rosalind found herself listening to a dial tone. She hung up slowly, and stood for a brief moment with eyes closed, her back pressed to the bathroom wall.

There was the sound of muffled footsteps, and then a voice asked, "What's the matter?"

The sudden intrusion caused Rosalind's eyes to flash open. She lifted a quick hand to remove any residual traces of tears. Not for anything would she let him see her cry.

"Nothing," she said, and turned blindly toward the sink. She hadn't heard him come in. For a big man, he moved very quietly. She turned on the cold water tap to full blast, and made an elaborate pretense of washing her hands.

"Is Tony gone?"

She felt him come to stand directly behind her. "He's down in the kitchen getting something to eat."

"Well, I won't be a minute," she said, and prayed

silently that he would just go away and leave her this small moment of privacy. But her fervent prayers were not answered. She felt his hands descend on her shoulders.

"Come," he said. And he turned her slowly to face him. Serious black eyes looked directly into hers. "You've been crying."

Rosalind blinked. She had been hoping against hope that he would either not notice, or have the tact not to bring it up.

"Is it all the work I've given you? You know, you can hire a housekeeper and all the staff you need to help you keep this place in shape."

He raised a thumb to rub the wet from the corner of her eyes, and before she could even guess what it was he intended, his lips had replaced his thumb. He stroked the saltiness away with the tip of his tongue. And the breath halted in Rosalind's lungs. Her immediate impulse was to pull away from him, but somehow her feet—her body—wouldn't obey her brain's frantic instructions. Her hands moved to rest against his chest, and beneath her fingers she felt the strong thudding of his heart.

"You know that you can tell me anything, Rosy."

Her arms slipped around his waist to hold him, and he folded her close, bringing her face into contact with his chest. Rosalind rested against him for a minute, forcing herself not to think about the reasons he was being so very tender with her. This gentle caring was what she needed from Ben and never got. And there was always a reason why not. It was never the right time. He was always too busy. Or too tired. Or not in the mood.

Sam's hands stroked the soft fall of wavy hair, his big fingers pausing to massage her scalp and then the shaft of her hair.

"I've been terrible to you," he said after a moment, "and . . . I'm sorry."

Rosalind lifted her head and stared at him. Sorry? He was sorry? That was a word she never thought that she would ever hear him say to her.

"Oh, it's not your fault. You've nothing to be sorry about . . . not really. If it hadn't been for you, Tony would've been—could've been—in very bad trouble. And I—I've been hostile toward you ever since the first. . ."

"I know," he said. "You don't like me."

Hearing him utter the very words that she herself had said so many times, gave them a certain cruel reality.

"No," she rushed to reassure him, "it's not that."

"You mean you like me?"

"I don't really dislike you."

His lips twitched, and she wondered what thoughts had caused that little reaction. "You have," he said, "the sweetest face I have ever seen. And that fiancé of yours is a fool to leave you alone for as long as he does." His fingers stroked lightly across her face. "If you were mine, I never would."

"Sam," she said, "you know you shouldn't say things like that to me. You promised that you wouldn't. Especially . . . since we have to live in such close proximity for—for such a long time."

His shoulders moved and he stepped away from her. "Will you answer me one thing?"

"If I can," Rosalind said cautiously.

He hesitated for a brief moment then said, "If Ben wasn't in the picture, would you have considered me?"

Rosalind's mouth opened and closed. She couldn't believe that he was serious. "I—I'm not sure what you want me to say."

"Is that such a hard question to answer? I'm not a

woman beater you know. . . . You can answer me honestly."

She grasped desperately for some escape. Her brain was in a thick fog. "But . . . what good will it do for me to answer that question? Even if you are serious . . . which I doubt."

"I'm completely serious," he said softly. "I need to know."

"Sammy," she said, using the affectionate diminutive without even realizing what it was she was actually doing. "I really think I know what you need."

He smiled. "You do? Tell me, then. What do I need?"

"I hadn't really spent a lot of time thinking about it before. But now I think I understand part of the problem." She paused for breath, and then rushed on. "You're lonely. But not lonely in a general way, maybe. You need a . . . woman."

He folded his arms across his chest. "Are you offering yourself to me?"

Rosalind bit back an immediate denial. He was back to that again, and she'd thought that she had managed very successfully to distract him.

"It's not me that you want—trust me. You just need to get out some more, you know? Have a little fun. You work hard . . . too hard even. You're still young. You should have some fun. Even if you weren't young, you should still have some fun," she said in a feeble attempt at humor.

A strange expression flickered across his face, and Rosalind tried hard to convince herself that it wasn't hurt that she saw for a brief instant in his eyes.

"I'm guessing that long-winded explanation of my needs is your way of saying that even if Ben were gone . . . I'd be the last person on Earth you would ever consider spending any voluntary time with."

Rosalind stayed silent, because she didn't know what to say in response. How could she explain that she had never thought of him in a romantic way, and probably never could? How could she tell him that his atheistic beliefs would forever be a stumbling block between them? Not to mention the completely unforgivable views he had about women.

"I'll meet you downstairs," he said after a moment. "I'll take your bags down." And with that he was gone.

Rosalind took a minute to straighten her hair and freshen her face, and then she joined him downstairs. She said a quick good-bye to Tony, who somehow in the short period of time they had been separated, had managed to wolf down an entire platter of tuna fish sandwiches, and polish off half a chocolate cake.

An hour later, the house had been closed up, and they were off to Newark Airport in Sam's black Lexus SUV. During the trip to the airport, Rosalind had tried in vain to decipher the expression on his face. She was unsure whether he was angry over the fact that she had not answered his question, as he would have liked. As they neared Newark, Rosalind ventured a question.

"Sam, this trip to Las Vegas . . . You haven't told me anything at all about it. What are we supposed to be doing there?"

He turned to look at her with his ultraserious eyes, and Rosalind had a very hard time holding his glance. His penetrating gaze seemed to be able to pierce tissue and bone, and it made her very uncomfortable to think that maybe he could guess at the turmoil that churned just behind her eyes. His earlier questions in the afternoon had disturbed her. He had appeared so very sincere. And when he had held her, she had experienced a strange belonging she had never felt with Ben or with any other man, for that matter.

"We're going to meet with various buyers. There's a lot of interest in the company's new line of sportswear. It's possible that a lot of high-end stores in Paris and the Caribbean might place substantial orders for the upcoming summer season."

Rosalind nodded. "And what will my role be?"

"You will help me put together a very attractive online presentation of the entire line. Each buyer will have a laptop in his suite. I want them to be able to preview the entire line of clothes before we go in for negotiations."

Rosalind's brow wrinkled. "That shouldn't be a problem. But I'll need time to put together something really attractive."

"We'll have about a week before everyone arrives." His brows lifted. "Is that long enough for you?"

"A week." And she did some very rapid mental calculations. "Do you have everything already scanned?"

Sam nodded. "You'll also have the help of a couple of Web page designers from the L.A. office."

"Ah," Rosalind said. "So there's going to be a group of people—of employees in Las Vegas?"

He swung the big truck into one of the long-term parking lots, parked it, and helped her from the vehicle before saying, "Don't worry. You won't be alone with me."

Rosalind was left to ponder that remark, all the way through first-class check-in. On the plane, a smiling stewardess showed them to their seats, and Rosalind, who had never flown is such plush luxury before, looked around her with admiring eyes. Sam sat in the aisle seat, allowing her full access to the view the window provided.

"We're staying at the Bellagio Hotel," he said. "You should like it there."

Rosalind smiled at him. She had heard of the hotel, of course, but had never thought that she would ever be able to afford to stay there.

"I know this trip is for work. But I really, really love Las Vegas. When I lived in L.A., I used to drive there once or twice a year."

He leaned forward to extract a glossy magazine from the circular blacktop table before them.

"Did you go alone?"

Rosalind shrugged. "Sometimes. But most of the time, it would be a bunch of us. Tony occasionally. I didn't want to encourage him to frequent Vegas . . . given the tendency he has for gambling."

"Hmm," Sam said. "Did he tell you that he's enrolled in a few programming classes?"

"He did?" And there was a momentary flash of happiness in her eyes. "That must be what he started telling me in the room."

"I think young Tony will be all right now. If you like, I can mentor him through this entire process."

"Would you? I didn't think you liked him very much."

"Now why would you have thought that?"

The plane started with a little bump, and Rosalind was spared the necessity of responding. She sat back with an expression of glee on her face, unaware that the man beside her was keenly observing her. She had decided on her way to the airport, that she was going to thoroughly enjoy herself in Las Vegas, even if she had to work. Her momentary upset over Ben's general attitude had faded. She understood that a surgeon's wife had to be stronger than average. Had to be willing to put up with the long absences of her husband, his irregular work hours, and occasional bad temper. But she knew that regardless of all outward appearances, Ben loved her. Just as she loved him. He was just very busy, and sometimes he forgot to show her how much he cared.

Halfway through the five-hour flight, Rosalind fell soundly asleep. Sam shifted her head so that she rested comfortably against him. She slept until they were a half hour outside of Las Vegas. She opened sleepy eyes and for a brief instant didn't remember where she was or whom she was with. She just knew that she had just had the best rest she had had in months.

Rosalind lifted her head from where it lay, and everything came back in waves.

"Oh," she said. "I'm sorry." She struggled to find the right words. She'd been practically lying all over him. What must he be thinking of her?

"You were tired," he said. "I was here. Don't worry about it."

For the first time, Rosalind noticed the faint shadows beneath his eyes. Shadows that undoubtedly pointed at lack of sleep. Concern rippled her brow.

"Why didn't you try to get some sleep, too?"

He said nothing for a moment, as though he was carefully feeling for words. "I've always had a hard time sleeping. And, of late, it's been harder than ever."

Rosalind looked at him, and Tony's words came back to her. *You haven't been behaving in such a Christianly way toward him. He did help us out, after all. Maybe he needs your help.*

"How many hours have you been getting a night?"

"One . . . on a good night, three."

She was incredulous. "One hour of sleep a night? You should go to a doctor about this. It's definitely not normal. No human being can exist on one hour of sleep a night."

"I know what it is I need," he said, meeting her eyes directly, "and it's definitely not something a doctor can prescribe for me."

A flash of hot blood rose to stain her cheeks. She was beginning to think that a lot of what Tony had had to say was correct. Maybe Sam Winter did find her physically attractive. Or maybe he just needed sex, and she was there.

The stewardess appeared with a sumptuous plate of smoked salmon, asparagus sticks, and seasoned rice.

"You must be hungry," she said. "We'll be landing in about twenty minutes, but that should give you more than enough time to eat."

Rosalind thanked the young woman and dug in heartily. She was feeling more than a little bit hungry. She sipped on the dark wine, and put her mind to work on how it was she was going to help Sam Winter. First of all, she would ensure that he got a good night's sleep. She wasn't at all sure of how it was she was going to do that yet, but that very night she would see what could be done. She was also going to try to get a handle on why it was he had lost his faith in God. Oftentimes, she knew, unrelenting hardships had a way of shaking a person's faith. It could also be that he had never grown up in the church, as she had. And without that formative belief system, once he was old enough, logic—and not faith—had probably helped to guide his thoughts and actions.

She swallowed her last bite of salmon, and decided firmly. She was going to help him—whether or not he welcomed her help. With her better understanding of things, she was sure that somehow she would be able to lead him back to the right path.

Her brow wrinkled as she bit into a warm roll spread with sweet butter. *Isn't that what a true Christian would do? Help someone in obvious need?*

Eight

The Bellagio was a sprawling hotel with an interesting blend of soaring Old World architecture and fine ultramodern symmetry. And their red carpet service was like nothing Rosalind had ever experienced before. Just minutes after landing, their luggage was gathered up and they were whisked away by limousine. At one point during the very short journey, Rosalind asked, with the beginnings of a worried frown creasing the smooth skin between her brows, "Sam, are you sure we didn't leave any bags behind? I mean, can we be sure they got everything? You had three . . . right?"

Sam turned to her with a little smile flickering about the corners of his lips. "You know, you really are a little worrywart. Just relax," he said. "They do this many, many times a day."

Rosalind gave him a tentative little smile. Her eyes drifted over the plush interior of the long car. There was every amenity anyone could possibly desire. Her glance skimmed over the TV, DVD, phone, laptop computer, and then darted back to rest on the phone. She gave her watch a surreptitious little look. Ben would be taking his afternoon break right about now. She didn't dare call him again on his cell phone, since he had been so unreceptive to it before. But she did wonder what he might be doing right then. She worried a bit about what kind of dinner he might be having. Sometimes he ate the unhealthiest of foods. He really needed her there to look after him.

"What do you feel like doing this evening?"

Sam's voice brought Rosalind back from deep thought. She glanced out the dark tinted windows. They were already at the hotel.

"I hadn't really thought about it. But maybe I'd better get a jump on all of the work that needs to be done to put the summer catalog online."

A liveried bellhop swept the car door open, and Sam climbed out and reached in to help Rosalind out.

"You don't have to plunge right into work," he said against her ear. "Take a few days to just enjoy yourself. There's a nice spa here. Maybe you'd like to do that tomorrow."

Before she could even think of a proper response to his suggestion, a tall and rather distinguished-looking man clothed in formal dress appeared at curbside.

"Mr. Winter," he said in a pleasant baritone, "allow me to welcome you and your wife to the Bellagio."

Rosalind's throat went dry, and she darted a quick glance at Sam, but his face was as impassive as it usually was.

"My name is Renard," the man continued. "I'll be your personal butler during your stay with us." He directed a polite smile in Rosalind's direction. "Was your flight a pleasant one?"

Rosalind returned his smile, and said a trifle breathlessly, "Yes, thank you. It was fine." Her brain was working furiously. How could there have been such a mix-up? Why in the world did they think that she was married to Sam Winter? And how would that assumption affect their sleeping arrangements?

But there was no time to even raise the problem with Sam. In next to no time, they were being ushered into a private elevator and taken to their suite. Renard chatted nicely all the way up to the penthouse, and Sam, who seemed not at all put out by the suggestion that she was his wife, responded to the man in an equally cordial manner.

The elevator doors opened directly onto a sumptuous white-and-gold foyer, and despite herself, Rosalind drew a startled breath. The elevator had deposited them directly in the suite. A beautiful spiral staircase, superbly finished with fine metal whorls, descended to a sunken sitting room of white and delicate mauve. Renard took their bags and proceeded ahead of them. Rosalind seized the opportunity.

"Sam," she hissed. "What . . . I mean is, they think we're married. Did you get that?" He shrugged big shoulders. "It shouldn't be a problem. I needed you close to me during these next two weeks, so for your sake I told them that we were married."

Rosalind took a breath. "You did what? You mean this was deliberate?"

He looked down at her in a patient manner. "Well, would you have preferred that they think you were a woman of uncertain virtue?"

Her brow wrinkled. If he was so very concerned about her virtue, why couldn't she have stayed in the next room down?

They were at the lip of the huge master bedroom, and Renard was pointing out all of the amenities in a cheerful voice. But everything he was saying was completely lost on Rosalind. Her eyes had gone immediately to the very large bed in a secluded alcove under a pair of sprawling floor-to-ceiling windows.

"You should find everything exactly to your liking," Renard was saying. "But just in case there's anything else you need, I'm here. I'll leave you alone now to get settled." He handed Sam what looked to Rosalind like a pager. "I'll be in the kitchen fixing you a snack. I hope you enjoy your stay with us." And with that he was gone.

Sam closed the bedroom door behind him, and Rosalind actually jumped.

He approached her slowly and stood looking down at her, hands resting casually in his pockets.

"Why're you so nervous?" he asked. "It's just me."

"We can't sleep in the same bed," Rosalind said. "Have you forgotten that I'm engaged? And not only that, you're my employer, for heaven's sake. What could you have been thinking of when you told them that we were husband and wife?"

Sam walked across to a door that Rosalind had completely overlooked. "There's a connecting room through here. You can have the big bed in here, and I'll take this one."

Rosalind gave him a grateful look. "Thank you. I hope you don't think I'm a prude, but this—all of this is highly irregular."

He gave her a very direct look. "We have a lot of work to do over the next couple of weeks, if we are to close this deal. So we're going to have to work very long hours. Sometimes into the wee small hours of the morning. And I felt much better knowing that you wouldn't ever have to walk back to your room at that time of the morning. This is a nice hotel, but we're still in Las Vegas. I'm responsible for you."

Rosalind felt suddenly very silly. She was always jumping to the wrong conclusions when it came to Sam Winter. But what was she supposed to think?

Surely any normal woman of moderate decency would have been similarly concerned.

"Get changed," he said. "If you like, we can go down to the casino for a while. By the way," he said, turning back toward her, "would you ask Renard to get us seats at the Ray Charles show tonight?"

Rosalind nodded, and gave him a very whisper-thin, "Sure." *Ray Charles? The Ray Charles?* He was her all-time favorite performer.

Very shortly, Renard was back carrying a tray of delicious snacks, which he placed on a smoothly lacquered center table that sat before a cozy gathering of sofas at one end of the massive room.

"Your husband is taking a shower?" he asked.

Rosalind tried to respond in a normal manner even though her heart thrashed at the very thought of referring to herself as Sam Winter's wife.

"Yes," she said. "We're going to go down to the casino in a little while."

"I can see how much he loves you," Renard continued. "Have you been married for very long?"

Rosalind gritted her teeth. "No. Not very long."

Renard smiled. "Yes, I can tell that, too. That passion that newlyweds feel for each other is strong. You are lucky to be cared about liked that."

For the first time, Rosalind noticed that Renard had a slight European accent, but she was so unnerved by what had just been said, that she made no comment about it, but instead plunged into rapid speech.

"Ah . . . we were wondering if you could get us into the Ray Charles show tonight?" She was desperate to get him off the track he was on.

Renard beamed. "Yes. I believe I can get you front-row center. Would that be satisfactory?"

Rosalind assured him that that would be perfect, and she was glad when she could again close the room door behind him. Having a butler at her beck and call was definitely a new and very unsettling experience.

She spent the next half an hour soaking in a languorously warm bath, her head wrapped tightly in a large white towel and resting against the very conveniently placed neck pad at one end of the tub. Such luxuries she was completely unaccustomed to, and she had to admit, she could begin to like living in this manner. If only Ben was already finished his residency. They hadn't been able to take a vacation together in years. And all of the fights they had been having of late were strong indications that they needed to get away from life for a while. Spend some quality time together.

She climbed very reluctantly from the tub when the water was finally too chilly for her to sit there in continued comfort. She toweled dry her long smooth legs, and spent several minutes over her hair. Then, wrapped in a thick white robe with the name Bellagio neatly embroidered across one lapel, she emerged. She was grateful to find that Sam was not in the bedroom. She dressed quickly in a pair of jeans, a vibrant burgundy T-shirt, and fashionable high-heeled sandals. Her hair spilled about her shoulders in a riot of blue-black curls, and she did her best to tame the ends, before putting one of the provided I Love Las Vegas caps atop her head.

She gave herself a critical perusal in the dressing table mirrors, turning this way and that so that she might see herself from every angle. She was beginning to gain a bit of weight, but it seemed to sit well on her hips and behind.

Her thoughts drifted once again to Ben, but just for a brief moment. Then she made a determined effort to put him out of her mind for now. Ben was busy. Too busy for her right then. So what was she to do? She was in Las Vegas to work, but there was nothing wrong with having a little bit of fun, too. Was there?

Nine

"I win again," Rosalind bellowed in glee. She reached forward to gather up an entire stack of hundred-dollar chips.

"I had no idea you were such a gambler," Sam muttered close to her ear. "Sometimes you never really know about people. Where'd you learn to play blackjack like that?"

Rosalind turned in her seat to laugh up at him. "You're just jealous," she said. Then on a generous impulse, she handed him one of her chips. "Here. Take this hundred and play it on . . . hmm . . ." She looked about the crowded room with bright eyes. "The roulette wheel."

Sam looked at her with raised eyebrows. "Roulette?"

Rosalind nodded. "Roulette. I think you'll be lucky there."

"What numbers should I play, madam?" Sam asked, a little smile beginning to twist the corners of his lips.

"Try our ages. Twenty-nine . . . and forty."

Sam laughed. "It's thirty-eight, woman."

And, Rosalind grinned back at him. For the first time in a very long time, she felt happy. Happy and free. And the feeling was intoxicating.

She went back to her game of blackjack, and soon there was an entire crowd of onlookers gathered around the table cheering her on. She had never been so good, so skilled, so absolutely unbeatable.

After what to Rosalind could only have been minutes, Sam came over again to whisper in her ear, "I think you're attracting the attention of the casino management. You know they have a rule about not allowing professional card sharks to play in the pits."

"I'm hot, baby. I'm hot," Rosalind told him, a feverish gleam in her eyes.

"No more cards for her," Sam said to the dealer. And he motioned to one of the pit runners that he was ready to gather her overflowing stack of chips.

"Oh, come on, Sammy . . . I'm not ready to go yet." Rosalind turned pleading eyes in Sam's direction.

"Come on, darling," Sam said. "Be nice. Don't scare the people." And he took Rosalind by the shoulders, and with gentle firmness steered her away from the blackjack table.

Once away from the crush of people, he fanned her with a hand. "You're sweating."

Rosalind stroked the tiny beads of perspiration from her top lip. "I know. It's really hot in here."

Sam bent toward her. "Can I have my daily kiss now?"

"But you just said I was all disgusting and sweaty."

Sam chuckled. "I said nothing of the kind . . . so can I?"

Rosalind looked around furtively, as though she expected an entire crowd of people to be watching. "Here? You want to kiss me right here?"

Sam traced a finger around the edges of her mouth. "No. Actually, I want to kiss you right there." And his finger trailed its way to the soft pouty part of her mouth, and froze to softly caress.

Rosalind met his eyes directly, and a strange thrill ran like quicksilver through her. "But . . ."

"But what?" he said. "No one knows us here. Besides, no one's paying any attention at all to us. They wouldn't care less even if we stripped naked right here, right now."

Rosalind hesitated for a moment more, then said, "Okay. But remember, you can't kiss me like you did before."

"No tongue?"

Rosalind shook her head, and a little smile peaked in her eyes. "Definitely no tongue."

"Hmm," Sam said in a husky undertone. "That could be difficult. I've never done that before. I might need some practice."

"Don't be silly," Rosalind chuckled, and she offered him her lips in a very pert and chaste manner.

Sam tilted her chin. "Relax your lips," he said. "I'm not your ninety-year-old grandmother."

Rosalind laughed then, in a hearty full-blown manner that caused Sam to chuckle, too. He raised a hand to stroke the side of her face. "You're the nicest girl I know," he said. "I've missed you so much these last six years."

Rosalind raised her eyebrows at him. "Missed me? I thought you hated me."

His hand had stroked its way to the round of her chin. "I could never hate you, babe. Not ever. No matter what happens between us in the years to come. Always remember that." And he tilted her head, and in a very natural, very warm, very right way, his lips covered hers.

The tight sigh that Rosalind hadn't even been aware she had been holding on to, escaped in a long sweet breath. And without coaxing, her tongue slipped into his mouth to softly, shyly stroke.

Sam froze for half an instant, afraid to move, afraid to do anything that might distract her from her purpose. Then slowly he folded her into his arms and deepened the kiss in a manner that caused Rosalind to clutch at his shoulders. Time and space ceased to have any meaning as his warm lips moved slowly and with infinite skill. Rosalind sighed again. She had never known. Never known that a simple kiss could be so good. She didn't care if the entire casino was watching them now. All that mattered at that instant in time was that the wonderful, beautiful sensation continue.

Her long, manicured fingers moved to caress his earlobes, and Sam uttered a soft sound of encouragement. And it was the near animalistic groan that he made that pulled Rosalind back from the sweet, nebulous place where she had been languishing.

"Oh, no," she gasped against his lips. "I'm sorry. I shouldn't have." She tried to move, but he continued to hold her.

"Shh," he said. "It's okay. You haven't done anything wrong."

"Ben . . ." she said in a desperate manner.

"Ben doesn't know the value of what he has. And when someone doesn't value what they've got, they deserve to lose it."

Rosalind's heart hammered in her breast. She was so confused. This was Sam Winter. Sam Winter, for heaven's sake. The man she had despised for such a long time. How was it that he had managed to rouse such deeply passionate feelings in her? Feelings that Ben had never even guessed existed. It couldn't be. It couldn't be. She had thought herself to be so strong. So resilient to Sam. Where were all of her fancy protestations now?

"Let's go have something to eat," Sam said. He recognized the signs of turbulence in her eyes, and he didn't want to give her a chance to overanalyze what had just occurred between them.

Rosalind was glad for the distraction. "Want to go to a buffet . . . or something more formal?"

Sam smiled at her. "Whatever you want," he said, and he extended a large palm. After a brief hesitation, Rosalind took it. What could it hurt after all? It was a crazy, wonderful night filled with crazy wonderful feelings.

Dinner was a hearty affair, filled with multiple helpings of an assortment of foods. Rosalind, who had a particular fondness for seafood, gorged on lobster tail, scallops, sweet crabmeat, and a particularly delicious smoked salmon.

Every so often, Sam would reach forward to sample the various niceties on her plate. But Rosalind was truly impressed by the sheer size of his appetite. In between swallowing mussels, scallops, and any of a number of other offerings, he somehow also managed to polish off two plates of fried rice, orange chicken, and a rather large helping of beef and broccoli.

When the waitress came to ask, "Would you like dessert?" Rosalind put both hands on her stomach and said with a genuine groan, "No thanks. I don't think I'll ever be able to eat anything ever again."

Sam, however, accepted a large slice of chocolate cake and tried in vain to convince Rosalind to try a piece.

After dinner, they went back to the suite to freshen up, and then Renard, who had anticipated their return, and had pressed and hung a suitable change of clothes for them both, called for the car, and waved them off with "It's going to be a wonderful show."

And it was. Rosalind sat through the entire performance as though spellbound, and Sam watched her with glowing eyes. She sang along with the audience when Ray Charles belted out his famous, "Hit the Road, Jack" And she became emotional near the end of the show when her favorite song, "I Can't Stop Loving You," was sung in that certain, completely soulful Ray Charles way.

Rosalind was the first person on her feet when the final curtain came down, bellowing along with hundreds of others, "More. More."

And when Ray came back out again, and sat to play "America the Beautiful" at his superb pristine white piano, there wasn't a dry eye in the house.

On the way back to the hotel, Rosalind looked across at Sam, and in a weepy way said, "I love Ray Charles."

He reached across to stroke a wisp of hair from her cheek, and said, "I know. I remember."

For perhaps the very first time, she looked with completely different eyes at the man seated beside her. She wondered about him, about his life. Wondered if he was happy. Wondered why it was he didn't have a woman in his life. She had always discounted his masculine beauty before. But there was no question about it. He was good-looking. In fact, he was very good-looking. Why had she never really paid attention to him before? There was a kind generosity in his eyes. And this was something that she knew could not be feigned even by a really good actor.

She turned pensive eyes toward the brightly lit Strip, not really seeing all of the many multicolored lights. She had to think of a way to help him. She had a small circle of friends, and most of her really close girlfriends were now married, or were soon to be. But there had to be someone. Someone she could set him up with.

She turned to look at him again and gave him a little smile. He was turning out to be such a nice man. And, incredibly, she was finding herself drawn to him, despite his atheism.

"Why're you so quiet?" His deep voice seemed to reverberate in the plush enclosure, and strangely the hairs on her arms stood at rigid attention and seemed to pulse with the sound of it.

"Oh, I always get really thoughtful after a great concert."

"Hmm," he said. Then he appeared to change course in an instant. "Are you cold?"

"No," Rosalind said, rubbing self-consciously at the raised gooseflesh on her arms. Goodness, but he had good eyesight.

She was saved the necessity of saying more by the car pulling to a smooth stop before the hotel. Sam helped her from the soft leather seats, and in next to no time at all, they were in their private elevator on the way up to the suite. Renard met them in the foyer with two long glasses of champagne.

"Did you enjoy the show?" he asked.

"It was the best performance I've ever seen," Rosalind said, accepting her glass of sparkling bubbly. "Thank you so much for arranging things for us. We had really great seats, too. Right up front."

Renard smiled. "I'm glad you enjoyed yourselves." Then to Sam, he said, "Mr. Winter, I've turned down the bed, and placed your shaving utensils in the large bathroom. What time should I wake you in the morning?"

"I'll be up. So don't trouble yourself," Sam said, and he rubbed a hand across his eyes. Rosalind felt a twinge of pity that she fought hard to suppress. He seemed so tired. Exhausted, really. The circles she had noticed earlier seemed to have deepened and darkened over the past several hours.

"Unless you need me for anything else, I'll say good night, then?"

Rosalind nodded. "Good night, Renard, and thanks again."

The butler nodded gravely, and said, "Thank you, madam. I'll be in again at about six in the morning."

Rosalind followed Sam across to the master bedroom suite. She was no longer at all worried about sleeping in the same suite as he. She was more concerned about the fact that unless she did something about it, Sam faced another essentially sleepless night.

"Sammy," she said, as he walked toward the connecting door, "Let me turn down the bed for you in the other room."

He turned, and looked at her with an expression of surprise in his eyes. "Don't bother. You must be tired."

"Don't argue with me," Rosalind said briskly. "You're the one who's tired."

He smiled at her in a slow, considering manner. "Okay. If you want to do it, I'm not going to resist you."

"Go on then," Rosalind said. "I'll be in after I change. And"—she said after a moment's pause—"tonight you're going to get a full night's sleep."

"Ha," he laughed. "Impossible."

Rosalind went into the bathroom, quickly brushed the tangles from her hair, and then changed into a pair of black leggings and an oversize white T-shirt. She slid into sturdy brown leather slippers, and then went into the kitchen to warm some milk. She did this after a few moments spent hunting for a carton of low-fat milk, the kind she knew Sam liked. Finding none, she settled on skim milk. In less than ten minutes, she was padding again in the direction of the master suite. She gave the large bed in the main room a guilty glance as she passed. She knew she should really have given Sam this one and taken the smaller bed in the other room. He was, after all, much larger than she.

She paused at the slightly ajar door and knocked softly. "Sam?" She could hear him moving around inside, so she stuck her head around the door and called again, "Sammy?"

"Bathroom," he said.

Rosalind pushed the door a little wider. "Can I come in?"

"Of course."

She entered, looking around for a place to rest the steaming mug of milk. She decided on the bedside table. He emerged almost as soon as she had rested the drink securely on the little wooden table. He was bare to the waist, dressed only in a pair of black cotton pajama bottoms.

Rosalind's eyes flickered over him. Suddenly, she was noticing everything about him now. The thick pelt of black hair that grew profusely across the wide expanse of his chest, and then tapered in the most incredible way to a fine silky line that plunged beneath the waistline of his pants. The long muscular sweep of his arms. The tight, trim waist. The blacker-than-night eyes that were looking at her now with a completely indecipherable expression.

"You brought me something to drink?"

"Milk," she said with a tentative smile. "Warm milk. It always helps me sleep."

He came across to the bed, and she peeled back the covers so that he might slide in. When he was comfortably settled, she handed him the mug.

"Drink it all," she said.

"Yes, nurse," he said.

He took the mug, sipped, grimaced, and then drank it all in one continuous swallow. When he was through, he wiped his mouth with the back of a hand and handed the empty mug back.

"I really don't think this is going to work."

Rosalind shook her head at him. "Don't be so negative. What kind of music do you like?"

"Any kind," he said.

She walked across to the compact stereo nestled in one corner of the room and knelt before it. There was quite a wide selection. There were the standards like Nat King Cole, Brook Benton, and Frank Sinatra. There were also several volumes of classical and Baroque music, and an interesting variety of contemporary hits from the seventies to present day.

She flipped through the CDs, then turned to ask, "How about some Nat King Cole?"

"Fine," he said.

"Come on, Sammy," Rosalind said coaxingly. "Keep an open mind. I have a feeling you're going to fight the sleep, even if you begin to get heavy-eyed."

He looked at her without comment for a moment, and Rosalind had to admit that he did look extremely wide-awake. But she wasn't nearly finished with him yet.

"It's going to take much more than a mug of milk and some music to break the back of this insomnia. I've had it for a long while."

Rosalind slid the CD in, then turned the melodic music down low.

"Now for the lights," she said with a perky smile. And she went about the room lowering them.

When she was through, and a soft sleepy mood hung over the room, he said, "I don't think it's working."

"It'll work," she said with a certain determination

in her voice. She kicked off her slippers and ordered,
"Move over."

She caught the flash of surprise in his eyes and said,
"Don't get any ideas."

"Oh, I never would."

She slid beneath the covers. "Now relax."

He flexed his shoulders, and despite her every effort
to prevent it, Rosalind felt an electric twinge in her
groin.

"Are you going to spend the entire night here?"

"I don't think it's going to take me that long to get
you to sleep."

He chuckled. "You're that confident then?"

"I am," she said. "Come here." And she extended
her arms.

He moved toward her in a cautious way, as though
he were afraid he might startle her into changing her
mind.

"You're going to lie in my arms, and you're going
to go to sleep . . . okay?"

"Wow," he said huskily. "Now what did I do to deserve this?"

"Be quiet," she admonished as he moved his head
onto the pillow directly beside her. "Now rest your head
against me so I can put my arms around you. . . ."

"Are you sure you can take my weight?"

"Come on now . . . I have a feeling you don't want
to go to sleep for some reason."

"Okay, young lady. But don't say I didn't warn you."

He shifted again so that his head was now nestled
just beneath her chin.

"Like that?"

Rosalind stuck her arms beneath his and pulled
without any success. "Move up a bit more," she said.

"I'm going to squash you."

"Let me worry about that." She shifted his head so

that she was now able to rest the side of her face against his. "Okay. That's perfect." She wrapped her arms about him and felt him tense. "Relax," she said again. "Now close your eyes."

"Are you sure I'm supposed to feel like sleeping?" he asked after a moment. "A beautiful woman in my bed . . . Sleep is really the last thing on my mind right now."

"Shh," Rosalind said. "Just trust me." She removed her arms from about him, and slowly, softly, began to massage his temples.

"Mmm," he muttered. "That feels really good."

Rosalind's fingers did not pause in their movement for even a second, but she bent to his ear to ask, "Sammy . . . ?"

"Mmm?"

She could tell he was beginning to get sleepy. His voice had thickened by several measures in the last little while.

"Why don't you have a girlfriend?"

His eyes popped open and Rosalind whispered against his temple, "Close them."

"So . . . why don't you?" she repeated.

"I'm too busy for that," he said after a momentary hesitation.

"Hmm," Rosalind said, considering his reply. "I don't believe that for a second."

"No?"

His eyes were open again, and Rosalind resorted to pinching him in the side to which he grunted, "You little vixen."

"Keep them closed and you'll suffer no pain whatsoever."

"That's what you think," he said beneath his breath.

"What was that?"

"Nothing. Never mind."

"Anyway," Rosalind continued, "as I was saying, I really think you should think about making time in your busy life for a woman. Someone nice. Someone who can really do all that it takes to make you sleep . . . whenever you can't."

"All that it takes?" He didn't open his eyes this time, but it was obvious that he was struggling against the urge to do so.

"You know what I mean. . . ."

"No. I'm afraid I'm a little slow. Tell me."

Rosalind shifted her position a bit, considered her words carefully, and then took the bull by the horns and decided that the best way was to just come right out and say it.

"You know that—that sex is good for getting anyone to sleep."

His eyes were definitely open now, and he shifted to regard her with eyes that had gone the most impossible shade of black.

"Sex . . . with you?"

Rosalind held onto the wave of embarrassment that threatened to swallow her whole. But she knew that he wasn't really to blame for the misunderstanding. It had been a very provocative thing to say, after all. But she had to get him to see that the manner in which he was living was unhealthy and unnatural. And probably largely responsible for the insomnia which she now had.

"I mean . . . with someone else. You don't want to . . . with me."

He turned his head and snuggled into the crook of her neck. "I don't?"

"No."

He sighed against her skin, and a wave of heat ran from the tips of her toes all the way to the crown of her head. She gritted her teeth and fought against the feeling. It was probably that she was missing Ben too much. It had been such a very long time since she had held him in this very manner. Her hormones had been neglected for far too long.

"You have someone in mind for me, I guess?"

His voice brought her back to the situation at hand.

"I might," Rosalind said cautiously.

"Hmm," he said. "Does she look like you?"

Rosalind's brow wrinkled. She had almost forgotten his preference for big-boned women.

"If you mean does she look horsey . . . then the answer is no."

"Horsey?" He appeared genuinely puzzled. "What do you mean, 'horsey'?"

"I know you prefer women who are of a certain physical type."

"You know what I like?"

"Some." *Strong horselike women with big butts, to be exact.*

He cuddled into her neck again. "This is very interesting. Go on."

A little chuckle bubbled out of her despite her every attempt to squash it. "You're just having fun with me, I know. But trust me, I know what I'm talking about. What you need is a woman. That's why you can't sleep."

He wrapped a long arm around her and said huskily, "It's more comfortable this way. In fact, I may not be able to sleep any other way ever again."

"Sammy . . . you're not paying any attention to me at all, are you?"

"About the women?"

She sighed. He was such a difficult nut to crack. "Not necessarily a whole pack of them . . . just one. Someone who cares about you."

"You care about me . . . don't you?"

"Yes. Yes, of course. But what I'm talking about, I can't do for you."

He seemed to get even closer to her, so close that she could actually feel the movement of his lips against her skin.

"Why can't you do it?"

It was her turn to sigh. "You know why not. I'm engaged."

He shifted so that he was now propped on the pillows looking down at her. "Engagements have been broken before. Especially if either party discovers that maybe they're about to make a horrible mistake."

She pushed the hair from her eyes. "I don't think I'm about to make a horrible mistake. I don't know why you would say that."

"Okay," he said. "Forget I said anything. Can I?" And he moved back into her arms. "I'm not sleepy yet."

"At this rate," Rosalind said, "I'll be asleep long before you. Come on. No more talking now."

She stroked the side of his face in a slow rhythmic way, and after several silent minutes, she heard his breathing thicken, and looked down at his face cautiously. Had he fallen asleep so suddenly? Or was he faking it?

Rosalind continued stroking his face, and watched him for any signs of wakefulness. But it would appear that he was really asleep. She tried shifting, but he was so completely wrapped about her that she couldn't possibly move without waking him. She stole a glance at her watch. It was just after midnight. She would stay with him until four. That way she would be sure that he had gotten at least that much sleep.

She shifted carefully so that she wouldn't disturb him, and then settled in to wait out the hours.

Ten

Eight o'clock? Rosalind stared in confusion at her watch. How could it be eight? She had only closed her eyes for a moment. She looked down at Sam and experienced a moment of panic. Why was he so very still? Had he stopped breathing?

She stuck her hand beneath his nose and released a relieved sigh. He was still alive. And apparently still very soundly asleep. She tried shifting away from him, and he muttered something unintelligible and pulled her back. Her brow furrowed. Well, it would seem that her sleep techniques had been a little too effective. But at least he had had a good night's sleep; four hours at the barest minimum. She had managed to stay up until then, and during that period of time, he had not stirred.

She watched him sleep for another half an hour, and then made a determined effort to free herself. She hated waking him because she knew how precious and rare this deep sleep was for him, but there was really no other way. She had to get up so that she might begin work on the online presentation, and she could also hear Renard moving around outside the bedroom. She hoped that the butler wouldn't decide to come in with a tray of coffee or some such thing, because although he thought they were man and wife,

Rosalind still felt a trifle guilty at being found in Sam Winter's bed.

"Sammy?" she said softly.

He moved closer to her and plunged a hand into the depths of her hair. Rosalind stroked the grizzle of new growth on his chin.

"Sammy . . . wake up."

He muttered again. Something that sounded very much like "Rosy . . . don't leave me."

"You're dreaming, Sam," Rosalind said. "Come on . . . it's time to wake up."

This time his words were distinct, and as clear as they would've been had he been completely awake. "An hour more. I need an hour more."

Rosalind sighed. Okay, she'd let him have an hour more of sleep. But why in the world couldn't he get that hour without being wrapped all around her like a large octopus? She cuddled him close again, and he sighed and settled back into full-blown sleep.

She closed her eyes, only for a second. But when she opened them again, it was to find that a pair of glittering fully refreshed black eyes was observing her.

"Good morning," he said in a manner that smacked of a strange happiness.

Rosalind blinked at him. Had she fallen off to sleep again? She glanced at her watch and sat up with a desperate "Oh, no. I tried to wake you three hours ago. But you wouldn't wake up."

He rubbed her cheek with the back of a gritty index finger. "What you did last night . . . is simply the kindest thing anyone has ever done for me. Thank you."

Hot blood rushed to Rosalind's cheeks, and he saw the heightened color and smiled.

"Did you sleep well?"

He wrapped a curl of hair about a finger and caressed its silky texture. "It's the best night of sleep

I've ever had. You've spoiled me now. I'm going to want to fall asleep every single night like that . . . from now on."

She smiled at him. What a nice thing to say, even if he didn't really mean it. Strangely she didn't feel much like getting up now. There was something peaceful and right about just lying there beside him.

"You need a shave," she said. And without conscious thought, she reached a hand to touch the new growth of hair on his chin. He lifted a hand to hers and pressed a kiss to the center of her palm. "I need many things." And with that cryptic comment he climbed from bed.

Rosalind stared thoughtfully at the strong lean lines of his back as he walked toward his bathroom, before deciding rather reluctantly that she had better get out of bed, too.

She took a quick shower and thought for just a moment about Ben. She knew that he would be finishing up work in the E.R. and then getting ready to go on rounds. Somewhere between the end of his E.R. stint and the beginning of his official duties as a surgeon, he would find the time to snatch a bite to eat. Eggs, toast, and coffee. He never varied from this routine. It was always eggs, toast, and coffee.

She brushed her hair vigorously, staring grimly at herself in the mirror. She was almost completely certain that Ben had not spared her even a moment's thought since she had last spoken to him. He hadn't even taken the time to ask her where it was she would be staying. He'd been more concerned about getting back to the E.R. Not that she didn't understand that his work was important and that his patients needed him. But wasn't she important, too? Wasn't he worried about her at all? For all he knew and cared, she might not even have arrived in Las Vegas safely. He hadn't asked her to call him once she got to her hotel, either.

"Rosy?"

Rosalind turned from her stern contemplation of herself.

"I'm in the bathroom," she said, and hustled to finish her hair before he decided to come in search of her.

"Feel like going to the spa today?"

She put the brush down on the side of the sink, smoothed her white T-shirt over her jeans, and bellowed at him. "The spa?"

She heard him approach the door. "Can I come in?"

Rosalind slid into her white sandals, and said, "Sure, I'm decent."

The door pushed open, and Rosalind stood firmly on the unexpected rush of pleasure she felt at seeing him standing there in the doorway, so tall and lean in his hip-hugging jeans and loose black cotton shirt.

"There's a nice spa in the hotel. Why don't you go down and see? Maybe you might want to do . . . whatever it is you women do when you get there."

She met his black eyes with a puzzled look in hers. "But I have to start work on the online presentation . . . don't I?"

He shrugged. "The L.A. team gets here tomorrow, so you can have another day of doing absolutely nothing or whatever it is you think you might want to do."

"Well . . . okay," she said uncertainly. "But what are you going to do while I'm having a pampered time at the spa?"

"Maybe I'll do something about finding that woman you were telling me about last night."

Rosalind's throat went dry. "What?" she almost croaked. Had he misunderstood her? She certainly hadn't meant that he should go out right then and pick someone up. He was a very wealthy man after all, and he had to be careful about who he associated with. There were women, maybe even many women, who would take advantage of him.

"Don't you remember what we were talking about last night?"

"Yes, but I didn't think you'd rush right out and do it today."

He came into the bathroom and stood looking down at her. "Well, as they say . . . there's no time like the present. This upcoming meeting is extremely important to the future of the company, so I need to get a good night's sleep for the entire time I'm here. Now that I know what the solution to my insomnia is . . . it would be irresponsible of me not to do something about it."

Rosalind drew a tight breath. Was he seriously thinking of bringing some strange woman into their suite?

"I really don't think it a good idea if you rush out and get just any woman . . . just so you can sleep through the night."

"I'll choose a nice one."

"I know," she said with the beginnings of a frown between her eyes. "A big-boned horse of a woman."

His chest moved in a silent chuckle. "What is with you with these horses and bones? This is the second or third time you've mentioned them."

Rosalind pursed her lips and gave him a considering glance. So he thought it was funny, did he? Well, he would have no success at all picking up any kind of woman if he intended to woo them gently with his talk of big horse-boned gals.

"I think you'd better focus on your presentation and leave the selection of hordes of women until later."

He raised thick eyebrows at her. "But what about my sleep? I really need to get more of that."

She knew what he was up to, of course. This was his way of asking her to sleep in his bed for the entire time they were in Las Vegas. Maybe her talk of women, sex, and sleep had triggered the wrong set of impulses in him.

"You'll be fine . . . on your own."

He laughed. "Okay . . . let's have breakfast, and then we'll sort out the itinerary for the rest of the day."

When they both emerged from the master suite, Renard greeted them with a bright "Good morning. I hope you slept well."

Rosalind smiled at the man as he led them to a nicely laid table in the breakfast nook, pulled out her chair, and neatly arranged a linen napkin in her lap. He handed Sam a copy of the *Wall Street Journal*, adjusted the slanting blinds so that the bright noonday sunshine would not slant directly across the table.

"I had a look at your meal preferences, and took the liberty of preparing an assortment of dollar-sized strawberry pancakes, waffles, and Italian sausages. But first we will start with a delicious iced fruit purée."

Renard busied himself for the next little while, pouring coffee and milk, laying down stacks of nicely buttered golden brown toast, and soft, slightly sweet, oven-warmed rolls. And despite Rosalind's every effort to prevent it, a small measure of contentment stole into a corner of her heart. It wasn't the first-class service that was getting to her. It was something else, something deeper, something decidedly more profound. She met Sam's eyes across the table, then looked hurriedly down at the half-buttered roll in her hand. She bit blindly into the bread and chewed for much longer than was necessary with her eyes fixed almost rigidly on her plate. If she didn't get a grip on herself soon, he would begin to suspect that her opinion of him had gone through a radical change in the last few days.

She ate her fruit purée with a delicate filigree silver teaspoon and thanked Renard nicely for the wonderful strawberry pancakes, and sausages.

Sam stole a glance at her from time to time from behind his newspaper, and what he observed caused him to hope just a little bit.

Near the end of the meal, Sam removed a platinum Visa card from his top shirt pocket and asked, "Did you bring any of the cards I gave you? Or do you need this?"

Rosalind finished the last swallow remaining in her glass of ice-cold apple juice before managing to croak incredulously, "Your platinum card? You want me to use that for the spa?"

He shrugged. "Only if you didn't bring any of the others."

She met his eyes for an instant. She had never known him to be this generous. He was definitely up to something. Of that much, she was completely certain. But what that something was, she was still unclear about. Her brow knitted. Maybe he was hoping to bribe her into having sex with him, since she was the most available female at hand.

"I don't think I'll need it." She patted the corners of her mouth with the linen napkin. "Maybe you should come to the spa, too."

He folded the newspaper in his hands and laid it beside his plate. "I'd be bored out of my skull. Spas are definitely not for me."

"You could get a massage or something like that."

He smiled at her. "I'm only interested in your massages," he said with a bright glitter in his eyes. And in that instant Rosalind knew that her newly formed suspicion was correct. He *was* planning to talk her into sleeping with him. There was no doubt in her mind about it now. She would have to think very carefully on how it was she would handle this new development. One good night of sleep, and he was as randy as a goat. God only knew what he would be like if he managed to sleep consistently well.

She stood. "Well, I'll head off downstairs for a few hours, then." She glanced at her watch. "I'll come back up around three."

"Take all day if you like. I won't need you. One of the lead Web page designers from L.A. is actually getting here a bit early. So I'll go get her from the airport . . . and then we'll probably spend the day catching up."

Her? Rosalind's brow wrinkled. So *that* was it. He hadn't been buttering her up with the devious intention of getting her into bed. He had really been trying to get rid of her by sending her off for a day of pampering at the spa. He wanted her out of the way so that he could spend hours of uninterrupted time with this woman from L.A. No wonder he hadn't been too concerned when she had suggested just the night before that he find himself a girlfriend. He already had one. But why hide it? Unless this woman he was carrying on with was herself married.

"Okay, then," she said. But there was a note of pique in her voice. She left him sitting at the shiny polished oak table and went quickly into the bedroom to collect a change of clothes and a pair of soft slippers.

Renard was clearing the table when she emerged again, and Sam had disappeared. Her brief glance about that part of the suite conveyed her confusion.

"Mr. Winter's in the first-floor library," Renard said.

And Rosalind was barely able to stifle the automatic denial that sprang to her lips.

"I'll go down and say good-bye to him before I leave."

Renard nodded. He understood the ways of newly-weds. "Will you require a snack after the spa?"

"Oh, I don't think so," Rosalind said before turning in the direction of the curving spiral staircase that led to the lower floor.

She hadn't really explored the lower level at all. There really hadn't been enough time since their arrival. She walked through the sunken sitting room with its soft white leather chairs and cushy thick pile carpeting. She nodded at no one in particular. Yes, it was really a beautiful suite. The design effects were impeccable. The absolutely perfect blend of whites and mauves and pastels was completely restful. It was the kind of suite that would be ideal for a honeymoon. *A real one.*

She knocked on a closed wood panel door, and turned the golden knob when she heard him call, "Come in."

He was on the phone, and she was about to turn around and leave him to his call, but he beckoned her in. "I'll be finished with this in a minute. Don't go."

Rosalind listened to him with one ear while wandering about the little library. It was stocked to the brim with books. All kinds. She paused before one of the bookcases and pulled a beautifully bound first edition of Richard Wright's *Black Boy* from the shelves. She turned it over in her hands, examining the smooth gilt-tipped pages and the deliberately gritty black leather cover. Richard Wright was one of her favorite authors, and *Black Boy* was probably one of the most gripping, disturbing, yet superbly written books she had ever read.

She turned to the first page and savored the first lyrical line of prose. It had been years since she had last read the book, but just as she had been the very first time, the skillfully woven words sucked her in, taking her immediately to the horror and desperation of Richard Wright's childhood. She was so deeply engrossed in the story that she actually jumped at the deep voice directly behind her.

She turned with the book in hand. "I'm sorry," she said. "What did you say?"

"I was saying that I had no idea you were a Richard Wright fan. He's one of my favorite authors. *Black Boy, Native Son, Twelve Million Black Voices* . . . they're all works of genius."

"Yes," Rosalind agreed gravely. "Great genius born of great suffering."

"We have a lot in common. Have you noticed that?"

Rosalind returned the book to its spot on the shelf and took a moment to adjust it neatly. She didn't want to think about how many things she and Sam seemed to have in common. Didn't want to think of the many things she and Ben seemed not to. As the days drifted by, she was finding that her life was getting more and more confusing. Things that had once seemed so clear, so easy to understand, now were not. And people she thought she knew were turning out to be entirely different. It was all too confusing.

"I just wanted to tell you I was leaving."

"Umm," he said. "After you finish up at the spa . . . maybe you might be interested in an afternoon of shopping."

Rosalind's jaw tightened. He really didn't have to be so absolutely obvious about it. She knew fully well that he didn't want her around. That he wanted to spend an uninterrupted afternoon with the woman from L.A. But there was no need to go overboard with spas and shopping.

"I don't think I'll feel much like doing any shopping once I finish downstairs. I'll probably want to take a nap," she said, and looked at him pointedly. If he were planning on spending the day in bed with his L.A. woman, he would just have to take her elsewhere.

"This must be a first." Sam smiled. "A woman turning down an all-expenses-paid afternoon of shopping." He paused, then continued. "Did I mention that you'd be free to purchase outfits from any of the top designers . . . ?"

"You know," Rosalind finally burst out, her eyes beginning to flash a little, "if you don't want me around at any point in time, all you have to do is say so. There's no need to come up with all kinds of inventive ways to get me out of the picture "

Pleased surprise shone brightly for a brief instant in his eyes.

Was she jealous? "I wasn't trying to get rid of you," he said with a carefully hooded expression. "I thought you might like to buy a little something to wear to the buyers' party on Saturday."

Rosalind's eyebrows rose. This was the first time she was hearing anything about a buyers' party. He was forever springing surprises on her.

"I wish you would tell me about these things well in advance instead of just a few days before the event," she said snappily.

"It just slipped my mind. I've been a bit overtired."

Rosalind made a determined effort to hold on to her temper. She didn't know why she was suddenly so angry with him. He had simply forgotten to tell her about a social engagement. He hadn't committed a crime, for goodness' sake. She was really becoming a cantankerous nag.

She had the grace to give him a rather shamefaced apology. "I'm sorry. It's my job to keep track of your many engagements, and I haven't been doing that." Her eyes said *forgive me*, and Sam stroked a large thumb across his lips in a thoughtful manner, but made no move toward her.

"Well, you'd better be off to the spa then. I'll have Renard save lunch for you."

He watched her, with the beginnings of a smile playing around his mouth. She was trembling on the brink. Just a little more, and she would be his. All his.

Eleven

When Rosalind returned from the spa, the first thing that greeted her on stepping from the elevator was the sound of well-modulated, distinctly female laughter. The tensions that had been massaged and soaked away in the superb European spa returned now in full force to settle just between her brows. She stood for a moment listening to the silvery sound of the other woman's voice. They were obviously in the library. She stood there uncertainly, and then decided that she would go and change first before going to see who this person was.

She went into the master suite, closed and locked the door, then went to the closet to choose something suitably flattering. She removed the little burgundy dress with the elegantly drooping back. It was a bit on the dressy side, but who would notice anyway? Certainly not Sam, now that he had brought his little piece of fluff in from L.A.

She spent an equal amount of time considering the shoes she would wear. *Open-toed? Closed? High heels? Flats? Suede? Leather?*

Rosalind finally settled on a matching burgundy pair with impossibly high translucent heels. In the bathroom, she gave her long smooth cinnamon legs a critical examination. For the past three hours, she had been massaged, wrapped, steamed, shaved, and plucked. Her skin was now as smooth and soft as a newborn's. And her legs looked particularly good, with or without stockings.

She stripped down hastily, and then wiggled her way into the dress. It was a stretchy kind, so it clung to her curves in the most pleasing way. She was of two minds whether or not to use any perfume. She didn't want the other woman to think that she was competing with her for Sam's attention, because she was most certainly not. She had no romantic interest in him whatsoever. He was simply her employer, and she had to make a good impression since she was supposed to be his executive assistant or some such thing.

She slid into the heels. Then she pressed a dab of fragrance to her temples and wrists. Her hair was softly wavy, and bounced healthily about her shoulders, but she still spent a bit of time brushing some more body into the glistening blue-black waves. When she was through, she ran a soft kohl eyeliner around the lower lid of her eye, and then stroked a matching shade of lipstick across her lips.

Rosalind gave herself another very critical inspection in the long floor-to-ceiling mirrors. Her brows furrowed. She had gained a bit of weight in the past few days, but maybe only she could really tell.

"I'll be back in a minute." *Sam's voice.* She stood quiet for a moment, listening to him. She strained her ears to hear what he was saying, and then almost jumped out of her skin when the door to the suite was tried and then rattled.

"Rosalind?"

"Coming."

She walked briskly across the stretch of carpeting, unlocked the door, and stood a bit uncertainly in the threshold. His eyes flickered quickly over her, and she felt sure that a gleam of amusement brightened them for just a moment.

"I thought I heard you come back. Had a good time?"

She stood back, allowing him to enter and shut the door. "It was relaxing. Thanks for giving me the opportunity to—to experience that."

"So formal." He smiled. "Is this the woman whose arms I slept so soundly in just last night?"

She met his eyes directly. "Well, you needed your sleep. I'm glad I helped . . . in some small way." She had never noticed before what nice eyes he had. Superbly black and smooth. Kind, too. Why had she not noticed that before now? Ben's eyes were just eyes. They were not particularly kind or unkind. They were just there somehow.

"Well," he said, looking down at her, "the rest of the L.A. team should be here by late tonight." He leaned back against the door. "Sue Perkins will be joining us for dinner. You two can catch up on all of the technical stuff."

"Is that . . . person out there Sue Perkins?"

He straightened. "She is, and actually, I've been wondering if it mightn't make more sense to have you two share this suite and—"

"What . . . ?" Rosalind interrupted. She had just gotten used to the idea of sharing the suite with him, and now he wanted to foist some strange woman on her, too? "What do you mean by have her 'share this suite . . . '? Do you mean you want to cram all three of us in here?" Was he completely out of his gourd?

Sam gave her a slitted-eye look. "You disagree with this plan?"

Without conscious thought, Rosalind's hands moved to rest on her hips. "Look, if you want to move that woman in here . . . go ahead and do it. But I certainly won't be a part of it."

Sam held onto a deep chuckle, and asked with exaggerated innocence, "But isn't it the most convenient solution to the working late-into-the-night problem?"

"Maybe you'd prefer it if I just moved into a totally different room? That might be even more convenient for you."

Sam's eyes gleamed. He hadn't expected this to happen so quickly. But there was no doubt about it. She was jealous. Hopping mad, and jealous of Sue Perkins whom he had absolutely no interest in.

"What would you suggest then? I was sure you felt uncomfortable staying here all alone with me. I was thinking of you . . . and of course, her."

"Of course," Rosalind muttered. And for the life of her, she couldn't understand why it was she was feeling so put out by the thought of the other woman staying in the suite with them.

Sam opened his arms and said in a very gentle manner, "Come here, Rosy." He didn't like teasing her in this manner. That she should still be uncertain of him, after all of this time was incredible.

"Come where?" She looked at him with suspicious eyes, not sure what he was up to now.

"I haven't had my contractual kiss today . . . and I'm a day behind on my massage therapy."

Rosalind did all she could to hold on to the chuckle brewing in her chest. But it was out before she could prevent it. "You know," she said with twinkling eyes, "I really think there's something seriously wrong with you."

He took her hand and pulled her toward him. "We'll discuss that later. . . . Now I want that kiss you promised me."

He tilted her chin up with a sturdy finger. "You

have the most beautiful lips I've ever seen," he muttered in a low undertone. Hot blood slashed red lines across her cheekbones, and Rosalind tried desperately to think of her fiancé as Sam's lips settled warmly on hers. Her breath sighed sweetly into his mouth. Maybe she'd been looking forward to this all day. Maybe she was losing her mind. But Ben had never ever been able to make her feel so much. So very much.

Her fingers went up to stroke the back of his neck, and Sam growled in a manner that caused a shiver of electricity to skitter across every hair follicle on her body. She was caught in a deep fog, a thick mist of pure feeling, which she couldn't get out of, which she didn't want to get out of.

"Sammy . . ." His name drifted from her lips in a broken moan.

He bit the full flesh of her lower lip in a manner that was deeply satisfying, and then gently stroked the exact spot with the flat of his tongue.

"Rosy. . . ."

His gritty voice pulled her back from the precipice and slowly, reluctantly, she opened her eyes. God, what was happening to her? This madness. This intense feeling that swept over her whenever he held her. It wasn't like this with Ben; it had never been like this.

She turned her face from him, her eyes troubled, conflicted. But his fingers found her chin, and she was forced to look at him again.

"Would it be so bad?" His voice drifted over her in a strangely disjointed manner, and her heart pounded with a mixture of trepidation and excitement. She knew his meaning. Maybe some deeper part of her had always known. Whatever his reasons, he seemed to want her.

"We—we can't," she managed after a momentary struggle to get the words past her lips.

"Why not?"

Rosalind attempted to pull herself away from him, but his arms about her were like twin bands of steel.

"You know why not."

His thumb traced the tender flesh of her lower lip and Rosalind did her best to remain unmoved by the soft caress.

"If I had a fiancée like you, do you think I would let her go off to Las Vegas with another man . . . employer or not?"

Sudden unexpected tears pricked at the backs of Rosalind's eyes. She had been wrestling with these very questions since she had left New Jersey. And she didn't like what some deeper part of her had been suggesting for a good long while now. Ben didn't care. He didn't care if she went off with one man or a whole pack of them. She just wasn't important to him. And maybe would never be.

"He doesn't love you, Rosy . . . not like—" But whatever he was about to say was interrupted by a soft tap on the door and a nicely modulated voice asking, "Sam? You okay in there?"

Rosalind stepped back from him immediately, but not before Sam said, "We'll talk about this later. . . ."

He pulled open the door, and Rosalind got her first look at the other woman. She was tall, as tall as she was herself, and, she was *drop-dead gorgeous*. There was just no other way to put it. High, beautifully sculpted cheekbones, an elegant Ethiopian nose, a full mouth that seemed to have been designed with just one purpose in mind. A medium-long bob of blue-black hair.

A slight furrow rippled like quicksilver across Rosalind's brow. The only thing that really detracted from the other woman's attractiveness was that she was perhaps a little on the bony side. Sam, she knew, liked women who had a little flesh on their bones.

"Oh, I'm sorry." Sue Perkins appeared genuinely startled to find another woman in Sam's private suite. "I didn't realize you had . . . company." And her voice petered out.

"Rosalind isn't company," Sam said in such a quick manner that a flash of anger heated Rosalind's eyes. She *was* his employee, but did he have to introduce her in such a way, especially after what had just passed between them?

Sue's eyes flickered over her in a manner that told Rosalind that she regarded her as a rival.

"You look sort of familiar," Sue began, and again Sam responded before she could even open her mouth.

"Rosalind used to work out of the L.A. office as one of our lead Web designers . . . years ago. Maybe you remember her from there."

Sue nodded. "Maybe that's it. Well," she said, extending a softly manicured hand, "nice to meet you."

Rosalind took the hand and shook it briefly. There was something about the other woman that irked her. She couldn't put her finger on exactly what it was, but she knew without question that this kind of woman would not be right for Sam. She would be interested in him only for as long as he remained wealthy.

"Well, I'll leave you two to get acquainted. I have a few calls to make." They both watched him disappear down the curving staircase, and there was a moment of uncomfortable silence as Rosalind tried to think of something to say to the other woman.

They both started speaking at the same time, and inherent courtesy made Rosalind say, "No . . . go ahead, please."

Sue smiled. "I was just saying that somehow Sam's never mentioned you before."

"I haven't worked for him in years. Not since L.A."

Sue nodded. "Well, that's good," she said, and then in a conspiratorial manner, she whispered, "Let's go across to the first sitting room. There's something I'd like to talk to you about."

Rosalind followed her through the dining room, and into the plushly furnished sitting area. Sue chose a soft love seat and patted the cushion beside her.

"Come and sit here," she said in a way that suggested Rosalind was the one who was the guest. Rosalind deliberately ignored the command and chose a small soft chair directly opposite.

"I guess you must be wondering about the online presentation." Rosalind began.

Sue laughed. "Oh, no," she said. "I already know all about that. What I want to talk to you about is . . . Sam."

Rosalind's eyebrows flicked upward. "Sam?"

Sue leaned forward. "Yes. Sam. I want to be clear on things. I don't know who you are, or what your relationship with Sam Winter is. But whatever it is, I think you should understand that it's going to end right here, right now."

The attack was launched with such velvety smoothness that for half a second Rosalind wondered if she had really heard the other woman correctly.

"Excuse me?" Rosalind said, and the beginnings of ire resonated in her voice.

"I think we understand each other," Sue said, without missing a single beat. "Sam Winter and I have had a long-term relationship over the past four years. But it's been a very volatile sort of thing. Fights. Lots of them. I wanted him back in L.A., and he would always refuse." She broke off to light a cigarette, and Rosalind watched her with a churning mind as she fiddled with the cigarette and then exhaled an acrid cloud of blue smoke. *Sam and this woman?* She couldn't believe it.

"I'm sure," Sue continued now with slitted eyes, "I'm sure you've noticed the strange resemblance between us."

Rosalind gritted her teeth. There was no resemblance whatsoever as far as she was concerned. The only thing that could perhaps be said was that they were both what Sam would probably describe as "big-boned gals." A reluctant smile curled Rosalind's lips. *This poor woman—does she know anything of Sam's views on women? Or anything else for that matter?*

The little smile playing about Rosalind's mouth seemed to get under Sue's skin for an instant, and her voice hardened a bit around the edges.

"You may think this is over because he's got you installed here in his suite. But take it from me . . . the only reason you're around is because he's temporarily interested in your . . . charms. But that will wear off soon enough." And she swept an arm in a half circle. "I was just trying to save you the ultimate embarrassment of being asked to leave this place. Because believe me, he will. You're no different from any of the—"

"Look," Rosalind interrupted. As far as she was concerned, things had gone far enough. "If you're as close to Sam as you say, I'm sure he'll eventually explain the reasons for my presence here. But let me assure you that since I have no personal interest in him, you have no cause to be concerned." Her eyes were flashing with silvery lights now, a clear sign that she had been roused to great temper. "But"—and she held up a finger—"let me also make it clear that were things different . . . and should I have had any sort of romantic interest in Sam, you for one would not have been able to stand in my way. You'd be no competition for me at all."

Sam, who had been standing just outside the sitting room for the last several minutes, decided that it was the opportune moment to intervene. He stepped into the room just in time to intercept Rosalind as she walked briskly from the room. He reached out to grab a hold of her arm, and said in a low tone that only she could hear, "Wait."

Sue stood, straightened her skirt, and said in a voice that very nearly purred, "Rosalind and I have had a nice little talk about things. I know we're going to be great friends now that we both understand our respective roles."

Rosalind opened her mouth to speak, but Sam's fingers squeezed her arm lightly, and she was just able to prevent the hot words from tumbling from her lips.

Sam's eyes flickered over the other woman in a manner that caused Rosalind to grit her teeth, and she waited with great impatience as he said in a very pleasant manner, "We'll meet you later for dinner. Go get rested . . . have Renard show you where your room is. You'll be sharing with one of the other female designers."

Sue appeared momentarily surprised, but she recovered herself quickly. "That sounds wonderful. It'll be nice to have a long warm shower." She gave him a cat-eyed look. "Where should I make reservations?"

"Renard will take care of that. I'll call you later."

And with that promise ringing in her ears, Rosalind watched Sue Perkins clip her way smartly to where the butler had suddenly materialized and stood waiting.

Twelve

Once the elevator had closed on her, Rosalind turned to Sam with snapping eyes.

"That woman," she said, "thinks that I—that I'm some sort of competition for her." Then she changed direction with a sudden swiftness. "I can't believe you actually had anything to do with her. What is the matter with you? I know she looks good and all that, but I mean . . . can't you see what she's after? What she really wants?"

He shrugged in a nonchalant manner that made Rosalind itch to slap him hard.

"What do you care who I spend my time with?"

But before she could think of an appropriate response to that, he added, "Besides, weren't you telling me just last night that I should get myself a woman?"

"A woman. Not a battle-scarred gold digger, for God's sake," she almost bellowed.

He held up a finger and wagged it at her. "Now don't take the Lord's name in vain. You're always telling me that."

Rosalind drew a filling breath. He had her there. Never had she done that before. But for some unfathomable reason, the thought of Sam with the woman she had just met made her angry enough to throw things.

"You do whatever you like then," she said in a tight little voice. "But don't come crying to me when she's taken you to the cleaners."

He laughed in a husky way that caused the hairs on the back of Rosalind's neck to stand at rigid attention. She yanked her arm from his grasp. "I'm glad you find it funny. I guess since you have more money than you can ever spend in a lifetime, you have no value for it. You'll just let any floozy come in and take it from you."

Sam's eyebrows rose, and he asked in a manner that Rosalind found a trifle too innocent, "So you don't think she qualifies as a possible matrimonial choice?"

"You know what your problem is?" Rosalind bit out. And she charged on before he could say a word. "You've always been way too willing to marry just any"—and she waved a hand wildly—"any woman at all, just so long as she has big bones and an even bigger butt."

Sam's eyes glinted at her. "Big bones . . . and a big butt?" he repeated, and Rosalind knew without question that he was laughing at her again.

"Okay, fine," she said, not seeing any humor at all in the entire situation. "You just go right on ahead. I have nothing more to say about it." And she walked rapidly into the bedroom, just barely managing to prevent herself from slamming the bedroom door, hard. If he wanted to make a total fool of himself over a woman who had no real interest in him, then . . . then . . . well, she would just have to do something about it.

She plunked herself into one of the small love seats arranged in the nicely designed conversation area, picked up the *TV Guide*, and began to thumb wildly through it. The bedroom door opened and closed with considerably more control than she had just exercised. She felt him come toward her, but she remained resolutely bent to her task.

Sam sat on the arm of her chair, and after a moment she was forced to look up at him.

"Have you ever considered the fact that you might be a bit spoiled?" he asked in a completely flat voice.

Rosalind's eyes flashed at him. "What?" *Spoiled? What in the world is he raving about now?*

He examined a nicely cut nail on his right hand before saying, "Well, just think about it. Not only do you not want me . . . for yourself . . ." And he held up the very hand he'd just been looking at with such studied concentration. "Wait . . . hear me out. Not only do you not want me the way a woman wants and needs a man . . . but you have a problem with me going out and trying to find someone who will actually want me back. . . ."

This time she was able to get a few words in, and she took full advantage of the opportunity. "I have no problem with you—with you having a normal healthy life. I told you that just last night, as you very well know."

"Right. If that's the case, why're you sitting in here sulking?"

"Sulking?" She was incredulous. "I have never sulked in my entire life. Not even once in my entire life. And as far as being spoiled goes . . . you know I've never had the privilege of that particular luxury. I've had to work hard all of my life . . . taking care of Tony and—" She broke off. For some ridiculous reason, she was very close to dissolving into sobbing floods of tears. He leaned toward her, and it was all she could do not to reach for him.

"I know it hasn't been easy for you. It hasn't been easy for me, either. But whereas I know about you . . .

you've never been interested enough to ask me about me. . . ."

Rosalind swallowed away the tremble in her throat. "You're not being fair," she said in hardly more than a whisper. Something very strange was happening to her. She wanted to put her arms around him, hold him, comfort him. He was right. She had never asked him any questions about himself. Not really. She had always been thrown by the fact that he didn't appear to believe in God, something she just couldn't seem to reconcile in her mind. She had been meaning to ask him about that, though. On and off she'd been thinking of the problem, but had not yet come up with the right way to broach the subject with him.

"Do you want me?" And his eyes wouldn't allow her to hide. But she played for time nevertheless.

"Want you? Of course I want you . . . as a—as a friend."

"That's not what I meant, and you know it."

"I—you know I can't. Ben . . ." she said with a hint of desperation in her voice.

"Ben is not a factor here," he said softly. "Ben's not important. Sue's not important. There's no one else to consider but you and me. There's no one . . . do you understand me? No one who can come between the two of us if you only have the courage to choose what you really want . . . and need."

Rosalind stared at him. She saw the raw emotion in his eyes and trembled at the intensity of feeling it stirred in her. She'd never known that she could feel so deeply, and it scared her.

"I don't know what you want from me." It was the best she could come up with under the circumstances. She was so confused now. What he was asking of her, she couldn't do without breaking forever whatever it was she had with Ben. It was just too bad that this madness had chosen this point in time to strike.

"You know what I want. You've always known. Six years ago, when you ran from me, you knew." He shook his head. "What would make you choose something so much less than what you could actually have? Why are you so afraid to take what is yours . . . ?"

"Because . . . you're an atheist." The words were out before she could rethink the wisdom of uttering them in such a completely bald manner.

He stood, and walked toward the closest bank of windows, and Rosalind watched him for a silent moment before saying, "That's what I mean. You can't even deny what I just said."

He turned to look at her, and his eyes were strangely haunted. "I can't believe in what I know is not there. Why can't we get past this little thing?"

"Because," Rosalind said with soft emphasis, "for me . . . it's not a little thing. My faith is very important to me."

"But . . . how important can it be?" he shot back at her, his voice hard, uncompromising. "You don't even go to church regularly. You gamble. . . . Aren't those huge no-no's for devout Christians?"

Rosalind thought this over for a second. He was right; she didn't go to church as much as she should. And, yes, she did gamble a bit. But that didn't make her a bad Christian. Being a good Christian, and developing a keen spiritual understanding, didn't mean that she couldn't enjoy a game of chance every so often. It also didn't mean, as far as she was concerned, that she had to go to church every single week. On the weeks when she didn't go, she always made sure that she read her Bible and entered into fellowship with others. True, she hadn't been doing that recently, but she'd been very disturbed about a variety of things.

Tony. Him. Ben. Her life. Where it was going. She'd been afraid, too. Afraid that maybe Sam was right. Maybe she had chosen the wrong man.

"Nothing to say?"

Rosalind uncurled from the chair. Nothing could be further from the truth. She had plenty to say.

She went to stand right next to him, and a sudden, completely unexpected tenderness for him filled her eyes. She placed a soft hand on one hair-roughened arm.

"Sammy. . . ."

He looked down at her. "Rosy."

"Listen," she said, "you don't have to be a Christian. . . . Whichever faith you choose is completely up to you. But I can tell you through personal experience that there is a God somewhere out there." She paused for breath. She was no theologian, so she wanted to make sure that she didn't push him even further away.

Unconsciously, her fingers drifted over his arm, pulling at the peppering of sleek hairs. He was listening to her, she could see that, but whether or not she was actually getting through to him was anybody's guess.

"What I mean is . . . in the Christian faith—and I can only speak about this one since I'm not familiar enough with any of the others. But in Christianity, you're taught that God is love. So really, in a very practical way . . . if you've ever felt love for anyone . . . anyone at all, you've actually experienced God."

The gold of evening slanted through the slatted blinds, kissed the ends of her hair, and turned her eyes a soft ebony. She stared up at him.

"Do you see that?"

He turned away from her for a moment, and she watched the struggle in his face. It was clear that he didn't want to hear what she was saying, but maybe because she was the one telling him this, he would at least listen.

"Sammy? Do you understand what I mean?"

"You're not telling me anything I haven't heard before." His black eyes were like chips of stone. "I just don't believe as you do. Does that make me a terrible person? I can tell you, I know many so-called devout Christians whom you wouldn't want to meet in a dark alley late at night."

"Hmm," she said. She could tell that it was going to be an uphill battle. But she knew now that he would at least give her a fair hearing.

"Maybe now's not the right time to talk about this. I'm going to go change."

He turned to give her a quick perusal. "You look fine to me."

Rosalind stuck a slim, elegant ankle before her and said with a slightly rueful note in her voice, "The heels are too high, I think. They're making my feet ache."

"If you come to me tonight, I'll give you a foot massage."

Rosalind chuckled deep in her throat, and Sam's eyes took on a thoughtful glint. "You'll be too busy entertaining that Sue Perkins person. You'll have no strength left over for me."

"You think so?"

She placed an unconsciously flirtatious hand on her hip. "I definitely think so."

He reached for her, and Rosalind felt a distinct thrill as he pulled her close. "Just for the record," he said bending to within an inch of her lips, "regardless of how it might look, Sue Perkins and I have never had that sort of relationship."

"Mmm-hmm," Rosalind nodded.

He laughed. "What? Are you saying you don't believe me?"

Rosalind stroked the snatch of chest that showed above the vee of his shirt. "I'm not saying that. I'm just saying 'Mmm-hmm.' "

"You," he said, bending to kiss the tip of her nose, "are a very suspicious woman."

"So you say, but that Sue Perkins woman is out to get you. That much is certain."

He shrugged. "Lots of women have been out to get me. But . . . as you see . . . I'm still here. Single, unattached, and completely available if you want me." He paused. "Do you want me?"

A bead of perspiration trickled the center of Rosalind's back. So they were back to that again. She'd been hoping that he might give up on that particular conversational direction, at least for the rest of the evening, but he was being very persistent about it.

"Well, Miss Carmichael? Are you going to give us the opportunity to experience that wonder everyone calls *love?*"

Rosalind met his eyes. There was no humor there although his words appeared to be lighthearted.

"What about Ben?"

"Give him up." And he bent to kiss her full on the lips. But before she could completely enjoy the sensation, he had broken the brief contact and was looking down at her again.

"So what're you going to do?"

"Are you serious?" She knew he was. But the question gave her the chance to gather her thoughts. What *was* she going to do? Never would she have ever thought that she could find herself in such a situation, and with *Sam Winter, too,* of all people.

"Look at me, Rosy," he said, tilting her chin up so that she couldn't avoid him. "I may not know or understand much about religion and this God you talk so much about. But I know this much. In life, you have to seize your chances whenever they occur . . . seize them with both hands. It's rough out here, you know? And love, real love is very hard to find."

She nodded, because she knew it to be true. She didn't have a lot of friends, but she did have a few, and she knew how much of a struggle it had been and still was for them all to find a *good* man. One who cared. One who wasn't psychotic, or a philanderer of some sort.

"It's hard to find someone who's right for you," she agreed.

The black eyes were unrelenting. "So at least we agree on that. So if you're ever fortunate enough to run into that right person, you don't send him away . . . do you?"

"Sammy . . ." she said, giving him a little pat on the arm. "Is it the sex thing that's making you so absolutely crazy?"

"There's no question that I want you in that way. You've always known that. But it's more. Much more."

"But . . . what you're asking me to do . . . How can I do it? He needs me."

"I need you more."

"He may even flunk out of his residency training if I spring this on him now."

"And what about me? What will it do to me if you go off and marry some other man? I may never sleep again."

"Don't be silly, Sammy. Men like you aren't a dime a dozen. Do you know how many women out there are looking for someone just like you?"

"And what's so special about me?"

"Well . . ." and she thought for a moment about it. "You're kind." Yes, he was that. He was definitely that.

"Mmm-hmm."

He seemed pleased by that, Rosalind noted. "And you're good-looking."

His brows lifted. "You think so? You've never let on for a second that you thought this. I even wondered at one point some years ago, if the reason you so obviously despised me was because I'm red-boned."

Rosalind blinked at him. "What?" He thought she had turned him down because he was light complexioned? Was he completely out of his mind? To even think that she would be so absolutely ignorant was completely ridiculous.

"It's what I thought. You know how you women have types. Tall men. Short men. Fat men. Skinny men. Brown-skinned men."

"How could you think that of me?"

"It just occurred to me that that might have been the reason. But now I know it's because of the religious question."

There was a discreet knock on the door before she could respond to him, and Renard's voice said, "Mr. Winter, you asked me to let you know when the phone call from Paris came in."

"Thank you, Renard. I'll be there in a minute." And then quietly, so that only Rosalind could hear him, he said, "Don't think you've gotten off."

Rosalind held his gaze as he turned at the door to look at her again. He mouthed the word *"Later,"* opened the door, and was gone.

Over a sumptuous meal of French cuisine at Le Cirque later that evening, Rosalind did her best not to pay any attention whatsoever to Sue Perkins's flirtatious advances toward Sam. She knew now that the woman probably had no chance with him, but as her brother had often told her, men—all men—were susceptible to the wiles of a determined woman. And Sam would be no different. No stronger at resisting, especially since she had not given him a reason to resist.

"So Sam was telling me that you're engaged to be married, Rosa," Sue Perkins was saying in a gushingly sweet manner.

Rosalind looked at the other woman in a calm manner. She hadn't heard Sam tell her that. *What is he up to now?*

"The name's Rosalind, Sue," she said. "And, yes, I am engaged."

Sue gave her a Cheshire cat smile and Rosalind gave the gleaming white teeth a look of complete distaste. *There was such a thing as having too many teeth.*

"Well, isn't that nice," Sue said, and leaned forward to press Rosalind's arm with an ultrasoft hand. "Congratulations to you. When is the happy event?"

Rosalind shot a pointed look in Sam's direction, before saying, "We haven't set a date yet. But it'll be soon."

Sue seemed satisfied with that response, and for the next little while as they ate their way through an indescribable creamy dessert of completely unpronounceable delights, she focused all of her attention on Sam, whom to Rosalind's way of thinking, responded like a dog in heat to every little flirtatious bone she threw his way.

Although the meal had been a sumptuous one, by the end of dessert, Rosalind knew she'd had enough. Her head was simply splitting open, and all she wanted at that point were two aspirins, a glass of water, and a comfortable bed.

She patted her mouth with a delicate white linen napkin, then pushed back her chair.

"I think I'll say good night," she said, standing.

Sue positively beamed at the suggestion, and

An important message from the ARABESQUE Editor

Dear Arabesque Reader,

Because you've chosen to read one of our Arabesque romance novels, we'd like to say "thank you"! And, as a special way to thank you, we've selected four more of the books you love so well to send you for FREE!

Please enjoy them with our compliments, and thank you for continuing to enjoy Arabesque...the soul of romance.

Karen Thomas
Senior Editor,
Arabesque Romance Novels

Check out our website at
www.arabesquebooks.com

3 QUICK STEPS
TO RECEIVE YOUR "THANK YOU" GIFT
FROM THE EDITOR

Send this card back and you'll receive 4 FREE Arabesque novels! The introductory shipment of 4 Arabesque novels – a $23.96 value – is yours absolutely FREE!

There's no catch. You're under no obligation to buy anything. You'll receive your introductory shipment of 4 Arabesque novels absolutely FREE (plus $1.99 to offset the costs of shipping & handling). And you don't have to make any minimum number of purchases—not even one!

We hope that after receiving your books you'll want to remain an Arabesque subscriber. But the choice is yours to continue or cancel, anytime at all! So why not take us up on our invitation to receive 4 Arabesque Romance Novels, with no risk of any kind. You'll be glad you did!

Call us
TOLL-FREE
at 1-800-770-1963

THE EDITOR'S "THANK YOU" GIFT INCLUDES:

- 4 books absolutely FREE (plus $1.99 for shipping and handling)
- A FREE newsletter, *Arabesque Romance News*, filled with author interviews, book previews, special offers, and more!
- No risks or obligations. You're free to cancel whenever you wish... with no questions asked.

BOOK CERTIFICATE

Yes! Please send me 4 FREE Arabesque novels (plus $1.99 for shipping & handling). I understand I am under no obligation to purchase any books, as explained on the back of this card.

Name _____

Address _____ Apt. _____

City _____ State_____ Zip_____

Telephone ( ) _____

Signature _____

Offer limited to one per household and not valid to current subscribers. All orders subject to approval. Terms, offer, & price subject to change. Offer valid only in the U.S.

Thank you!

AN072A

Accepting the four introductory books for FREE (plus $1.99 to offset the cost of shipping & handling) places you under no obligation to buy anything. You may keep the books and return the shipping statement marked "cancelled". If you do not cancel, about a month later we will send 4 additional Arabesque novels, and you will be billed the preferred subscriber's price of just $4.00 per title. That's $16.00 for all 4 books for a savings of 33% off the cover price (Plus $1.99 for shipping and handling). You may cancel at any time, but if you choose to continue, every month we'll send you 4 more books, which you may either purchase at the preferred discount price. . . or return to us and cancel your subscription.

THE ARABESQUE ROMANCE CLUB: HERE'S HOW IT WORKS

ARABESQUE ROMANCE BOOK CLUB
P.O. Box 5214
Clifton NJ 07015-5214

PLACE
STAMP
HERE

Rosalind very nearly sat again, splitting headache or not. But the pain was beginning to affect her vision, and she knew that she was in for a migraine of magnificent proportions.

Sam's eyes flickered across her face, and he stood immediately. "Yes, I think we'd better all call it a night. Tomorrow we begin work on the presentation and we're going to need everything we've got."

Sue's eyes flashed between them both. "But . . ." she began. "Sam, there's no reason for you to leave, too. Rosalind's a big girl. She can find her way back to the suite on her own. Surely?"

Rosalind gritted her teeth, and a flash of white-hot pain nearly made her bend double. Sam was looking at her in a very concerned manner now, and he didn't even bother to respond to Sue's comment. Instead he rapped out an abrupt "Charge the dinner to my suite, Sue. I'll see you in the morning."

Rosalind was grateful for his support as she tried her best to walk in a dignified fashion from the room.

"What is it? Something you ate?" Sam whispered against her temple. And some part of her brain registered the fact that he was concerned. Very concerned.

"No," she said in a voice that was completely unlike her own. "It's a migraine. I don't get them often, but whenever I do, it's always really bad."

They were almost to the door of the restaurant, and Rosalind wondered how it was this horrible pain had come upon her so very suddenly. Why it had was another matter entirely. Her head was swimming now, and there was a sick sensation in her stomach that made her feel as if she might not make it all the way to the suite without losing the wonderful dinner she had just eaten.

"Should I carry you?"

A sheen of cold perspiration glinted on her fore-head. "No. I'll be fine. I'll be fine.

He wrapped a strong arm about her waist, and Rosalind leaned heavily on him all the way into the elevator. It seemed an eternity before the doors were opening again in their suite. Once inside, Sam ignored her protests and swept her into his arms.

"No one can see us now. I gave Renard the night off."

In two strides he was in the master bedroom. He laid her carefully on the bed and began to loosen the tiny buttons running down the front of the dress. Feebly Rosalind tried to stop him.

"No . . . wait . . ." she muttered.

He put her hands aside with a gentle "Come on, Rosy. What kind of man do you think I am? I'm not likely to ravish you in this state."

She squinted up at him, trying her best to focus on his face. "This is so silly," she said. "I haven't had one of these in years. I really don't know what brought it on."

"Shh," Sam admonished. "Don't talk. I'm going to get you some painkillers. I'll be back in a moment."

Rosalind's eyes sagged shut as soon as he left the room, and she uttered a prayer that the throbbing, spinning pain would stop.

He was back again in only moments, lifting her head and slipping two white tablets into her mouth, and then tilting a glass of water to her lips and saying softly, "Drink." She did so obediently and then sank back against the white pillows.

"Where're your night things?" he asked after what seemed like an interminable stretch.

"Top shelf. Closet."

She turned on her side, drawing her legs up toward

her stomach and curling into a protective fetal position.

"Turn over, sweetheart," she heard him say from a distance. She felt his hands on her shoulder, and she allowed him to roll her onto the flat of her back without putting up any resistance.

"Lift your arms."

She followed his instructions like a sleepwalker, allowing him to remove her dress, and then slide her arms into the silky pajama top. The bottom he didn't bother with, and Rosalind couldn't have cared less about that particular formality at any rate. All she wanted was for the pain to stop.

She felt his hands on her temples and tried to open her eyes a crack.

"Relax," he said. "This is an old technique my grandmother taught me." He pressed the balls of his hands against both temples and squeezed. Hard. Rosalind made a little sound of protest, and she heard him say, "If you can stand this, I promise you the pain'll be gone in no time."

He squeezed again, and Rosalind suppressed a little grunt. Was he trying to crack her skull?

"Just a few more times now," he promised. And he squeezed and released. Squeezed and released. Then began the most vigorous massage of her temples with the flats of his thumbs.

A few minutes into it, Rosalind opened her eyes. She was actually beginning to feel a bit better. The pain was still there, but it was not nearly as bad as it had been before.

"Stay still now."

Rosalind closed her eyes again and gave herself up to the wonder of his strong hands. She had to admit, they were amazing. Hard and soft at the same time.

Touching all of the right spots, seeking out the pain and massaging it away.

After more than half an hour, Sam finally moved his hands, pulled the blankets up to cover her, stroked a wisp of hair from her face. Rosalind stirred as the weight of his body left the bed. She turned to look at him, and said in a slightly mournful manner, "You're going?"

Sam smiled down at her. "Feeling a bit better?" Rosalind nodded. "Much. What you did with your hands was just amazing."

"Old trick. But works every time."

Rosalind met his eyes, and she forced herself to ask the question before the sane, logical, part of her brain could take over and talk her out of it. "Can you stay?"

The expression in his eyes became indecipherable, and Rosalind added hastily lest he misunderstand her, "I meant . . . just to sleep. Nothing else."

"I knew I couldn't be that lucky. But I'll take what I can get. I'll be back in a minute."

Rosalind scooted over to the left side of the bed and the minutes that he was gone were spent worrying about whether or not she should put on her pajama bottoms. The top was quite long and covered her to a very respectable midthigh.

By the time he had returned, she had come to terms with the idea of not wearing the pajama bottoms. She had also come to terms with the idea that she was probably going to have to break it off with Ben. But she wouldn't tell Sam of her decision until after she had made it clear to Ben that their strange engagement was at an end.

"Giving me the right side of the bed?" He stood over her, looking absolutely splendid in a pair of black silk pajama bottoms. Rosalind tried to prevent the rush of blood to her cheeks. It was really too unbelievable that he was standing where he was now, preparing to get into bed with her. If anyone had told her a month ago that this would be happening to her, she would have laughed her head off.

"You sleep on the right, don't you?"

He peeled back the blankets and climbed under. "I'm very flexible. Right or left is fine with me."

When he was properly settled, he turned to regard her with deeply hypnotic black eyes. "So, how's the migraine?"

"It's bearable now."

"Come," he said, "lie against me, and we'll see if we can't get rid of it all."

Rosalind moved into his arms, and she lay absolutely still as he brought her into close contact with his chest. Through the thin cotton of her pajama top, she could feel his heart beating solidly, consistently. And she found herself drifting off to sleep. Never had she felt so very safe before. Never so content.

Rosalind slept soundly, making hardly any noise at all. And in the darkness of the room Sam watched her, until finally he, too, slept. Sweetly.

Thirteen

Rosalind awoke just before dawn to find herself completely wrapped in Sam's arms. For a minute, she didn't understand why he was there, but then she remembered. The migraine. It had been quite possibly, the worst attack she'd ever had, and she would be forever grateful to him for the way in which he had helped her.

She shifted slightly, turning so that she might see him. In sleep, his face was relaxed, almost boyish. Definitely not the face of the hard-nosed tycoon she knew him to be. A little smile curved the softness of her mouth. Life was indeed a funny thing. She had really thought that she despised this man, yet here she was not despising him at all. In fact, she was really beginning to like him. A lot.

She reached a hand to turn out the bedside lamp, and as she did, his eyes opened. She drew back immediately.

"Sorry . . . didn't mean to wake you."

He smiled at her. "I'm a light sleeper. How's your head?"

"No pain whatsoever. I feel fine. Thanks again for . . . what you did."

His eyebrows lifted. "So . . . now that we're both awake, what're we going to do?"

Rosalind chuckled. "Is it true what they say about men . . . and sex?"

"Hmm, this is interesting," he said, propping himself on an elbow. "So many things have been said. Which thing in particular were you thinking of?"

"Well, I've heard it said that men think about sex several times a day. Is it true?"

"A day?" he said with a bark of laughter. "That's definitely a very conservative estimate."

"You mean . . . more than that?"

He stroked her cheek. "Definitely more than that. I think it might be fair to say that we . . . with a few exceptions here and there, think about sex . . . pretty much all the time."

Rosalind absorbed this bit of information with a smile. It was nice just lying beside him, talking about everything and nothing.

"Sammy . . ." She trailed a finger down his arm, following the run of a blue vein. "What happened when you were small . . . to turn you against religion? Is it okay to ask?"

He stilled the progress of the finger down his arm and drew her close to him.

"You know you can ask me anything."

She settled on the pillows and said, "Okay, I'm ready."

He settled his head beside hers and his eyes became turbid. "I haven't thought about any of this in years. I don't even know where to start. . . ."

"Start wherever it's easiest to," Rosalind said, and gave him an encouraging pat on the arm.

"I grew up without a father. But I didn't really notice it that much because in my neighborhood most of the other kids were fatherless, too. When I was about . . . I guess five years old, I went to live with my grandmother. It was supposed to be just for a little while, you know, until my mother got herself on her feet. But the weeks stretched into months, and every single day I would ask when she was coming back for me. My grandmother was a devout Baptist. So every time I would ask, she would tell me to pray."

Rosalind's brows furrowed. "And you did?"

He nodded. "I did. As much as, if not more than, a little child of that age could. I was very intense for such a small child. I didn't play like other kids my age."

Rosalind "Hmm'd" sympathetically.

"Anyway," he continued in an emotionless way, "before I knew it, an entire year had passed and my mother still hadn't come to get me. Finally, one day, my grandmother sat me down"—he laughed in a harsh humorless manner—"and in the gentlest way she could, she told me that my mother was never coming back. I remember sitting there like a block of ice. Not moving, not feeling. She told me that I'd see my mother again . . . in heaven. She was hit by a drunk driver while she was crossing the road. I learned this years later."

"I'm sorry," Rosalind said, reaching out to press his hand. "So you gave up on God because your prayers weren't answered then?"

"No. It took almost ten more years. Ten years of unbelievable hardship and suffering before I was completely convinced that there was no one up there, or anywhere else for that matter, who cared whether I lived or died. By the time I was fifteen, I had lost my mother, grandmother, my home. . . ."

"Your home?" Rosalind sat up, and in the early-morning light, with her raven-black hair in a glorious tumble about her shoulders, she was softly beautiful. And Sam's eyes flickered over her before he continued. "My home. When my grandmother died, I was left with no one. No one who cared enough to take me in anyway. I became a street child."

Rosalind stared at him for a moment, shocked into speechlessness. She'd thought that she and Tony had had a hard time of it, losing their parents as they had. But a life on the streets? And as a child, too? It was almost too incredible to be believed.

"But . . . there must've been someone . . . I mean what about child welfare services?"

He shook his head. "I was big for my age. Tall. At fifteen, I looked about twenty-one. Besides, by then I'd heard all the horror stories about foster care. So I decided to go it alone. I had to learn the language of the streets in L.A. I ran numbers, did just about everything. Any scam going, I found a way to be part of it. The only things I didn't do were drugs . . . and of course prostitution. But I did just about everything else." He smiled at her in a distant sort of way, and Rosalind felt a surge of pity that very nearly had her reaching for him.

"I had a plan, you see. I was determined that somehow I was going to make it to college. Throughout all of the losses I suffered as a child, I still somehow managed to maintain a very respectable grade point average."

Rosalind nibbled on the side of her lip. She was almost too afraid to ask. "Did you make it to college?"

He nodded. "I did, but only for one year. After that, the money ran out and so did my grades. I was put on academic probation, and then asked very nicely . . . to leave."

"Oh, no," Rosalind said softly.

"Oh, yes. All of the hard work, the prayer, the suffering . . . everything in vain. As I walked out the gates of that college, I vowed that I would never say another prayer in my life. What for?" There was anger in his voice now. "There's no one there."

Rosalind propped her chin on the round of her palm. She was beginning to understand how she could help him.

"Sam," she said, and then paused for a moment before going on. It was really important that she choose her words carefully. "Have you ever wondered why you were able to make it through all the really horrible things that you went through? Look at you now. You're successful, rich . . . All of the things that most people think they want, you have. And you managed to do it . . . and come out on the other side . . . in one piece."

She paused for breath, her expression earnest. "So many street kids become victims of their environment. You didn't—"

"The only reason I didn't," he interrupted, "was because I made up my mind that no matter what life threw at me, I wasn't going to go down. I would fight, any way I could. I was completely without any scruples. I learned to do anything—anything at all to survive . . . to win."

Rosalind reached forward and cupped his face between the palms of her hands. It was abundantly clear that the task ahead was not going to be an easy one.

"Sam Winter," she said, and she looked directly into his eyes, "you've developed a reputation for being a difficult businessman. Am I right?"

He smiled. "Right."

"And you never listen to anyone. Right?"

"I listen . . . if it makes sense to me. If it doesn't . . ." He shrugged. "I trust my judgment and the judgment of a select few."

"Well," Rosalind said, "I know you don't trust mine, but you're going to listen to me anyway."

His eyes glittered at her. "I am, huh? And if I don't listen, what're you going to do to me?"

She gave him a little wink. "I'll think of a suitable torture for you. Trust me."

He laughed, and the husky sound echoed around the room. "You know I don't give in easily. So be careful."

"Come here," Rosalind said in a manner that surprised even her. She bent and kissed him softly on the left and then the right corner of his mouth. He moved immediately to take her lips, but she prevented him with a hand.

"Something else to consider," she said with a wicked note in her voice. And she gave him an all-too-brief kiss on the blunt of his mouth. "I'm a Christian woman."

"Mmm-hmm," he agreed in a distracted manner, and tried to return her lips to his again.

"And you say you want me . . . for a time."

He kissed her cheek. "I do."

"Have you considered why it is you seem to want me . . . and not some other woman whose beliefs aren't as strong?"

"It's simply because I want your body," he said huskily.

She tapped him on the nose. "That's not it."

"And how would you know this?"

Rosalind chuckled despite herself. "I have my ways, and I know for sure . . . that's really not it."

He looked at her with an unusual gentleness in his eyes. "Okay, tell me what it is."

"Maybe"—and she hesitated a bit—"maybe God caused you to choose me."

"That's an interesting thought if I've ever heard one. But as nice and as comforting as that explanation might seem . . . take it from me, *that's* really not it."

Rosalind wrapped her arms about him, and he cuddled her close.

"I give up," she said against the skin of his neck. She hadn't, but she had decided to approach him in more of a subtle manner. The direct, frontal approach was not working at all.

He kissed the fold of her ear and said, "Well, don't trouble yourself about it. If I'm wrong, and there really is a God . . . then I guess my evil soul will burn forever in the flames of damnation."

"Mmm-hmm," Rosalind said in a noncommittal manner. Not if she had anything to do with it.

The next several days went by in a blur. The buyers' party, where she wore a little black dress with a high neck and a low back, was a mixed success. Sam introduced her around and somehow managed to skillfully answer the many questions about who exactly she was without saying anything much at all. Throughout the party, Rosalind was keenly aware that Sue Perkins was watching her with undisguised interest. And near the end of the evening when she finally launched her offensive, Rosalind was ready for it.

"I'm not sure I understand what your game is," Sue had said as Rosalind touched up her makeup in one of the many powder rooms.

Rosalind finished applying her lipstick and closed the compact before saying in a very calm voice, "I'm afraid I don't know what you mean."

Sue came to sit beside her, and Rosalind had to force herself to remain seated. Never before had she ever felt such a strong revulsion. The woman literally made her feel ill.

Sue checked her makeup before saying, "You have a fiancé back in Jersey, and you're in Las Vegas, carrying on with your boss." She rolled a new coat of color onto her cherry-red lips. "Know what I mean now?"

Rosalind closed her purse, and stood, but Sue curled long fingers about her wrist, and yanked her back onto the padded stool. "I'm not finished with you yet," she said, black eyes glittering like pointy bits of stone.

Hot blood rushed straight to Rosalind's head, and it was all she could do not to turn on the other woman like a tigress. She drew a steadying breath, and said in a voice that would've made anyone with half a brain back down, "Let go of my hand. Now." Sue's hand however, remained wrapped about Rosalind's wrist. "Not until I've said what I intend to."

Rosalind stood again, but this time she yanked her hand away in a sharp movement that broke one of the beautifully manicured acrylics on the other woman's hand.

"Oh, no, you didn't," Sue shrieked, and Rosalind was just able to dodge the blow that seemed to be aimed directly at her face.

The missed slap caused the other woman to lose her balance, and she toppled to the floor in an unladylike sprawl of arms and legs. Rosalind looked down at her in disgust, and then turned on her heel and left the powder room.

Sue shrieked at her departing back, "I'll get you. Mark my words if I don't. Sam Winter will never be yours. I'll see to it."

Rosalind paid her no attention whatsoever. As far as she was concerned, Sue Perkins was quite probably psychotic, or maybe she drank. At the very least she was severely unstable, and because of that, Rosalind could only pity her. She had to wonder, too, at the quality of Sam's judgment. Hiring a crazy woman like that. Surely she was exactly the kind of employee who, if sufficiently roused, could come in one day, and for no apparent reason, blow the entire office away.

The party broke up soon after, and Rosalind was grateful that she didn't have to remain there for hours on end, with a forced smile glued to her face. She was noticeably quiet in the elevator on the way back up to the suite. She was of two minds about whether to let Sam know about her altercation with Sue Perkins in the powder room. So deep in thought was she about the matter, that it was a while before she realized that Sam had asked her a question and was awaiting a response from her. She looked at him and said, "I'm sorry . . . What?"

"I was asking if there was anything wrong. You seemed so far away."

"No. Not really. I was just thinking." She gave him a brave little smile. "The party seemed to go well. Think the buyers from the Caribbean and Paris will place orders?"

"There's a good chance, I think. But the online presentation and mini fashion show will seal things."

The elevator doors opened smoothly, and Rosalind was never happier to see the suite she had called home for the past week and a half. Renard met them with a tray of snacks and steaming cups of coffee. Rosalind accepted the coffee, but declined anything to eat. She'd really had her fill at the party, but even if she had been tempted to eat anything, the incident with Sue Perkins had certainly quenched any possible appetite she might have had.

Sam followed her into the bedroom suite after saying a brief good night to the butler. He closed the door behind and turned the lock. Rosalind went immediately to the bathroom. She spent several minutes taking the hundred and one pins from her upswept hair, and then began the nightly routine of brushing the tangles from her hair. Sam came and stood at the door.

"Need some help?"

Rosalind turned, and the surprise in her eyes was bright. No man had ever made such an offer before. Such a thing as brushing her hair would never have occurred to Ben. It was beneath him somehow. And she wasn't at all certain that Sam wasn't having some fun with her, too.

"You want to brush my hair?"

He loosened the first few buttons on his shirt, and Rosalind's eyes were immediately drawn to the dark profusion of hair at his collar.

"Don't sound so surprised," he said, taking the brush from her. "I do have a couple of uses outside of the boardroom."

Rosalind met his eyes in the mirror. "Sam Winter, you're a man of many faces. I never would've thought it possible."

He stroked the brush through her hair, gently massaging her scalp before stroking again.

Rosalind's eyelids drooped as he bent her head this way and that, moving the brush through her thick mass of hair with consummate skill. Finally, when she was sure that she would fall asleep if he kept to his purpose, he bent her head forward, and very naturally began to massage her neck. His fingers moved over her muscles in the most amazing way, and she sighed slowly, deeply contented.

"Oh, you do that so well," she said, opening her eyes again to look at him.

He bent and placed a very warm kiss at the edge of her hairline. "I do many things . . . well. See what you've been missing all these years?"

Rosalind drew in her bottom lip to prevent the smile

she was feeling from curling its way across her lips. It would appear that she had made a poor choice, selecting Ben over Sam. But how was she to know that the face Sam Winter showed the world was not his true face?

He turned her to face him, and Rosalind raised her eyes slowly to his. "Do you want me just because I said no to you . . . all those years ago?"

He tilted her chin and lowered his head to taste her lips. "Is that what you think?" he asked between biting little kisses that brought Rosalind's arms up and around his neck.

She chuckled. "Yes. I think you like the chase. If I'd shown any interest at all in you earlier . . . you probably wouldn't want me now."

He bit the side of her mouth, and Rosalind gasped at the absolutely exquisite feeling.

"You'd be wrong there," he muttered. "If you'd said yes to me . . . we'd probably have at least fifteen children today."

"Ha. Not me, buddy," Rosalind said, pressing her hands against his chest and attempting to put some distance between them.

"Ten children?"

She grinned. "Try again."

"Five?"

"Well, at least that's closer to reality."

He pulled her close again. "We would've had a little girl who looks just like you do. Same big beautiful eyes. Sweet face. Gorgeous lips."

"You say the nicest things. Even if they're not true."

"They're true. So," he said, changing direction on her, "what're we going to do about Ben?"

Rosalind's forehead wrinkled. She'd been dreading that very question. She'd already decided to break things off with Ben, of course, but felt it would be highly unwise to let Sam know that at this stage.

"You have to give me time, Sammy," she said, stroking his arm.

The expression in his eyes grew suddenly very pensive. "Time? How much time?"

"Everything's just happening so fast. I need to be sure I'm doing the right thing. . . ."

"What're you so afraid of? I don't understand."

She stroked the hair at his neckline, and felt him relax a little. "I'm not afraid. Not of you. Not anymore. Maybe I was once. But not anymore."

"Well, then . . . just tell Ben it's all over. It's as simple as that. Don't make it more than it has to be."

"He'll be crushed, I know it."

"He deserves to be crushed. But I'm grateful for his stupidity."

Rosalind rested her head on his chest, and Sam wrapped his arms about her and murmured close to her ear, "I want you. Tonight."

There was no mistaking his meaning, and Rosalind didn't bother to pretend that she had misunderstood his soft command. Her heart pounded heavily in her chest. She was beginning to wonder if he had had this plan in mind from the very moment she'd asked him to lend her the two hundred thousand dollars needed to bail Tony out of trouble.

"You know I can't," she said softly.

He nuzzled her neck. "Why not? Haven't I waited long enough for you?"

She met his eyes, and for a brief instant, madness fired her blood. *Oh, if only I could say yes to you.* But she couldn't do it. Not yet. Not until she had officially broken her engagement.

"We can't," she said, and there was a heartier note

in her voice. "It wouldn't be right. I'm still officially engaged to Ben."

"But we've slept together in the same bed now for several nights."

"Just slept," Rosalind said. "Nothing else. We have nothing to reproach ourselves for."

"I wouldn't reproach myself even if something had happened. I wouldn't have a problem with you, either."

"How about a massage?" Rosalind asked hopefully. There was a restless energy about him tonight, and she knew intuitively what it was he needed. She had been with him for over two weeks, and he had quite obviously not had a woman in all that time.

He sighed in a long and mournful manner. "Is that all I can have?" Rosalind took him by the hand and led him back to the big bed. "Lie down," she said.

He gave her a simmering look. "Undress me."

Rosalind drew a tight breath. He was back to that again. "Sammy . . ."

"What harm will that do?"

"Are you sure you'll behave?"

He flicked two black brows toward his hairline. "Don't I always?"

"Can you wait until I change my clothes?"

He smiled. "Can I watch?"

She gave him a playful slap. "No, you can't."

She left him sitting on the side of the bed, and in the bathroom she changed quickly, having selected a pair of satiny white pajamas. She gave her face a quick glance. There was a flush in her cheeks and an unusual happiness in her eyes.

She padded back to him on bare feet, and in an intensely focused manner that set her heart to pounding in her chest, he watched her approach. He remained seated, and for that Rosalind was grateful. At least she'd be able to maintain a modicum of control over the proceedings without him towering over her.

Her fingers went to the buttons on his shirt, and he flexed his shoulders slowly, all the while never taking his eyes from her even once. Rosalind willed her fingers not to tremble as they made their way down the front of his shirt. At the line of his belt, she paused to pull his shirt free.

"Mmm," he said in a low groan. "I've waited such a long time for this."

"Behave," Rosalind said softly, and her hands dipped beneath the cloth to push the shirt from his shoulders.

"That's all you ever say to me."

Her fingers went to his belt again, and this time they hovered for a bit. It was still a trifle nerve-racking to perform so intimate a duty on him. Especially when he was watching her in such a very intense manner.

"Would you prefer to keep your pants on?"

He chuckled. "You don't get off that easy, young lady."

She hadn't really thought that he would've agreed to that. But she had decided to give it a try anyway.

Her fingers stumbled over the silver buckle, and he eased back onto his elbows to give her more room. A rash of perspiration beaded her nose as she pulled back the leather and then plucked at the buttoning at his waist. She darted a look at him, and caught a tiny smile flickering about the corners of his mouth. He was enjoying her discomfiture. The beast.

On a wicked impulse, she reached out a hand and pinched him on the side.

"Ach," he said. "You vicious woman."

"I'll do even more than that if you don't behave. Now, lift your hips," she said in as clinical a manner as she could manage. He did her bidding with a smile flickering in the depths of his eyes.

Rosalind yanked his pants from him, tossing them over her shoulder in one smooth movement.

"I really like the way you do that," he said, and Rosalind waved a warning finger at him.

"Move up onto the pillows and turn over."

"I want you to start with my chest."

Rosalind bit her lip. Such a very difficult man he was. Well, okay, she would show him that she was definitely up to the task.

She picked up the bottle of baby oil and poured a small puddle into the scoop of her palm.

"What? No argument out of you?"

Rosalind rubbed her hands together. "Well, you are my employer. Besides . . . you don't scare me."

He laughed. "That's certainly a new development. You were certainly scared to death of me six years ago."

"Is that what you thought?" Her hands drifted to his shoulders and began to move in ever-widening circles.

"Yes. Among other things. But definitely that. You would almost run in the opposite direction whenever you saw me coming."

"I wasn't running away from you because you scared me. Believe me."

"Why did you disappear at the first sign of me then?"

Rosalind massaged a bit more vigorously. Had he actually forgotten his treatment of her? How hard he had worked her? Finding fault with everything she did? Working her to the very point of total exhaustion? Insulting her at every possible opportunity?

"I was trying to keep out of the line of fire."

"Line of fire?" He was looking at her intently now. "I never treated you badly."

Rosalind looked up at him. "You haven't had a head injury or anything like that in the last six years, have you?"

He chuckled. "So now we get to the heart of the matter. You thought I was punishing you by keeping you with me late into the night."

"I was the only one you singled out for such treatment. And no matter how hard I tried to please you, you were never satisfied. I know you remember."

He stilled one of her busy hands with one of his. "Didn't you wonder—even once—*why* I'd taken such a keen interest in you . . . at the time, a very junior Web designer?"

Rosalind frowned. "I didn't have time to think about it. I was too busy working. Other people in the office noticed, of course, and there were rumors flying about the place, that I was attempting to sleep my way up the ladder." She paused, remembering those very difficult years. "You didn't make it easy for me."

He stroked the hand that he'd taken possession of. "I didn't realize you were having such a hard time. I felt sure you knew why it was I went out of my way to create special projects just for you. Didn't you guess why I did it?"

"I figured it was probably because you thought you could push me around."

He brought her hand to his lips, and proceeded to kiss every digit. "Not because I liked you?"

Rosalind rested her free hand on his chest. "Liked me? I felt certain you despised every bone in my body. The only thing I had going for me . . . which is why I felt sure you hadn't just up and fired me . . . was the fact that I was tall, had big bones and a big butt."

Sam threw back his head, and guffawed. Rosalind

looked at him in silence. Well, it was nice that he could be so amused about it. She certainly hadn't been at the time.

Sam pulled her to lie beside him, and she went with the tiniest bit of resistance.

"Let's get one thing straight," he said, his eyes still holding back residual traces of laughter. "You're tall, but you certainly don't have big bones." He paused, and his hand slid to just below her waist. "Now the butt . . . that's another story all together."

Rosalind sat up with a flourish, her hair sloping silkily to her shoulders.

"I always knew I was right."

"About your cute little derrière?"

She pushed at his chest. "I'll never understand why it is you men seem so absolutely fascinated by that particular part of a woman's anatomy."

"I'll show you why . . . once you break it off with Ben."

She looked down at him. Six years before, such confidence would've severely irritated her. But now she was just vaguely amused by it.

"You're so certain I will—break it off with him, I mean?"

He sat up, and pulled her to sit close to him. "I know one thing."

She turned to look at him, and a warm feeling filled her at the expression in his eyes.

"What's that?"

He played with a twist of hair before saying. "You're not the kind of woman to play with a man's emotions. You're too kind-hearted."

She smiled at him. "That's probably one of the nicest things anyone has ever said to me."

He pulled the shoulder of her pajama top down to expose the round of her shoulder. Her heart thudded heavily in her chest as he bent his head to kiss the smooth skin.

"Listen to me, Rosy . . ." he said, lifting his head again to look at her. "I know exactly the kind of man you need. And believe me, you don't need one like Ben."

"No?" She lay back, and he leaned over her.

"No. You need the kind of man who'll have time for you . . . always. But more than that. You need a man who'll spoil you rotten . . . someone generous to a fault. Someone . . . like me."

Rosalind pulled at the sleek hairs on his chest, and was fascinated by the sudden totally unexpected appearance of goose bumps on his arms.

"What about this Sue Perkins woman? Where does she fit in the picture?"

A black brow flashed upward. "Sue Perkins? She's an employee . . . and a friend. But she has nothing to do with you and me. She understands the situation."

What does he mean she is a friend? How good a friend? "Are you sure she understands? She seems to have other more interesting ideas in mind."

"You think so?" he said in a manner that made Rosalind regret the fact that she'd brought the subject up in the first place. Maybe he hadn't fully discerned the other woman's interest in him, and now that she had pointed it out, this would kindle an interest in him. Sue Perkins was very attractive, after all.

"She's a very strange woman," she said, peeping at him from under her eyelashes.

His brows wrinkled. "No stranger than any other, I guess."

"Hmm," she said, and his eyes flashed to her face. "You two haven't hit it off well."

Rosalind folded her arms before her. "That's one of the biggest understatements I've heard in a while."

He turned to look at her with serious eyes. "I want you two to get along. It's important to me."

Rosalind sucked in a breath. Get along with Sue Perkins? Impossible. First of all, the woman hated her guts. And to be perfectly honest, she wasn't overly fond of her, either.

"Why's it so important that I like her?"

"That's something I'll tell you about later. Just try to like her for now. Everything will eventually become clear to you. It's just too soon to go into all of that now."

He settled his head beside her on the pillows, and with only a brief whisper of "good night" in her ear, he was soon sleeping deeply.

Fourteen

It took Rosalind a while to settle into full-blown sleep, and when she finally did, it was with a niggle of worry. She was not normally a jealous person, but as far as she could see, there was obviously a deeper relationship between Sam and that Sue Perkins. Rosalind was certain now that he hadn't told her the whole truth about their relationship.

She slept and woke the next morning to find that Sam had already gone. She showered and dressed, had a quick breakfast of toast and orange juice, and then decided to take the bull by the horns. In all of the time since she'd been in Las Vegas, she hadn't tried to call Ben even once. He hadn't attempted to contact her, either. But this morning, she would give him a call, and on his *emergencies-only* cell phone, too.

"Where's Mr. Winter?" she asked Renard.

"He left very early this morning. At about six. He didn't say where he was going, but he said to tell you he'd be back no later than ten, and that you were to sleep in if you felt like it."

Rosalind thanked the man, closed the bedroom door, and went to sit on the side of the bed. The simple thought of calling Ben made her hands damp with nervousness. She was just beginning to realize that all of what Sam had said was quite probably true.

Not only did Ben not love her, but she was beginning to feel that she had never really loved him, either. What a horrible mistake she would be making if she actually went ahead with the marriage.

She gave the phone a glare, then steeled herself, picked it up, and dialed. She wasn't going to break up with him on the phone, of course, but what she was going to do was let him know exactly what she thought of his treatment of her. It was really incredible that he hadn't even tried to get in touch with her even once since her arrival in Las Vegas.

The phone rang once, twice, and then it was answered abruptly with a "Ros?" The anxiety in his voice was so pronounced, that for a moment Rosalind almost didn't answer.

"Hello, Ben," she said in a lukewarm voice.

"Thank God. I've been worried sick about you. Why haven't you called me, left me a message, or anything?"

Call him? After the kind of reception she got the last time? Was he out of his mind? And why hadn't he called her?

"I didn't think you'd have the time to talk to me. Besides, I felt sure you would call . . . eventually."

"You didn't tell me where you'd be staying in Las Vegas . . . so I couldn't call. I tried to get it out of your brother, but he told me that he didn't know where you were, either."

Rosalind's brows lifted. Now that was a likely story indeed. Tony knew exactly where she was in Las Vegas. He even had the direct number to the suite.

"Well," she continued in a very flat voice, "it probably doesn't matter anyway." She had lost her desire to have it out with him on the phone. Strangely she found that she didn't care at all about his reasons for not calling her. "I just wanted to let you know I was okay." She paused for a beat, and then forced herself

to go on. "When I get back to New Jersey, we have
to talk . . . about things."

"I couldn't agree more, baby. There're so many
things we have to talk about. I've . . ." And suddenly
he sounded hesitant, almost afraid. "I've been doing
a lot of thinking myself, these past few days, and some
of the things I've come to realize about myself aren't
very complimentary. . . ."

"Well—" Rosalind attempted to interrupt, but he
shushed her.

"No . . . please, Ros, let me finish. I have to say
this while I still have the courage."

Rosalind took a breath and waited. So he was also
of the same opinion. They weren't right for each
other, and probably should never have gotten involved
in the first place. But was the phone the appropriate
medium by which to say it was all over? After all they'd
gone through together? After all she'd done for him?
Didn't she deserve just a little more consideration?

"Ros . . . I've treated you badly. Yes I have," he
said, as though he expected an argument out of her.
"But not only that . . . I've also taken you for granted,
and I haven't been nearly as loving as I've wanted to
be. You know I love you, don't you?"

Rosalind actually bit her tongue in her anxiety.
"W-what?" she stammered. What was he saying to
her? She was confused. Totally confused.

"I said . . . I loved you," he said with a hurt little
note in his voice. "And I'm sorry that I've been so
preoccupied with things at the hospital."

Again Rosalind rushed into automatic speech. "I—I
know how important your training is."

"It's important, of course. But not nearly as important as you. I've never told you that before. I always
assumed that you understood. But I've been a fool.

This is exactly the way that two people who really love each other can drift apart."

Rosalind gnawed at her lip. She hadn't been expecting this. What could she say to him now? She would have to wait until she saw him in person. She'd be able to handle things better then. She'd be able to explain that things were all over. All over for good.

"Are you still mad at me, Ros? I behaved like a jerk when you called me last time." He cleared his throat. "Forgive me?"

"Yes," she said. He always expected her to forgive him, no matter what it was he had done. But not this time. She had finally come to her senses. He would get over the temporary damage the breakup would cause his ego. Of that much she was completely certain. She was fully convinced now, that he had always been more in love with himself than with her.

"Ros," he said, and his voice crackled for a bit in a sudden storm of electronic disturbance, "do you still love me?"

Rosalind swallowed. She really didn't want to go into it on the phone. "We'll talk about everything when I get back," she said again, and hoped he would take the hint and not press her to express a sentiment that she no longer felt for him.

The door opened behind her, and her pulse rate went up. *Sam.* She'd hoped to be through with the call before he returned.

"I've got to go," she said hurriedly.

"Ros . . . wait . . . your number. What is it?"

Rosalind covered the mouthpiece and looked behind her. Sam stood in the doorway, a cluster of bags in his hands. But it was the expression on his face that had her saying very hastily, "I'll have to call you again later." She hung up without saying good-bye, and felt a double twinge of guilt as she replaced the receiver.

Sam closed the door, and took the many parcels in his hands and laid them at his feet. "Ben, I guess?"

Rosalind tucked a leg beneath her. "I hadn't called him at all since I got here," she said almost apologetically. "I thought I should."

He looked at her for a long moment before asking, "So does he understand the lay of the land now?"

"I'll talk to him when I get back to Jersey. It was kinda hard to do that on the phone."

He came to stand beside her. "You promise me you will?"

She met his eyes for a long moment, and then took the plunge. "I promise you I will."

He smiled at her, and extended a hand to help her to her feet. "I bought something for you."

Her eyes darted to the cluster of bags by the door. "You did?"

"I did. Come and see."

Rosalind followed him across the room to the bags, and stood watching as he removed several large satiny-looking boxes from them. He handed them all to her, and said with a note of anticipation in his voice, "I wasn't sure what your exact size was, but I described you to the lady in the shop, and she felt that these might be just right." He stroked a hand across his jaw. "Although I am in the urban gear business, I haven't a clue when it comes to women's clothing."

Rosalind opened the first box, peeled back the delicate wrapping, and stared. For an instant, she was completely robbed of speech. Clearly it was a dress of some sort, but it was probably one of the ugliest items of clothing she had ever seen. She pulled it from its cocoon of wrapping, and tried to think of something complimentary to say. But the words failed her.

Sam rubbed his hands together. "So . . . what do you think? Nice isn't it?"

Rosalind nodded. "Yes . . . it's really . . . ah . . . interesting." *For a tablecloth, or maybe a nice set of curtains.*

Sam beamed at her. "Well . . . if you like this one . . . wait until you see the next one." And without waiting for her to get around to the next box, he whipped the second dress from its packaging and held it up to the light.

"Oh, God. . . ." Rosalind said, unable to prevent the exclamation from spilling into sound. What in the name of heaven was it?

"It's the latest thing, the lady told me. I really wasn't sure about this one, but . . . what do you think? Is it you?"

Rosalind took the thing from him, and gave it a close inspection. It seemed to be a curious mixture of burlap and silk, with hanging multicolored threads of some other fabric she couldn't quite discern.

"This one is . . . is quite unusual"—she gestured with a finger—"with all of the hanging threads and beads." She turned it again. "And feather things . . ." She hoped to God he hadn't spent a lot of money on it.

Rosalind laid the two dresses carefully on the bed, then tried her best to smile at him. He seemed extraordinarily pleased with himself.

It was the thought that counted, after all. What did it matter that the dresses looked like something out of a masquerade show? She went to him, wrapped her arms about his middle, and placed a quick kiss on his cheek. "Thank you for thinking of me."

He lowered his head to rub his nose against hers. "I'm glad you like them . . . but you haven't seen the rest of what I got you."

The hairs on the back of Rosalind's neck stood at rigid attention. *Oh, please, dear God, no more.*

"Sammy . . . you really shouldn't buy me so . . . so many things."

He gave her a lightning glance. "I haven't started buying you things yet. This is just the beginning."

Rosalind swallowed. *Oh, no.* She gave him a trembling smile, and waited with a fluttering stomach as he lifted out a couple additional boxes. He handed her a long flat one, and Rosalind muttered a prayer before opening it. She pulled back the lid, reached in, and removed an even smaller box. She opened this one, and gasped. There, lying on a bed of softest black velvet, was an eighteen-inch strand of glittering white diamonds.

"Oh," she said softly. "It's . . . it's beautiful." There was wonder in her voice. Her eyes flashed to his. "But . . . it's not real? Is it?" Something like this would cost the world. A small fortune, easily.

He lifted the strand from the box, draped it around her neck, and spent a moment fastening the clasp.

"I'd never buy anything else for you."

He stood back to admire the hang of glittering stones. "Nice," he said, "but something's missing." He opened another package and extracted two dangling earrings of matching beauty. He held them up to the light, and a rainbow of colors shimmered and danced across each multifaceted teardrop.

Rosalind stood absolutely still as he carefully fastened each earring in place. She looked up at him with bemused eyes. Was this real? Was he?

One of her hands moved to touch the glittering drops at her ears. Things like this just did not happen, not to her, anyway. Soft tears misted her eyes, and she struggled to speak, but couldn't. She had never been so touched. It wasn't the fact that he had bought her such an expensive gift. It was the fact that he would even think to do it. No one before would have cared enough. . . .

She sniffled, and Sam stroked a tear away with a

large gritty thumb, and then gathered her close. "You weren't supposed to cry," he muttered in her ear.

Rosalind's throat clenched as he kissed each eyelid in a delicate flowering caress, his tongue gently stroking away the crystal tears at the curve of each eye. She offered him trembling lips, and he kissed them in a slow and satisfied manner, his tongue dipping into the hot center of her mouth to sample, stroke, worship . . .

The feeling was like none other she had ever experienced, and she clung to him with head thrown back. She had read of this, had seen movies about this, but never, never would she have thought that sensations like these actually lay in wait for her.

Soft, warm breath sobbed out of her, and she murmured his name in a broken way. Without conscious volition, her thoughts went back to the day six years before when he had asked her to marry him. She had thought him to be such a beast then. Had been so insulted by his offer. Her uppermost thoughts had been primarily: An atheist? A die-hard chauvinist with nary an ounce of compassion in him? How dare he think that she would even consider him? But had she been the one in need of a little compassion, a little understanding? She had been so self-righteous. So absolutely inflexible. So uncaring.

She was so ashamed.

She opened midnight-black eyes that were bright with a new knowledge, a different light. God had given him to her so that she might help him, lead him back to the path. He was essentially all that every true Christian struggled every day to be: *Kind. Generous. Caring.* How could she have been so very blind?

For the first time without any encouragement from him, she kissed his eyelids, his face, the furled skin of his ears, and he laughed against her face and said,

"Now, if I'd known that I'd have gotten this kind of reaction, I would've bought you diamonds ages ago."

"Thank you," she said simply. But her words held more meaning than they appeared to have. And, she wondered if he would guess at the depth. *Thank you for showing me my true self. Thank you for touching my heart and showing me how to really feel again. Thank you for so many things that are only now being born. . . .*

Fifteen

The online presentation took several days of effort, but since most of the work had already been done in Los Angeles, all that was really required was for Rosalind to pull the many fashion pages together into one cohesive package. Sue Perkins, Rosalind was very happy to observe, was conspicuously absent from the entire process. Since their little altercation in the ladies' room on the evening of the buyers' party, Rosalind had gone out of her way to avoid the woman. And so far, her tactics of avoidance had worked perfectly. Sam had helped in this process, too. And Rosalind was grateful that he hadn't attempted to force them both to work together.

"Rosy?" Rosalind looked up from the computer screen, a smile in her eyes. *Sam.* He had been an absolute rock through the long days and nights of work, bringing her things to eat and drink, rubbing her shoulders and neck when her bent position at the computer screen began to make her muscles ache.

"How's it coming?" Sam came to stand beside her. Rosalind pointed to the screen with the back of her pen. "It's just about done. If this doesn't get you the business, then those guys need their heads examined."

Sam nodded, and Rosalind noticed the tired shadows around his eyes. Her brows furrowed for a moment. For the past several days they had slept in separate beds, and she had been so preoccupied with the development work that she had not asked him whether or not he was managing to sleep well.

She touched the side of his face, and he turned his lips into her palm for a brief contact of flesh.

"Have you been sleeping okay?" she asked now, her eyes large and concerned.

He shrugged. "I sleep better when you're with me." He chuckled in a self-conscious manner. "I guess you're my security blanket."

She made a clucking sound with her tongue. "You poor thing. What about the fashion show preparations? Everything set?"

Sam sank into a sprawl on a nearby couch, placing his head on one of the armrests. "I'll be glad when this is all over. But, yes . . . I think we're ready." He stretched a hand, and Rosalind went to sit beside him. With a gentle finger she touched the circles beneath his eyes.

"Have you eaten?" she asked.

"Not yet. I wanted you all to myself tonight, so I gave Renard the night off." He smiled. "Will you cook for me?"

Rosalind leaned forward so that her hair curtained one side of his face. "I'll do more than that."

His eyes gleamed. "This sounds interesting."

Rosalind reached for the first button on his shirt. And as she undid the buttons, she caressed the sleek hairs just beneath with the back of her index finger.

"I'm going to make you your favorite dinner. . . ."

His eyebrows lifted. "But you don't know what that is."

She leaned forward to kiss the exact spot where her finger had just stroked, and she felt his heart leap in his chest. Between kisses, she said, "Medium-well steak, stuffed portobello mushrooms, macaroni and cheese, corn bread . . . spicy collards with a dash of green onions." She had worked her way down to just above his navel, and he eased onto his elbows to watch her.

"Did I miss anything?" Her eyes danced with little lights.

He reached long hands for her. "That's way too exact to be a guess. Have I been talking in my sleep?"

She laughed. "I asked Renard."

"Ah," he said. "So you're going to do this for me? And what else will you do?"

She thought for a moment. "What about a nice warm bubble bath?"

"A bubble bath? A hard-nosed businessman like me in a bubble bath? Imagine what would happen if word of that got out. My reputation would be ruined forever."

Rosalind pulled his shirt closed. "Okay," she said. "No bubble bath for you, then."

Sam swept her from the spot beside him, and placed her to lie directly atop him.

"You know, you give up way too easily," he said with a trace of wicked humor in his eyes. "Don't you know yet that there's little I wouldn't do for you?"

She sat up and straddled him. "You say the nicest things." And she was beginning to believe that by some strange and wonderful miracle, the things he said he might really actually mean.

His hands came up to grip her waist, and he moved her slowly, provocatively against him. "Let's just skip the dinner and go straight for dessert."

She chuckled. "You're not getting that kind of dessert."

He sighed in an exaggerated manner. "Come on, babe . . . please."

She swung her leg from across his chest and stood up. "Now, you promised me you were going to be good."

He sat up slowly, his shirt pulling open at the waist. "Me and my promises. Whenever I make them, I always get myself into trouble."

"Not this time," and she winked at him. "There'll be absolutely no trouble for you this time."

"So you keep telling me, but I'm the one who can't sleep at night."

She interlaced her fingers with his. "You'll sleep like a baby tonight. I promise *you* that." And she pulled him along with her. "Come and help me cook."

On his protestations about not knowing how to properly boil water, she wrapped him in an apron, and tied it behind him with a grand flourish and a big bow.

"Now, Mr. Winter," she said after she had removed all of the necessary items from the fridge. "You're going to chop the greens and the onions. Then I'll show you how to stuff the mushrooms."

She handed him a rough wooden board and a knife, which he accepted as though she had just handed him a piece of moon rock.

Rosalind tried her best not to laugh as he began to chop the greens in the most wild and uncoordinated manner. "Try not to lose any of your fingers," she said with an unbelievably straight face.

"Lose my fingers? You'll be lucky if that's all I lose."

Rosalind stifled a laugh with the back of her hand, and with her knife, pointed to the huge hunks of greens. "Cut those bits smaller."

"You're giving me all the hard stuff to do," he grumbled. "Let me see what you're doing."

He came over and had a look at her hands as they chopped, diced, mixed, and spiced the stuffing for the mushrooms.

"Hmm," he said after a moment spent watching the speed and skill of her hands. "Where'd you learn to do all that? You cook like one of those professional chefs on TV."

Rosalind gave him a sideways glance. "I love cooking. I find it very relaxing."

He went back to his chopping, and between the hacking sounds the knife made each time he whacked the board, he said, "I can really think of several other things I would prefer doing for relaxation."

"Oh, stop fretting like that," Rosalind said with a coaxing note in her voice. "When you taste the meal, you'll understand why all this preparation was worth it."

He gave her a hooded look, tossed the severely mangled greens into a bowl, and then started on the green onions with the same wild abandon.

After a few minutes of the banging, Rosalind took the knife from him.

"I don't think you have any talent at all in this area," she said after having a look at the onions, which were now very close to a fine mush.

He nodded. "I won't argue with you there. I told you that I had no skills at all."

Rosalind patted him on the back. "Don't worry about it. You can just sit and watch me, then." And she went about the kitchen like a whirlwind, chopping, mashing, whipping, stirring. In next to no time at all, everything was in the oven baking nicely.

She turned to him, wiping her hands on a wet towel. "You look really tired. Are you going to be able to make it through the meal?"

He pulled her to sit on one of his knees and rested

his head on her breast. "Don't forget my bubble bath."

She stroked his head and felt the beginnings of something deeply profound flutter in a corner of her heart.

"I'm not sure you need that anymore. You seem about ready to drop."

He raised his head to look at her, and his eyes did look very tired. "I need you tonight," he said.

She stroked the side of his face. "I'll stay with you."

She met the dark gaze, and felt that she had never seen eyes more beautiful. A mouth more perfectly built for kissing. A spirit more tenderized by life.

"Thank you," he said, and she bent to kiss him gently on the mouth. And for the next several minutes, what had started out as a simple caress, deepened to sweet warm kisses that felt so deeply right somehow. It was only the smell of something catching on the stove that finally tore them from each other. And Rosalind scampered up with an "Oh, no."

She had so completely lost herself in him for the moment, that she had neglected the greens on the stove. She stirred them now with sweeping, stirring strokes, scraping at the bottom of the pan. Sam came to stand behind her.

"Is it ruined?"

Rosalind stirred it a bit more, and then turned the fire down. "No. It should be okay. It just got a bit singed. But no real harm done."

"I have an idea." And he spun her into his arms again.

"Hmm?" Rosalind said, looking up at him.

"Why don't we leave the bubble bath thing for New Jersey? After you've told Ben."

She massaged his back with both hands. "Too tired?"

"Not enough self-control," he said, a smile curling about his mouth.

"I now see that every word you were telling me before about men thinking about sex at every available opportunity . . . every word is true."

He rocked her back and forth. "And it's especially true in my case. But only in relation to you."

She tilted her head. "What's so very special about me? I'm just an ordinary big-boned gal."

He laughed. "You're back to your bones again. You have a slim build. Why do you keep harping on the fact that you have big bones?"

Rosalind was tempted to tell him why it was she was still so hung up on the subject of her bones. But it all seemed so very silly and inconsequential now.

"From now on, I won't mention my bones."

He massaged the fat of her earlobe. "Don't feel restricted if you feel you must talk about them. I'm more than willing to discuss them with you . . . or anything else you feel the need to talk about."

Rosalind felt herself getting tearful again, so she turned back to the stove and busied herself with the pots, and the oven. She stuck the tip of a fork into the macaroni and cheese, nodded in satisfaction, and then checked the two steaks. They were both browned to simmering perfection, and she spent a moment spooning gravy from the sides of the pan over them both.

She straightened again to say, "Well, everything's done except the mushrooms."

Sam shrugged. "Let's forget them." He took her hand in his and walked her across to one of the large floor-to-ceiling windows. He pointed to the shimmering city below.

"Isn't that an incredible sight?"

Rosalind nodded. She had seen these very lights so

many times before but somehow there was something special about them tonight. Spread out like a blanket of diamonds, white, red, blue, green, and yellow lights played with each other in a beautiful symphony of color. It was a breathtaking sight.

She rested a palm on the flat of the glass, and Sam's hand came up to cover hers. He softly stroked her hand.

"Rosy," he said, "will you stay with me . . . beyond the term of our contract?"

She turned, so that her head rested on the glass.

Stay with him beyond the term of the contract. In the past days, she'd been hoping that he would ask her that very question, but she had been afraid that maybe his interest in her was no longer a long-term one. But regardless of how long Sam's interest in her continued, she had firmly decided she was never going back to Ben. Not that Ben would want her, either, after this.

He bent to rest his forehead against hers. "Does your silence mean no?"

She moved her nose against his. "It means I can't believe you want me for longer than the contracted period."

He turned his head so that his lips were just inches above her own. "You're the hardest woman to convince. What do I have to do to show you how much you mean to me? How much you've always meant to me?"

"I guess I'm insecure." She tried to joke. But the truth be known, it probably wasn't that much of a joke. She still couldn't believe that he really wanted her in a long-term way. After the years of separation. After . . . everything.

He kissed her once, then again and again in short little unsatisfactory kisses. "Don't worry," he murmured against her mouth. "By the time I'm done with you . . . there won't be an insecure bone left in your body."

Sixteen

Dinner was delicious. The steaks had been done to absolute perfection. The meat was tender, succulent, with just the right amount of browning to make it almost melt in the mouth with just the barest minimum of chewing. The macaroni and greens were ideal companions to such culinary extravagance. And the gravy possessed just the right degree of thickness to encourage sopping with the sweet corn bread.

At one point in the meal, Sam raised his wineglass, and after taking a sip, said, "I think I may have some culinary talent after all. My greens and onions taste pretty good."

Rosalind sampled another forkful, and then said, "I would never have expected it, after what you did to those poor leaves."

He laughed, and their eyes locked. A deep, warm smile wrapped itself about her, and Rosalind reached forward to pat the corner of his mouth with a linen napkin. She hadn't been this happy in a long time. . . . Maybe she had never been this happy. She liked him. She really did.

He finished the meat on his plate, wiped the remaining gravy away with the soft back of a hunk of corn bread, and polished off the remaining greens with a very satisfied "Time for bed."

Rosalind rose to begin clearing the dishes, but Sam reached a hand to forestall her.

"Leave those. Renard will get them tomorrow."

"But it won't take a moment."

He stood, hands in pockets. "You look about ready to drop, too. Come to bed and I'll rub your feet for you."

Rosalind looked at him from beneath lowered lashes. It was a tempting idea.

"Are you sure you feel up to it?"

He smiled. "I'm never too tired for you. And especially after the kind of dinner we just had. You definitely deserve a treat."

She followed him into the bedroom, feeling only the slightest twinge of guilt over the dishes, pots, and pans left sprawling all over the kitchen, and dining table.

Sam sat on the side of the bed and began to remove his shirt. "Do you mind if I sleep without pajama bottoms tonight?"

She was halfway into the bathroom, and turned back to look at him. Did he mean sleep completely nude? "Ah . . ."

But he answered the question in her eyes before she could properly put it into words. "I didn't mean naked. I'll keep my shorts on. It's just a bit warm tonight."

Rosalind felt the blood surge in her cheeks. Had her panic been so immediately apparent to him?

"Should I turn the air lower?" She tried to ask the question in as normal a manner as possible.

"Won't you be cold?"

"No. I'll be fine." She was already looking at the thermostat on the wall, and adjusting the setting. "Is sixty-nine okay?"

"Perfect," he said. Then, "When the online presentation and fashion show are over, do you feel like going to see Cirque du Soleil?"

Rosalind scrubbed her teeth over the sink, rinsed with a glass of water, and then straightened to say, "The production here at the Bellagio is called 'O,' isn't it?"

"Mmm."

"I'd love to see it."

She emerged, dressed in a silky burgundy pajama set. He was already lying beneath the covers, with the sheets pulled to his waist. And an errant thought ran through Rosalind's head. He looked as though he belonged there in her bed. As though he had always been there.

She went to him slowly and he watched her come. Bedside, she looked down on him.

"You're way too generous with me. You know you're really going to spoil me for anyone else."

He sat up, and his chest muscles rippled. Rosalind's eyes were pulled to the hard stomach and lean waist. He really was the most gorgeous man. Had she been completely out of her mind six years before when she had turned down his proposal of marriage?

He stretched a hand to pull her to him. "Is there going to be someone else . . . after me?"

Rosalind pushed at his shoulder. "Do you want me to become a nun after you finish with me?"

He stroked the leg of her pants toward her knee, folding the cloth as he went. "Who says I'll ever be finished with you?"

Rosalind leaned back on her elbows. There was really no response to that. And she was afraid to really press him on the matter. He had already asked her to stay longer than the agreed-upon year. But how long would he really want her for? After the newness of having sex with her had faded, would he still feel the same way he did now? Or would he begin to grow restless and start to look around again for a new challenge? For that was all she had been to him these past six years—of that she was sure. His personality was such that he would chase and conquer anything he could not immediately have.

His fingers roamed her leg, from the sole of her foot to her calf, massaging in the most superb way. Without conscious effort, her eyelids sagged shut. The languor deep within her spread like a sweet tide of feeling, and she actually gasped as she felt his mouth close on one of her toes. The soft sound she made deepened to a ragged moan as he suckled on each toe, giving each one his full attention. His name stumbled from her mouth in a rush of broken breath.

"Sammy . . ."

He raised his head to look at her. "Do you want me?" His voice sliced through the haze, but only enough for her to get a grasp of what it was he was asking her.

"Yes." Her voice was a squeak of sound, hot and desperate, yet somehow afraid now that she had had the admission wrung from her.

"Tell me how much."

She squirmed beneath his mouth. And as her heart thrashed in her breast, her brain screamed a frantic warning: *Don't let him know. Not now. He'll have too much power. Too much.* But for once she paid her brain no attention, and groaned, "So much. Very much."

"More than Ben? Tell me." He started on the other leg, and her blood pressure went up another willing notch.

"More than Ben."

"More than any other man?"

Oh, God. What was he asking of her? But the feeling

was so incredible. She had never known she could feel so—

"Yes." The sound sobbed from the back of her throat.

He kissed the scoop of each foot, and then kissed a wandering path up one calf and down the other. Rosalind sighed his name again, and he muttered hers in a rough and aching way.

"Tell me what you want, babe."

She didn't know what it was she wanted. Why did he set fire to her blood in such a strange and wonderful manner? She had to stop him. Stop him before it was too late.

With superhuman effort, she reached for the strength. "Sammy . . . we . . . we can't."

He pulled himself above her, balancing himself on his fists. His eyes glittered with wild passion. "Don't stop this, Rosalind. We both want it. It is the right thing to do." He hardly ever called her by her full name. The fact registered like a soft footfall somewhere in the back of her mind, and in response, she wrapped her arms about him in silent entreaty.

He sighed against her neck, "I know. I know. It's just been such a long time for me. And having you here like this is stretching every ounce of self-control that I possess."

Rosalind stroked the deep furrow running the center of his back. What did he mean? It had been a long time for him? Surely not that?

He rolled onto his back, turning her neatly to lie atop him. She looked directly into his eyes and asked the question that she had to have answered.

"Sammy . . . what did you mean 'it's been such a long time' for you?"

His fingers played with the ends of her hair. "I was hoping you didn't notice that."

She touched one of his eyebrows and traced the thick black line from one end to the next. So, what he'd said had been significant and not just a slip of the tongue.

"Why shouldn't I have noticed that?"

He gave her a deeply hooded, dark-eyed look. "I do have a reputation to maintain, after all. How would it look if it got out that Sam Winter was . . . whipped?"

Rosalind chuckled heartily. "Whipped? You? Could never happen."

"Well, how would you explain away the fact that I haven't been with a woman in years?"

She touched his face, suddenly serious. "Years?"

He shifted her slightly so that they now lay side by side. "I got tired of imagining that all the women I went through after you left L.A. were you."

"Oh." Her voice was soft. Humble. Was he really serious? Had he wanted her that much even then? When he'd asked her to marry him?

He touched the tip of her nose with his index finger. "Is that all you can say? Oh?"

"Sammy," she said, and without warning, there was a cluster of warm salty tears just behind her eyes. "I'm sorry. I—I didn't know you felt like that. I thought . . ." What had she thought? The plain unvarnished truth of it was that she had barely spared him a thought back then. So absolutely prejudiced against him had she been. It would never have occurred to her that he might have had deeper feelings for her. Not after his comments about having a particular preference for horse-boned, squid-faced women.

He was smiling at her, and there was a sadness somewhere deep in his eyes that she hadn't noticed before.

"What did you think?"

Rosalind thought about it for a second, and tried

to put together the right combination of words that would somehow cause him the least amount of hurt. "I—I figured you'd gotten tired of looking for the right woman, and . . . and you chose me because I fit your particular physical requirements."

He leaned on an elbow. His eyes flickered over her face then went to settle again on her lips.

"Very few men ever choose women to marry just because they look good. Not if they're wise, anyway."

"Why did you choose me?"

He took her hand and laid it directly above his breastbone. Beneath, she felt the strong thudding of his heart, and was bemused by the sudden change in its rhythm as her fingers moved to play with the dusting of hairs.

"If there is such a thing as being meant for each other . . . I believe we were meant to be together. I felt it the very first time I saw you."

"The very first time?" Did he really remember the very first time he had seen her? The day she'd been standing outside his office, eavesdropping . . . through no fault of her own? She remembered quite clearly the stunned look he had given her. At the time she had chalked the look up to simple shock. Shock and confusion regarding her presence just outside his door, as he unburdened himself in the most unrestrained manner.

"Why's that so surprising?" And he bent to run a warm tongue just inside the soft inner curve of her lip. "You're a very sexy girl."

She held his head in place and kissed him back with warm enthusiasm. "You know very well that there're lots of very sexy girls all over the place. In fact, in L.A., sexy girls are a dime a dozen. Nothing unique there."

He bit her softly, and she squealed in protest.

"Maybe . . . I'll tell you the real reason soon. But meanwhile, you'll just have to be satisfied with the sexy-girl explanation."

"Okay," she said, and her eyes sparkled. "I'll let you off the hook."

"Thank you, ma'am." And he pulled the blankets up to cover them both. "Now I face another sleepless night."

"You always sleep when you're with me. Come here. . . ."

He came to rest his head on her breast, and she held him gently, tenderly, her fingers playing with the softly curled hairs at the base of his neck.

They both slept soundly, and morning found her wrapped in his arms, her long legs intertwined with his. Sam woke as the first rays of sunlight crept into the room, and for long moments, he just watched her sleep, and then for the first time in decades, he closed his eyes and uttered a silent prayer to the God he was almost sure was not there. . . .

Seventeen

"Well, we did it," Sam said to the small group of staff assembled in the hotel suite. "Our line will be carried by some of the biggest stores in not only Paris, but Italy, Spain, the Caribbean and Africa."

A cheer went up and Renard took this opportunity to hand around glasses of champagne and tiny, exquisitely made hors d'oeuvres. The fashion show had been a great success, and the online presentation had just been the icing on the cake. Rosalind was proud that she'd had a part, albeit a relatively small one, in helping pull the entire thing together. She sipped at her glass of sparkling bubbly and listened with a certain measure of pride as Sam wrapped up his speech. What an incredible man Sam Winter had turned out to be.

"And," Sam was saying, "in addition to the little bonus you'll all find in your paychecks at the end of the month, tonight—dinner, and any show you choose to see—are on me."

Out of the corner of her eye, Rosalind saw Sue Perkins edge a little closer to her, and she made herself continue to sip her drink. Surely the woman wasn't crazy enough to start anything with her right there in front of Sam?

"He'll never marry you . . . you know."

Rosalind finished the last swallow remaining in her glass, then turned to give the other woman a measured look.

"I'm sure you're completely right about that. So I wouldn't let it worry you."

She moved away before any response could be made. She was not at all interested in standing there, trading barbs with Sue Perkins.

The other woman watched her go, a strange little smile playing about her lips. She looked across to where Sam stood, and winked at him. Sam gave her a little nod and then followed Rosalind into the little alcove just off the dining room. He pulled the screen door closed behind him.

Rosalind rested her empty glass on a little round table.

"Sammy," she said, "I don't think I really ever thanked you properly for helping Tony . . . and me— lending us that sum of money I mean."

He came to stand right before her, a smile glinting in his eyes. "What is this? An attack of conscience? Or are you planning to leave me . . . so you're getting a last thank-you in . . . ?"

"Leave you?" she said with softly shining eyes. "Not unless you want me to."

He stretched an arm for her. "Come here." And when she was comfortably settled in his arms, he tilted her chin and bent to rub his nose against hers. "There's something I've been wanting to ask you for a while now."

She looked up at him. "Hmm?" Her heart tripped a soft rhythm in her chest as he stroked a gentle hand down the center of her back.

"We're leaving for Jersey tomorrow. . . ."

"Mmm-hmm." She knew what was coming, she was sure of it.

"When we get back home . . . and after you settle things with Ben, what're we going to do about the sleeping arrangements?"

Rosalind hid a little smile and met his dark gaze. So very much had changed in just a little over two weeks. How incredible life was.

"What do you want to do about them?"

"I want you with me. In my bed. Every night." He bent to press a kiss to her lips. "I think I can manage to wait two more nights for you. But that's about it."

"You are," Rosalind said, "one of the most determined men I have ever met."

He laughed. "I came to Jersey to get what's mine. And I intend to have it."

His words registered softly with her. What a sweet-talker he was. She didn't believe him for a second, of course. She had been the one to get in touch with him, so that couldn't possibly be true.

"So you came to New Jersey for me?"

"I did." And he bent again to take her lips in a long sweet kiss that left Rosalind breathless.

"You're such a liar," she said against his mouth.

He chuckled. "You didn't believe for even one minute, that you'd escaped me six years ago, did you?"

She tilted her head to look at him. Sometimes she couldn't tell if he was kidding her or not. But he had somehow ended up in New Jersey, not ten minutes away from where she lived. So maybe he *had* followed her. . . .

"I felt sure you would've been married with an entire legion of kids . . . by now."

He turned her face toward him. "So you did think of me then . . . from time to time?"

"Every so often you would pop into my head," she lied. The truth be known, she had made a very determined effort not to think of him at all in all of the years that they had been apart. But she couldn't say that to him now for she knew that he would be hurt by her words. He appeared so tough on the outside, but he was really so easy to hurt, and to hurt deeply.

"Hmm," he said. And she wasn't sure if he believed her or not. "Well, there was no chance that I was going to marry someone else and have kids with them. It wouldn't have been right."

"Not right? But one woman is much like any other." She thought to play with him. He had, after all, said this very thing himself.

He looked at her for a long moment. "It wouldn't be right to marry one woman . . . and constantly need another."

"Oh." She hadn't expected him to say that. She had been sure that he would've given an equally playful reply. But she could see by the expression in his eyes that he was completely serious.

"No one else will ever be able to make love to you . . . the way I will."

Sudden tears misted her eyes. She didn't deserve him. She didn't. What had she done in her life to warrant such devotion? It was unbelievable. It couldn't be real. Could it?

"But . . . what if I don't please you in bed? What then?"

He smiled at her, and his eyes became, if possible, darker than ever. "Do you really think there's any chance of that happening?"

"You never know. You may have built this experience up in your mind into something I can never live up to."

He stroked her cheek with a finger.

"It's not the experience. It's you. Yes . . . you," he said as she was about to say something to dilute what he had just said. "As long as you're the one in my arms . . . the experience will be the best I've ever had."

A knock on the door disturbed them, and Rosalind removed herself from his arms and went to stand at one of the windows. She stood looking blindly out at the teeming city as he spoke to Renard. She heard him say, "Front row seats for 'O.' Tonight. The seven-thirty show is fine."

Rosalind's brow rippled. She wanted to believe him. She wanted to believe him. But she was still afraid. Afraid of what it might mean if she came to care for him deeply. There were still so many things that sepa-rated them. Well, one thing mainly. His lack of belief in God was a major stumbling block between them, and of course, although he appeared to want her now, she really had no idea how long his interest in her might last. He said that she was the important element in whatever fantasy situation he had built around her, but she had a sneaking suspicion that it wasn't her at all. It was simply the sex. Since he hadn't had it in a while, it had probably assumed an unbelievable level of importance.

The door closed, and she half turned to him, her expression still pensive. He placed a hand on either side of her and bent to kiss her on the side of the neck.

"Thinking about what I said?"

She wrinkled her nose at him. "I hope I don't dis-appoint you."

He touched the tip of her nose. "You won't."

Later, at the Cirque du Soleil performance, dressed in a brand-new gown of soft blue silk, with diamonds glittering at her ears and throat, Rosalind sat beside Sam and thoroughly enjoyed one of the most splendid theatrical performances she had ever seen. Sam held her hand during the entire performance, and only relinquished it from time to time so that she might applaud with the rest of the audience. When the show was through, he whispered in her ear, "Since this is our last night in Vegas . . . what else would you like to do?"

She gave him a quick look. "I saw a nice little church somewhere around here a few days ago. How about if we go there for the evening service?"

His eyes became turbid, and he seemed to go somewhere far away from her for a moment. He took her elbow and maneuvered her through the crowd. When they had finally reached an empty patch of space, he said, "A church. That's where you want to go now?"

She nodded. "Yes." *Maybe stepping back into that environment might have some sort of an effect on him.*

His eyes flicked over her. "You're a little overdressed for church, I think. Why don't you wait until you get back to Jersey?"

Well, she'd tried. She hadn't really expected him to go for the idea right away. But maybe with a little coaxing, a little time . . . he might.

"Will you go with me in New Jersey?"

"I can't promise you that I will." And the hard edge in his voice reminded her of the Sam Winter of old. But that Sam was not real; she knew that now. And she also knew how to handle him when he got into his little moods.

In the middle of the still-very-crowded lobby, she put her arms about him and kissed him. Tenderly. Warmly.

He muttered a surprised "Oh" against her lips, and his arms folded about her without hesitation.

Rosalind stroked the rough velvet of his tongue with the tip of hers, and then proceeded to caress the roof of his mouth in a manner that caused a hair-fine shudder to ripple through him.

Someone passing close by made the half-joking comment, "Why don't they get a room?"

And Sam reluctantly pulled himself from her to say in a husky undertone, "I think we'd better go up to the suite . . . before we get arrested."

Rosalind followed him into the elevator and as soon as the doors closed, he moved closer to her.

"I felt sure you'd be mad at me."

She smiled at him. "Why? Because you don't want to go to church?"

"It's important to you. You told me that yourself."

"Yes," she said, and there was a soft, teasing note in her voice. "Well, I guess we'll just have to have a short and torrid affair . . . and forget about anything more meaningful . . . since you're so absolutely opposed to anything of a spiritual nature."

But he didn't laugh as she had expected him to. All he said was "Hmm" as the doors opened on to the suite. Rosalind gave him a sidelong glance as she left the elevator. Boy, was he having some strange mood fluctuations tonight. Happy and cheerful one moment, almost completely depressed the next.

"Go get changed into something less dressy," he said as soon as they were in the bedroom.

Rosalind's eyebrows lifted a little. "Changed? Why? Where're we going?"

He walked into the first bathroom, and over the noise of the tap being turned on, she heard him say, "Church."

Eighteen

The flight back to New Jersey was smoothly uneventful. Last night had been an interesting one, to say the least. They had found a little church somewhere just off the Strip, and had been drafted into what appeared to have been an impromptu wedding. The bridegroom had been so severely sauced, that he had spent the majority of the ceremony leaning, quite heavily, on Sam's shoulder. The bride, a very brittle yet determined young woman, was herself in such a high state of nerves, that after the entire affair was over, she was sick all over Rosalind's shoes. Rosalind and Sam were forced to return to the hotel to get cleaned up. And Sam had remarked to Rosalind on the way back, "I don't ever remember church being so much fun . . . somehow."

Rosalind had tried to be angry, but after a momentary struggle had seen the humor in the whole thing and had responded laughingly, "I'm pretty sure that poor guy's going to wake up tomorrow and wonder what in the world happened last night."

Sam turned to her now as the Fasten Your Seatbelt sign blinked on. "Hard to believe that we were only there for two or so weeks, isn't it?"

Rosalind nodded. Just two short weeks, and everything had changed. Her entire world had been turned upside down. All of her carefully laid plans, out the window.

Their good-byes to Renard too had been particularly wrenching for her. She had somehow managed to grow very attached to the butler during their short stay, and had found herself very near tears as she had thanked him very sincerely for taking such good care of them both while they were there. Renard had smiled and asked them to return again to the Bellagio as soon as they possibly could.

"I'm really going to miss him," Rosalind said as the plane taxied to a smooth stop.

Sam snapped back his buckle. "Renard?"

She nodded. "I somehow got really used to having him around."

"We can always go back there, you know. And if you have a particular preference for a certain member of the staff, I can make sure that person is part of the package."

He extended his hand to help her out of her seat, and within minutes, they were walking briskly through the terminal building.

Rosalind's mind turned inevitably to the upcoming situation with Ben. She wasn't looking forward to it at all. In fact, if there had been any way that she could think of to avoid the confrontation that she knew was possibly only hours away, she would've opted for that.

Their VIP luggage service met them at the car with their bags, and before long they were on the highway, pointed toward home. *Home.* Rosalind's brow rippled in thought. It was strange that she now thought of Sam's house as hers, too. Her apartment had been pushed to the very back of her mind. All of her things were still there, of course. Her furniture, her pots and pans, paintings, most of her clothes. But somehow, none of those things seemed important now.

She sucked in a breath. She was in such deep water now, and she couldn't even explain how it had happened. Or why. But in a totally unexpected way, she had come to care about Sam Winter. How much she cared she wasn't clear on. But she no longer felt any antagonism toward him. It had all been foolish anyway.

She turned to look at him now, and found to her chagrin, that he had been observing her all along.

"Happy to be back?" he asked, and in his eyes she read uncertainty.

She covered his hand with her own. "It'll be great to see Tony. . . ." Her voice tapered off.

"And . . . Ben?"

She turned to look out the window at the passing scenery. "I'm not looking forward to that." He was silent for a bit. "You know," he finally said, "whenever you have anything to do that's not pleasant, it's always best to do it right away. The longer you wait, the harder it'll become."

"Hmm," Rosalind agreed. There was certainly some truth to that. But what was she going to say to Ben? How was she going to tell him that things were just not going to work? Wouldn't he want to know why not? And if he asked her that question, what would she say? Sam Winter had happened? Or would she tell him that she had gotten fed up with his offhand and uncaring treatment of her? Just thinking about it caused her stomach to flutter a bit in anxiety. She was absolutely sure that he would not take it well. Ben had grown so accustomed to her always being there for him. To her always taking whatever it was he dished out—and never complaining.

"I'll come along with you . . . if you want me to."

Rosalind sucked in her bottom lip and chewed on it for a bit. That would be the coward's way out, and

Ben would definitely think that she and Sam had been sleeping together in a very real sense in Las Vegas.

"No," she said. "This is something that I have to do alone. I owe him at least that much."

Sam swung the big vehicle into the long curving driveway. "You owe him nothing. Nothing at all."

As the car came out of the final bend and the house came into view, Rosalind's hand came up to cover her mouth. "Oh, no." Ben. What was he doing parked in the driveway? Why wasn't he at work?

She cast a lightning glance at Sam, and noticed that his face had tightened. It was an almost imperceptible reaction, one that she would not have noticed weeks ago.

"Did you tell him when you might be getting back?"

"No . . . I didn't. I actually hadn't called him again. Not since that first time." Rosalind rubbed the damp away from her palms with a tissue. She'd been hoping to hold Ben off for perhaps another day or two. She had never imagined that he would have taken it into his head to meet her at the house.

Sam brought the car to a smooth stop, and as soon as he did, Ben was at the passenger side door, pulling at the handle. Rosalind barely managed to release the lock, before he was pulling open the door and wrapping her in a bear hug. Rosalind tried her best to remain stiff and unresponsive in his arms, for she could feel Sam's eyes on them both.

"Ben," she said a bit breathlessly, attempting to free herself from his grasp. "What're you doing here? How'd you know when I'd be back?"

He gave her a resounding kiss on the lips, and said, "Tony. I had to resort to making threats before he would tell me that you were due back today."

He lifted her from the car seat and spun her about. "God, you won't believe how very much I missed you."

He hugged her again. "I will never, never let you do that again. The next time you go anywhere, it'll be with me. On our honeymoon."

Rosalind pushed at his chest with her hands. Out of the corner of her eye, she saw Sam go to the trunk of the car and begin unloading the luggage. But she was very aware that he was watching them both very closely.

"Let me get my breath back, Ben," she said, and he looked down at her with slightly puzzled eyes.

"What's the matter? What kind of a welcome is that for your fiancé . . . whom you haven't seen in weeks, I might I add. I thought you'd be glad that I'd managed to get out of work, just to see you."

"I'm glad to see you, of course . . . but as I told you on the phone . . ." Her eyes followed Sam as he walked to the front door of the house, inserted his key, opened the door, and disappeared inside.

"I know we have a lot to talk about." He gave her the kind of look that had always managed to melt her resolve in the past. But this time it left her completely unmoved. "But . . . let me look at you first." And he grabbed her about the waist and spun her about.

"Yes," he said with some satisfaction. "You've gained a bit of weight. But"—he grinned—"all in the right places. I guess the boss man is treating you well?"

Treating her well? What would he say if she told him how well?

"Yes. We're getting along fine . . . now."

He smiled at her. "Where're your bags?"

Rosalind looked around her. The luggage had disappeared. "I think Sam got them all."

Ben wrapped an arm about her that very nearly constricted her breathing. "You two're on a first-name basis, huh?"

Rosalind tried to escape the arm about her, but it

was near impossible. "We've always been on a first-name basis. You'll remember that I've known him for quite a while."

He shook her a little as they walked toward the house. "Ros, Ros, Ros . . . come on now. Put some life into your voice. Are you jet-lagged or something?"

"No," she said in a quiet voice.

He looked down at her, and then said brightly, "Well, the evening I have planned should cheer you up. When's the last time you had me all to yourself for an entire evening?"

"I . . . don't—"

"That's right," he interrupted. "You can't remember. I can't even remember myself. It must be years. But . . . tonight, we're going to do whatever you want. Dinner. Movies. You get to choose the one you want to see for once." He laughed. "Then we'll go and sit in some nice secluded spot and make out. How's that sound?"

Rosalind swallowed. "Ben . . . before we make any plans like that . . . I think we need to talk about things. . . ."

He looked down at her as though he had only just heard her. "Things? What things?"

"Us," she said. "We have to talk about us."

"Oh. Yes. The wedding date. That's right. We never did set one, did we? Well"—and he paused by his battered old car to remove a huge drawstring cloth bag—"I'm ready to do that now. I think we can safely say that I'm going to make it through my residency with flying colors. You're going to be a surgeon's wife, dear heart. Isn't that exciting? We'll be able to buy a house very soon—nothing fancy, of course, but it'll be ours."

They walked through the open door, and Rosalind wondered where in the house Sam had disappeared to. She looked around the entry foyer. Her bags weren't anywhere in sight, so she guessed that he had taken them up to her room.

"Ben," she said now, "let me go get freshened up. I'll be back down in a little while. Do you mind waiting here?"

He beamed at her and removed the large bag from his shoulder. "I think I should come with you. Don't think you'll be able to carry this huge bag of laundry. I have more than two weeks of stuff in here. I'm completely out of socks, and almost out of shirts. Don't know what I would've done if you hadn't come back when you did."

Rosalind gave the bag of laundry a look. Yes, this was why he wanted her. Probably the only reason he did want her. He didn't want a wife; what he really needed was a servant, and maybe an occasional bed partner. She was not willing to be either any longer.

"Rosalind's not here to do your laundry for you." The voice just behind caused them both to turn. Sam stood in the corridor leading to the office, his face a hard uncompromising mask.

"You have no say in this, Winter," Ben said, his voice equally hard. "This has nothing to do with you. I'm having a private conversation with my fiancée."

Rosalind swallowed. She hated scenes, but she could see one looming directly ahead, for she knew Sam well enough to know that he would not back down.

"Ben . . ." she began. But he hushed her with "Just a minute, Rosalind. You're not a part of this."

Sam straightened from his lean against the wall. "Come here, Rosy," he said.

Ben's eyes flashed between them both. "Her name is Rosalind. Stay where you are, Ros. This man doesn't own you."

"Ben, please stop it. Sam didn't mean—"

Sam's eyes were like chips of ice. "I did mean it.

You're not going to do another piece of his laundry. Not ever again."

And he advanced toward Ben in such a threatening manner, that the shorter man took a few cautious steps backward.

"What is this?" His eyes darted from Sam to Rosalind, and then back to Sam. "What right have you to tell me how I can or cannot treat my own fiancée—the woman who's going to become my wife in no less than a year?"

Rosalind's brows drew together. Less than a year? A month ago such an admission would've made her deliriously happy, but now she felt nothing, nothing at all.

"I have every right to," Sam said, and he went to stand between Rosalind and Ben. "This woman is not your personal maid. She's not here to wait on you. If you need your laundry or anything else done . . . you'll just have to go to a Laundromat and toss a couple of quarters into the machines . . . just like the rest of the medical students you work with."

"Rosalind," Ben said, attempting to step around Sam, "have you been discussing our private affairs with your employer?"

Rosalind cleared her throat. Things were very rapidly getting completely out of hand. Sam, she knew, if sufficiently roused, would not be averse to knocking Ben flat on his face. And by the danger signals flashing in his eyes, she could tell that he was not very far away from doing exactly that.

"Let's go up to my room, Ben," she said hurriedly, and tried not to look at Sam as she did. She needed to get them away from each other until she could adequately explain to Ben that their engagement was at an end.

"Rosalind, I'd like to see you in my office for a

moment." His tone brooked no argument, and she left Ben standing in the middle of the floor and hurried after Sam. He stepped back to allow her to enter the room, which she did with some amount of trepidation beating in her chest. He couldn't be angry with her, surely? She was doing her level best to handle the situation.

With the door closed, he pulled her into his arms and bent his head to take her lips in a very warm—and equally surprising—kiss. Rosalind gasped against his mouth, for he had very nearly driven the breath from her.

"Oh," she muttered as his tongue mated with hers in the most supremely satisfying way. Her hands lifted to cling, and he raised his head to say thickly, "Has he ever made you feel like this?"

She answered without hesitation. "No. Never."

"Remember that when you're alone in your room with him."

She touched the side of his face. Was he actually worried that she wouldn't be able to do it? That maybe Ben would be able to talk her out of it?

"Absolutely nothing will happen once he's in my room. I—I just think I need to tell him . . . explain things to him alone. I've been trying to tell him all along, but for some reason, he's not been getting any of my hints."

"Oh, he's getting them. I'm sure he's getting them. He's just trying to manipulate you into taking him back." He tilted her chin up with a finger, and she looked deeply into black eyes that were suddenly soft, gentle.

"Don't let him bully you, Rosy. Or make you feel guilty. Because you have nothing at all to be guilty about. You haven't left him. He left you . . . ages ago. He doesn't care for you. I do. I always have"—he

stroked her bottom lip with the flat of his thumb—
"and I always will."

She rested the blunt of her forehead against his
chest. "Sammy," she murmured, "you're too good to
me. Sometimes I think I don't deserve it." She looked
up at him. "I really thought some very . . . unkind
things about you."

"Maybe you were justified in some of the things you
thought of me. Six years ago I was a slightly different
man. There were a great many things that I didn't
understand or even care to understand. But"—and he
bent again to sample her lower lip—"thank God . . .
I came to my senses."

Rosalind looked up at him. *Thank God?* Did he realize what he'd just said? He stepped back from her
and for a moment her hands still rested on his chest.
He was such a strong man in every way, and yet, somehow, he needed her. And little by little, day by day,
she was starting to need him, too.

"I'd better go. . . ."

"If you need me . . . just shout. I'll be in my room."

Ben was sitting in one of the chairs in the entry
foyer when she emerged from the office. He stood as
soon as she came into view.

"I'm beginning to think that maybe you shouldn't
be living here with that man. He seems to have a more
than professional interest in you."

"Come on," she said, ignoring his little comment,
"let's go on up."

In the elevator, he attempted to pull her close, but
she held him off with "Not now, Ben." And for the
first time he seemed to realize that there was something wrong. That she wasn't responding to him as
she usually would. That she wasn't panting after every
little crumb of affection that he deemed to toss her
way.

"Are you mad at me . . . or something?"

Rosalind suppressed a sigh. He was so completely clueless. The fact that he hadn't seen any of this coming was really incredible.

She walked briskly down the corridor to her room, inserted her key, turned, and said, "This is where I sleep."

Ben trailed in after her and dropped his laundry bag in the middle of the room.

"This is where you sleep? Here?"

"Yes," Rosalind said, and she walked briskly about the room, drawing back the curtains and throwing open windows.

"This is definitely not the kind of room you let your average employee have." He sat on the edge of the bed, and Rosalind knew he was looking directly at her, even though her back was turned.

"Is there something going on between you two?"

Rosalind threw open the final window then turned to face him across the plush expanse of carpeting. Her stomach was beginning to flutter again.

"Ben," she said, deliberately avoiding his question, "for a long time now . . . things haven't been exactly right between us."

She had his full attention. He was staring at her as though he was seeing her for the first time.

"Not *right* between us? What do you mean?"

"I mean," she said patiently, "our engagement hasn't really been one . . . has it?"

"I know I've been a bit busy these past months," he interrupted, "but I—I never realized that you weren't happy."

"That's the whole point, Ben. You've always been too wrapped up in your own affairs to even care if I was happy or not."

He wiped a hand across his face and said in a bemused way, "Where is this coming from, Ros? This isn't you at all. This just isn't you."

"This is me," she said firmly. "I just never let you see this side of me before." She went to sit beside him. "We're not right for each other, Ben."

"Don't say that," he said, and Rosalind swallowed the dryness away from her throat.

"I'm not the right woman for you, Ben. It may be hard to see it now. But . . . really, it's true."

He got up to pace the room. "God, I don't believe this. I don't believe this is happening to me. And now when I'm so close to finishing up my residency, too." He laughed in a wild way. "I guess I should've seen it coming, though. A simple surgeon is no competition for a multimillionaire. . . . Isn't that right, Ros?" And he returned to stand over her in an almost belligerent manner.

"That's not fair, Ben," Rosalind said, and she attempted to stand to face him, but he was suddenly down before her on his knees, his head in her lap.

"Please don't do this, Ros. I . . . Maybe you're right. Maybe I've—I've been blind. But give me another chance. Things can be as they were before."

As they were before? Rosalind looked down at his bent head, and her heart felt curiously empty. Somehow over the past weeks, she had come to understand that she actually deserved more than what Ben was willing to give her.

"It's best this way, Ben," she said, and he lifted his head to look at her. There was a hard expression in his eyes.

"Best? Best for whom? You and Sam Winter?"

"You know Sam Winter was never one of my favorite people. In fact, I never would have come here at all if you had lent me the money to help Tony."

"Of course," he said, and there was an unpleasant

tone in his voice. "It's all my fault, isn't it? Everything's my fault. Your wastrel of a brother steals from the Jamaican mob, and you expect me to ride to the rescue like Sir Galahad. Well, sorry I wasn't able to oblige you there. That money is mine, get it? Mine. And no one, not even you, will be getting your hands on it."

"Well," Rosalind said, pushing herself away from him and standing. "That about says it all, doesn't it?"

She opened the little velvet pouch hanging from around her neck. "Here's your ring," she said in a flat little voice. She hadn't worn it at all the entire time she was in Las Vegas.

He gave the ring a vicious look, then turned and picked up the bag of laundry. "Don't expect me to wish you the best," he said. "And when you're through with this situation"—he swept a hand in a wide gesture—"I'm sure you'll have time enough to think on how much you've lost. Because if you're hoping that Sam Winter will marry you"—and he gave a bark of laughter—"don't fool yourself. He won't. I've met his kind before. He'll wine you and dine you until he gets you into bed. And once he does, he'll tire of you. Then Rosalind Carmichael, where will you be? What will you have then? In your greed, you would've lost your only sure thing: me. But I won't want you then. I don't like secondhand goods."

And without another word, he walked from the room. Rosalind slid the engagement ring back into the pouch. Her fingers were trembling, and there was a sick feeling in the pit of her stomach. She knew that what he'd had to say about Sam was quite probably true. She had had these very thoughts herself. Sam wanted her—yes, but just for sex. And, yes, she also knew that he would tire of her once he got her into his bed.

Tears misted her vision. She suddenly felt com-

pletely lost, and terribly alone. Ben, despite his many
flaws, had been a constant in her life over the past
three years. What was she going to do without him?
When Sam no longer wanted her?

She sank onto the corner of the bed. What had she
done? What had she done?

"Come . . . Rosy darling." And suddenly she was
being wrapped in strong arms. "Don't cry," he muttered against her temple. "It won't be so bad with
me."

She sobbed brokenly against him. His gentle words
had caused the floodgates to open.

"Maybe . . . maybe I did the wrong thing," she said
brokenly.

"Shh," he said. "It was the right thing. The only
thing you could have done." He tilted her chin so
that she had to look at him. "Listen, life is too short
to be miserable. I realized that a few years ago. I was
living my life . . . going through the motions, but I
was empty . . . unhappy. That's when I decided that
I had to do something about it. None of us knows
how long we're going to be here on this earth . . .
hmm? So . . . we should be happy . . . every day if
possible. And don't ever settle for someone who's too
selfish to even try to make life a joy for you. Darling . . ." And he kissed the wet spots beneath both
eyes. "Choose me."

"I'm afraid," she sighed against him.

"What're you afraid of?"

She couldn't put her feelings into words. Everything
was too tangled. Too confused.

"That—that you won't want me . . . after."

He cradled her close. "That will never happen.
Trust me a little. Hmm? I am the man you need. *You*
are the woman I need. What could be better than
that?"

"I don't know." She sniffled. "It just seems too unreal. . . . Things like this don't happen. Maybe we're not compatible, either."

He sat on the edge of the big bed and pulled her to sit on his knee. "You worry too much," he said. "Do you know how . . . happy I am whenever you're anywhere around?" He pulled playfully at the lobe of her ear. "You're my little piece of sunshine. No matter how I might be feeling at any given point in the day, no matter what's going on . . . all I have to do is see you, hear you, and suddenly things don't seem so bad."

A tear rolled from the corner of an eye. "You say the nicest things. I think you have a much better understanding of true spirituality than I do."

"Hmm," he said. "Tell you what, why don't we go visit Tony tonight? Would you like that? It might cheer you up a bit."

He handed her a square cotton handkerchief and she dabbed at her eyes and blew her nose heartily. She was being silly, she knew. But Ben's words still beat a frantic tattoo in her brain, and try as she might, she couldn't make the doubt go away. *I'm sure you'll have time enough to think on how much you've lost. Because if you're hoping that Sam Winter will marry you, don't fool yourself because he won't. He'll wine and dine you . . . until he gets you into bed. . . .*

"Yes, that'll be nice," she said. "I got so wrapped up in Vegas with—with everything, that I didn't even give him a call."

"Well, that's settled, then. We'll spend the evening with Tony. I'll call him." And he shifted her from his knee and stood. "You'll feel better about things tomorrow . . . once you start working on fixing up the house. And remember, you can buy anything you like."

She gave him a watery smile. "Let me give you his number."

"That's okay," he said, "I know it."

And Rosalind watched him with the beginnings of puzzlement in her eyes as he went to the phone on her bedside table, picked it up, and dialed. She'd had no idea at all that he and Tony were even on speaking terms. How was it that he knew her brother's number off the top of his head?

She listened as he said, "Tony, Sam here. We're back from Vegas. Yes. Fine. We'd like to come over tonight. You doing anything? No, that's not a problem. About eight, then. Right."

He replaced the phone in its cradle. "He's going to be at home. Said he's watching the neighbor's children."

Rosalind's brows wrinkled. "He's what?" Tony, watching the neighbor's children? She hoped to God he hadn't figured out a way to use the neighbor's kids in some sort of dastardly scam.

"That's what he said. Baby-sitting."

Rosalind chewed at the corner of her nail. "Did he say whether the neighbor gave him the kids voluntarily?"

Sam laughed. "You don't think Tony's kidnapped some kids, do you?"

"Don't laugh," Rosalind said, and a frown of worry wrinkled the skin between her brows. "You don't know what he's capable of doing. I mean, I don't for a minute think that he would ever hurt the children, but . . . he might find a way to use them . . . you know, in one of his schemes. Did he ask to speak to me?"

"He asked how you were. But I could hear the kids in the background, so I suspect he probably didn't have much time to talk. I thought I heard things crashing and breaking."

"Well, that probably means that he's afraid to talk to me. And that's never ever a good sign."

Sam glanced at his watch. "Well, I wouldn't worry too much about it. You have about four or so hours to unpack and relax. Why don't you take a nap . . . or go down to the pool for a swim?"

The pool. She'd forgotten all about calling the pool service company.

"I meant to get the pool all cleaned up before we got back. I don't think it's in good shape for swimming right now."

"I took care of that before we left for Vegas. So if you feel like it . . ." And he let the rest of what he'd been about to say taper off.

Rosalind met his dark gaze, and for a minute she didn't know quite what to say. He was being so very good to her. Had been so good to her these past weeks. Why? And what had she really done for him? Helped him sleep. Talked to him a bit about his lack of spiritual beliefs. Listened to him talk about the horror that had been his childhood. She had done nothing for him. Not really.

"Why don't you come with me?"

A faint smile came and went in his eyes. "I'd love to come with you, but I have some work to do. With these new lines opening up around the world . . ."

Rosalind came to stand right before him, and she moved to wrap his arms about her. "Sammy," she said in a coaxing manner, "there are other people who can handle the mechanics of that for you. Right?"

"I've always handled these things. That way, nothing goes wrong."

She stroked the back of his arm. "But you told me yourself that you only hire the most competent people. I know your senior executives can handle this . . . if you let them. And," she said as he was about to speak, "you can conference-call them weekly for progress reports . . . if that makes you feel better."

He smiled at her. "And I thought you were feeling down. And now here you are, bossing me around."

"Well," she said, and there was a perky little note in her voice now, "Maybe I'm finally coming to my senses . . . about things. So will you come and swim?"

"Only if you promise to wear something really scanty."

Rosalind chuckled. She really was beginning to feel much better about the breakup with Ben. It was just striking her now how much she laughed when she was with Sam, and how little she had even smiled when she was with Ben.

"You have an extremely one-track mind."

He bent to press a quick kiss to her mouth. "Always. But only with you."

And with that little comment ringing in her ears, she went into her closet to find something suitable to wear.

Nineteen

Two wonderful hours were spent in the gleaming navy pool. Sam, with very little encouragement, had spent the entire time lounging on one of the inflated water chairs, a pair of very jet-settish black sunglasses perched on his nose. Rosalind had drifted beside him in a similar chair, clad in a stringy but elegant black bikini. They had said very little to each other, but had been simply content to enjoy the warm sunshine, one another, and the acres of blissful quiet.

A few minutes after six, with the heat of the day slowly beginning to burn off, Rosalind slid back into the water, did a leisurely crawl from one end of the pool to the next, and then pulled herself from the water to towel herself dry in brisk strokes. Sam paddled his chair around to where she stood, and lifted his glasses to inquire, "Ready to go up?" His gaze flickered over her long, long legs, and then lifted to settle on her face.

She was ridiculously pleased by the frank appreciation on his face. His body was pretty splendid, too. Long, muscular legs. Flat washboard stomach. Trim athletic hips. He was certainly a beauty.

"Yes, I think I'll go take a quick shower, maybe wash my hair before we go."

He stretched a hand to her. "Help me up?"

"Just a minute." She dropped the towel onto a lounger, then reached to grab his outstretched hand. She yanked at him with both hands, but he pulled back, and she teetered, then fell with a resounding splash into the pool. She surfaced, shrieking, "Oh, I should've known you were going to do that."

He laughed heartily, and she tipped him out of his chair. He swam beneath the water and came up right beside her, his eyes gleaming with deep humor.

"Sorry. I couldn't resist that."

She threw a handful of water at him. "I'm gonna get you."

He wrapped long arms about her and pressed her against the side of the pool. "When? Tonight?"

She chuckled at that for she knew his meaning. "Maybe tonight."

He kissed her neck with lips that were almost fiery hot. "You promise?"

She pressed a soft kiss to his chin, and then another to the corner of his mouth. "Only if you're good."

"I'll be good," he said. "Very, very good."

Later that evening, Rosalind and Sam pulled up outside Tony's brick-faced two-story town house in Madison. It had been a little while since Rosalind had visited, and she was surprised by the many little improvements about the place. The yard, which was usually overrun with weeds and untidy grass, was neatly cut. The bushes were trimmed to a decent height, and the garbage cans no longer overflowed with an assortment of refuse. There was also what appeared to be a brand-new sports car parked in the garage.

Rosalind climbed from the SUV, closed the door behind her. A sudden thought occurred to her as she looked around at the general state of the yard and at everything else. And the very possibility that it might be so, scared her so much that her heart began pounding in her chest. She darted a little glance at Sam, but he appeared blissfully unaware of what the new car and the very visible improvements about the place might mean.

"Nice car," he said as they walked by what Rosalind knew to be at the very least, a fifty-thousand-dollar vehicle.

"Yes," she agreed in a scratchy voice. Had Tony actually put the two hundred thousand dollars back? Or had he spent every penny she had given him?

She waited with her heart in her throat as Sam leaned heavily on the doorbell. Within moments, the door was flung back, but not by Tony. A little girl of about six stood on the threshold, her face covered in camouflage paint.

"Hello there," Sam said, bending to muss her hair. "Who're you?"

"Cindy." Large black eyes looked curiously at them both.

Sam smiled at her. "And where's Uncle Tony, Cindy?"

"Hiding," the little girl said. "We're playing war. Can you play, too?" And she grabbed a hold of Sam's hand and pulled.

Rosalind stepped into the modest sitting room and she bit down hard on her bottom lip. *New furniture.* Every single piece she'd ever bought for him was gone, replaced with very stylish, ultramodern leather settees and love seats.

Tony?" Sam bellowed as the little girl pulled him along with her.

Two more children rushed by at top speed, armed with huge water guns, and Rosalind just barely managed to avoid the smaller of the two as he clambered over a chair, shrieking with laughter and falling almost directly at her feet.

"Oops," she said, and bent to pick the toddler up. But he was none the worse for his little tumble, and he squirmed from her grasp and disappeared into the bowels of the house, bellowing at the top of his lungs.

"Where in the world is Tony?" she asked, looking at Sam.

He shrugged. "Might be best to get into the spirit of things. Feel like playing war?"

Rosalind's brows lifted. *Sam Winter playing war with a bunch of hyperactive kids?* How very little she had really known of this man.

"Come on," he said. "Cindy . . . this is Aunty Rosy, Uncle Tony's sister. Can you put some paint on her, too?"

"Sure," Cindy said, and she had both Sam and Rosalind sit on the chairs. Within a few minutes, Rosalind's face resembled something out of a Halloween freak show, and Sam's was not much better.

"Good," the little girl said after a moment of close inspection of both faces. "Now you're both on my team," she said. And proceeded to explain the intricate rules associated with the game.

Fifteen minutes later, while hiding in a closet, the door was yanked open and Rosalind found herself looking directly at her brother. She grabbed one of his arms and pulled him into her little hiding place. He wrapped an arm about her waist and gave her a giant hug.

"Ros, I'm so glad you're back."

"So glad that you didn't even want to speak to me this afternoon on the phone when Sam called," she hissed at him.

"Is that what he told you?" In the darkened closet she could just barely make out his eyes.

"Forget all that," Rosalind whispered. "I'm more interested in where you got the money to buy that car I saw outside . . . and all of the new furniture and stuff."

"I got all those things with money I earned. Legitimately."

"Oh, please spare me, Tony. Do you take me for a fool? You've spent the money I gave you. Haven't you?"

"Spent the money? Of course not. How could you think that? I would never do that."

Rosalind shook her head. "I knew it. Tony, I can't believe you did this to me. You've spent Sam's money on—on toys. Ben was right about you. God." And she covered her face with both hands.

He wrapped both arms about her. "Sis, I promise you . . . on a stack of Bibles that I didn't spend the money you gave me. I know I've done some terrible things over the years, but I'm really trying to change. I really am." And he gave her such a very earnest look that she almost felt ashamed for doubting him. But she knew better than anyone else whom she was dealing with.

"Okay," she said after a moment. "But if it turns out that you've lied to me . . . yet again, I won't forgive you. Not this time. And not only that, but I'll let Sam deal with you himself."

The door was pulled open before he could respond, and two gleeful children fell upon them both with shrieks of "We got you. We got you."

Rosalind got completely into the spirit of things over the next hour or so, and threw herself wholeheartedly into the madcap game of water tag. At the end of it all, the hair that she had so painstakingly washed and curled was soaking wet and stringy. She finally collapsed in the little backyard under the only available leafy tree.

"I give up," she said as one of the children made a beeline for her.

"Do we win then?" the little boy asked.

Rosalind nodded. "You win."

She relaxed against the tree trunk and laughed in a deep and hearty manner when Sam, who was still tearing about the place, got a thorough double-barrel dousing from the three-year-old. After a brief skirmish, which resulted in Sam being blasted again, he came across to where she was sitting and flopped down on the grass beside her.

"I haven't had an evening like this one in a very long while."

"I know," she said, grinning at him. "Who would've thought it? You, of all people, playing water tag like that."

He wiped a smear of paint from the side of her face. "I love kids. I've always wanted to have a whole bunch."

"Yes, I remember you telling me that. Ten or fifteen, didn't you say?"

He chuckled. "Well, I'm willing to be reasonable." He gave her a simmering dark-eyed look. "But at least one or two."

Tony appeared in the back doorway. "Pizza," he bellowed.

Sam got lithely to his feet and extended a hand to help her up. "Pizza," he said.

As the evening wore on, it became clear that Tony was baby-sitting the neighbor's children for the night. Something Rosalind would never have thought him capable of doing. She watched in some amount of bemused fascination as he settled the three-year-old neatly into his booster seat, then went from one child to the next, making sure that they all had enough to eat.

"This is amazing," she whispered to Sam between bites of pizza. "I've never seen him like this. It almost worries me. I wonder if he's coming down with something."

Sam dabbed at the corner of her mouth with a paper napkin, removing a bit of shine. "Any man can change if he really wants to." And he gave her a hard-to-decipher look before turning to say to Tony, "So how's the new job coming along?"

Rosalind's eyes flashed between the two, her mind churning as Tony and Sam settled into a long discussion regarding emerging trends in urban fashion. How had Sam known of Tony's new job, and better yet, why hadn't he told her anything about it? Her brow wrinkled. There definitely was something very odd going on.

She munched on her pizza and bent her mind to figuring out exactly what was happening. Sam had asked her just before they left for Las Vegas if she would like him to mentor Tony. Maybe he had helped her brother get a job? But that had only been a mere two or so weeks ago. Even if he had made some calls that somehow resulted in Tony being hired somewhere, that still wouldn't explain the presence of the new car and furniture, not to mention the other things that she had also noticed about the town house.

"Aunty Rosy."

Rosalind turned to smile at the child seated next to her. "Yes, sweetheart?"

"Can I have another slice of pizza?"

"Sure you can manage another one? You've had two so far. Sure you won't be sick?"

"Oh, no," the child said, patting her stomach, "I can eat an entire pizza myself."

"Well," Rosalind said with a little laugh, "I'll give you one more piece. I don't want you to explode."

The other two children chortled merrily at that, and also held out their plates for more pizza. Somewhere near the end of the impromptu meal, Cindy asked, "Aunty . . . next time you come, can you and Uncle Sammy bring your kids so that we can play war again?"

Rosalind glanced at Sam quickly, and intercepted a fleeting smile in his eyes.

"Uncle Sammy . . . and I don't have any kids, Cindy," she said. And for some unknown reason, a faint flush stained her cheeks at the admission. It was silly to feel any embarrassment at all over the child's innocent assumption.

"No kids?" And Cindy actually paused in her pizza eating for a few moments. "How come you don't have no kids?"

"Any kids," Tony corrected.

Rosalind looked helplessly at Sam, who she could tell was enjoying the entire situation immensely.

"How many kids do you want us to have, Cindy?" Sam asked, giving Rosalind an all-too-innocent stare.

Cindy gave the matter some thought before saying, "Five. Can we have five?"

Sam leaned forward to tweak Cindy's nose. "We'll have to talk to Aunty Rosy about that. But"—and he winked at her—"I'll see what I can do."

With that settled, the children went back to their eating, and Rosalind tried her best to avoid looking at Sam. There were many things she had to ask him, but she would save all of the questions until they were alone.

Later they all sat around watching cartoon videos.

Cindy, who had developed a huge crush on Sam, cuddled in his lap and refused to budge even when it was finally time to go to bed. Tony got the two boys into bed with promises of bedtime stories if they were absolutely good. But when he returned to coax Cindy away from Sam, they were all subjected to a session of very loud tears.

Rosalind patted the little girl's face dry and said, "It's okay, honey, Uncle Sammy will put you to bed. Don't cry."

Sam followed Rosalind to the little bedroom where Tony had put the boys. He placed Cindy gently in bed beside them, but when he tried to straighten, she still clung to his hand.

"I've never seen anything like this," Rosalind whispered to Sam. "Do you usually have this kind of an effect on kids?"

Sam chuckled and sat on the edge of the bed. "Aunty Rosy and I have to go home now, darling."

"Tell us a 'tory," the three-year-old, named Jimmy, pleaded.

Sam looked at Cindy, "What kind of story would you like, Cindy, honey?"

The little girl played with his fingers for a bit, then said in a voice that was still dangerously close to wailing tears, "A Bible story. The one about Jesus, the bread and the fish."

"Ah . . ." And Sam's eyes darted to Tony, and then Rosalind. "How about a fairy story instead?"

"No." And a note of truculence crept into Cindy's voice. "Don't want a fairy story. Want a Bible story."

Rosalind hid a smile behind one of her hands. "She wants you to tell it, not me," she said at Sam's pleading glance. "Isn't that right, Cindy? You want Uncle Sammy to tell the story and not me?"

The child nodded, propped herself against the pillows, and folded her arms in a very adult manner. "Tony . . ." Sam said. "Do you have a Bible?"

Twenty

At about ten P.M., the children finally settled down for the night. But not before the telling of numerous stories, all of which Sam did with amazing ability. With very little help at all from Rosalind, he, after reading various snatches of scripture from the Bible, was able to quickly assimilate and then retell the story in a manner in which the children found hugely entertaining. He did this so very well, that even she found herself hanging on his every word. And she was forced to wonder, on more than one occasion, how it was he could retell the scriptures with such ease and understanding, and yet not believe in any of them himself. He was without question, she realized yet again, a very complex man. And so very hard to figure out.

When it finally came time to go, Rosalind gave Tony a big hug and whispered in his ear, "We still have to talk. Call me tomorrow."

She was determined to get to the bottom of whatever it was that was going on. And she wasted no time in getting right to the heart of the matter as soon as Sam had settled himself behind the wheel and pulled away from the curb.

"Sammy," she said. "Did you help Tony get a job? One that pays a lot of money, I mean?"

He blended smoothly back into the traffic before saying, "Remember I told you I would help him?"

"So you got him a job, then?"

He stared straight ahead without looking at her. "He's working for me."

"You?" Well, that explained a few things.

His eyes slid over her and then went back to the road. "Me."

"What kind of job did you give him?" She refused to let the matter drop because she still had the sense that somehow something wasn't exactly right.

"He's the senior consultant on new fashion trends. He advises our designers . . . you know, helps point them in this direction or that. He's very familiar with the trends on the street, so . . . he actually helps make sure that our clothing remains fresh . . . real."

"Oh," she said, and sat back to consider what she had just learned. Well, that might explain where Tony was getting the money and the things.

"Does he have a car allowance, then?"

Sam turned the car onto Beaumont Road, and in the darkness, his expression was even harder to read than normal.

"A young man needs a nice car."

"You gave that car to him?"

"He pays me for it every month. Part of our agreement."

He swung the car into the circular courtyard, cut the motor, and turned in his seat to regard her with glinting midnight-black eyes, one arm resting along the curve of the steering wheel.

"So . . ." he said, "have I made you happy?"

She touched the side of his face with a gentle hand. "I don't know how Tony and I will ever repay you for all—all that you've done for us. But"—and she stroked the curve of his lower lip in much the way that he would usually do with her—"I'm going to give it a try."

She pressed a soft kiss to the base of his neck, and then another and another, moving higher, up over his Adam's apple, then to the round of his chin, and finally settling on his lips. His arms folded about her and he kissed her hungrily.

"Are you still sorry that you broke up with Ben?" he asked against the side of her face.

"I was never really sorry . . . in that way," she said, pulling back to look at him. "It's just that . . . I was used to him always being around. So—so I got scared. It's hard to find someone these days. . . ."

"Well, now," he said between little kisses across the rise of her nose. "Now you have me. And you don't have to worry about being scared anymore. Do you believe me?"

She rested her head on his shoulder. Did she believe him? She should believe him. Anyone in their right mind would believe him. He had helped her. Had helped Tony, and had asked for precious little in return. Why would he do this? Did he care for her in a deeper way? On a deeper level? Surely sex could not be the single solitary motivator?

"I believe you," she said. And with a slow settling certainty she realized that she really and truly did believe what he said to her. She trusted him.

And as she struggled to come to grips with that he smiled at her and said, "Let's go inside."

He paused at the door to her suite, an uncertain expression on his face, jingling the keys in his pocket. A flood of tenderness for him swept over her. He was still unsure of her. And no wonder, too, since she had never once volunteered a single jot of information on how she actually felt about him. But all that was going to change.

She opened the door, pushed it wide, and said, "Do you want to stay with me tonight?"

His fist clenched in his pocket, and as she looked directly into the deep dark depths of his eyes, emotion unfurled somewhere deep inside her, emotion that had been locked away in cold storage, perhaps forever.

"No one has ever made me a nicer offer."

Her lips curled in a smile. "Come on in, then."

He walked in and perched on the side of the bed, watching her as she removed her shoes. She turned to regard him, feeling suddenly strong, powerful, vibrant. Look at what had fallen into her lap. This man, this wonderful, wonderful man. Yes, he was flawed, but so were so many others. And so was she herself. And maybe as he had helped her, she might help him, too. And for as long as he wanted her, she would be his. Completely.

She caught sight of herself in the mirror. Because of the dousing she'd received at Tony's house, her hair was flat, without any body at all, and yet, he sat there on her bed, looking at her as though she were God's most beautiful creation. What had she done to deserve this? To deserve him? So many women searched for exactly what she now had. Why was she so fortunate?

She held out her arms. "Come, baby."

She had never called him that before, and the happiness that radiated from him, amazed her, touched her, swept her up. His arms wrapped about her, and he bent to rub his nose against hers.

"What have I done to deserve this? Me . . . the man you couldn't stand. . . ."

She kissed the warmth of his mouth. "I'm sorry about—about that. I was wrong. Blind. Stupid."

"Not about everything. But you forced me to take a good long look at myself."

She played with the hairs at the nape of his neck. "You mean you're not stubborn and opinionated anymore?"

He laughed. "No. I'm still that. But at least I recognize now that I am. And that's a start. Hmm?"

Her fingers went to the buttons on the front of his shirt. "Well, that deserves some sort of reward, don't you think?"

"What do you have in mind?"

The first three buttons were open, and her fingers went beneath the fabric of his shirt to caress the hair, then the hot skin. He bent slightly to take the fat of her earlobe in his mouth, and her fingers curled against his skin at the rich, yet somehow raw, aching sensation that filled her.

"Oh." She had never felt this way with Ben. Never felt this way with any man at all.

"Do you like that?" he asked, his voice a mumble against her heated skin.

"Yes." She would have been unable to say that to him before. In fact, she had always been a bit inhibited about expressing how she felt about sensual matters.

She pulled the rest of his shirt from where it was tucked beneath his belt. "Remember that bubble bath?"

His chest moved in a silent chuckle. "Is that my reward?"

"Only part of it."

He kissed her neck. "What's the other part?"

"You'll have to wait and see." And she took him by the hand and led him into the bathroom.

Twenty-one

"You know," Rosalind said as she poured a trickle of liquid soap into her cupped hand, "you have one of the nicest chests I have ever seen." She reached forward and began to slowly massage his shoulders, and then his arms, her fingers moving with exquisite skill over his muscles.

He lay back in the warm soapy water, his eyes half-closed and brilliantly black.

"You think I'm attractive . . . then?"

She ran the soft peanut-shaped sponge over his torso, and then dipped below the water line to massage the area just above his elastic briefs.

"Not only do I think you're attractive . . . you're also very, very"—and she snapped the elastic at his waist—"sexy."

He laughed in a deeply pleased manner, his fingers folding about her wrist. "Well, it's a good thing I kept myself in shape. After you left me in L.A., I could've let myself run to fat."

"And why would you have done that?"

She dipped the sponge back into the water, then squeezed warm water from his neck all the way down to where his lower body disappeared beneath the water.

"Because"—and his eyes were suddenly serious—

"when you left, I felt as though the light had gone out of my life. And I had no idea where you had gone."

She had stopped squeezing the sponge, and was staring at him with wide contrite eyes. "Oh, Sammy . . . I'm sorry. I—I didn't think it would've made a difference. I felt sure you hated me anyway."

He stroked the side of her wrist with a long index finger. "Hated you? And I had just asked you to marry me?"

"That's exactly why I knew you probably wouldn't care if I lived or died. Where I went I was sure wasn't important to you."

He lifted a hand from the ledge of the bath and touched the first button on her blouse, working it through the buttonhole. "Maybe I was arrogant at the time, but you surely cut me back down to size. I'd never had a problem getting women before. Any woman I wanted, I knew I could have. So I knew without question that I could have you, too. I didn't exert myself too much. I just expected you to fall into my lap. After all . . . why wouldn't you? I was a great catch. Wealthy. Many had told me I was good-looking . . . but"—and he laughed in a derisive manner—"none of that meant anything to you. I actually thought I was doing you a favor . . . asking you to be my wife. It's only after you left that I realized that, if you had accepted me, you would've been the one doing me a favor."

"Oh, don't say that. You were a great catch. *Are* a great catch. I just didn't—didn't think we were compatible."

His fingers played with the second button on her blouse, undoing that one, too. "And now? Do you still think we're incompatible?"

Then the third and fourth buttons were undone,

and the smooth golden tops of her bosom were softly visible. Rosalind's heartbeat picked up a notch as his hand stroked gently over the frilly lace of her bra.

"Well . . ."

"Yes?" And he bent his head to kiss the rise of one breast.

Her throat clenched. "We seem to be getting along a lot better now."

He pushed the strap over the round of her left shoulder and peeled back the white cup with fingers that felt somehow, divinely right.

"But . . . you're not completely sure . . . yet?"

The breath caught in her throat as he removed the other cup and then bent to pull the dark heart of a quivering nipple deep within the hot cavern of his mouth. He pulled on the heated nub so strongly, and so exactly in the manner in which she had always known it should be done, that Rosalind cried out. A tiny burst of sound that brought an answering moan from him.

He transferred his attentions to the other breast, and her hands went up to hold the back of his head, pressing him closer. His teeth closed on the tip of the dark circle, and an electric shudder raced through her. Never had she felt like this. How could she have known that such sensation existed? It was unbelievable. Unreal. Beautiful.

"Are you sure yet?" His voice was a husky growl against her skin.

She opened clouded eyes. She couldn't go through her entire life being afraid of things. Afraid of being hurt. Afraid of being left alone after the relationship was at an end. Life was short. Too short in some cases. And life was meant to be lived. Yes, life was meant for living, and she would live it. Right now, not later.

"I'm . . . sure," she said, and held his head to her

with trembling fingers as he kissed and suckled every inch of flesh from her shoulders to her waist.

He pulled her into the water right atop him, and she didn't even care that she was still clothed from the waist down. His mouth drifted across her chin, and then went unerringly to the petal softness of her lips.

"You're not afraid of me . . . still?"

She bit his bottom lip, and then soothed the spot with the blunt of her tongue. "I don't know. . . . What're you going to do with me?" she asked teasingly.

"What do you not want me to do?"

"Ah . . ." And she cast about in her mind for the appropriate limitations, but she could find none. Everything he was doing was so absolutely, perfectly right.

"I can't think of anything," she husked in his ear.

He turned her smoothly and removed her jeans with such skill that she hardly noticed they were gone. He looked down at her with eyes that were bright with excitement.

"Tonight," he said, "is going to be like nothing else you've ever experienced."

"It is?" She chuckled, playing with the lobes on both of his ears.

"It is." And he stuck a finger beneath the strap of her underwear, and pulled an inch. "Your skin is so smooth . . . so beautiful," he said with something very like wonder in his voice, and before she could even guess at what he intended, he scooped her into his arms and stood. Her heart raced in her chest as he stepped from the tub, paused to wrap her in a large towel, and then carried her across the soft expanse of carpeting to the large bed.

When her back touched the fabric of the comforter,

she made a whisper of sound and he looked down at her with tender eyes.

"It's going to be okay, Rosy. I promise you."

She watched him as he dimmed the lights and came to her. It was truly not to be believed that she was here with him now. In this way. She stretched her arms for him, and he was there in an instant, his lips moving warmly across her cheekbones, eyelids, nose, and then coming to rest again on lips that trembled just a bit. Rosalind stroked a finger across the line of each strong eyebrow.

"I can't believe this is happening. . . ." she said.

He rested on his elbows, looking down at her. "I can." And there was a smile in his eyes. "I would've moved heaven and earth to get us here . . . to this moment."

"You're an amazing man," she said. "And sometimes I think—I think that maybe . . ."

"That maybe what, sweetheart?"

She swallowed. "That maybe, whatever this thing is between us, it won't last. That something will come along—some thing or some set of things will happen to destroy what you feel. Whatever that is."

He parted her legs, and lowered himself to her. "Nothing will happen to us, sweetheart, because I won't let anything happen." He kissed her again, and she surrendered herself to the tide of feeling that swept over her. Maybe he was right. Maybe nothing would come between them. Maybe they would be among the lucky few. The blessed few.

Her fingers gripped his shoulders as he kissed a heated path down the flat of her stomach, and his name stumbled from her lips in broken entreaty as he peeled away her bikini briefs and kissed the soft triangle of hair. His tongue, hot and sure, moved in and out of every crevice, tasting, stroking, touching, until she was in such a fever of need that salty tears sprang to her eyes and she demanded in a voice that was several shades huskier than normal, "Now, Sammy. Right now."

But this one time he did not obey her. He removed the black briefs, slid on adequate protection and lowered his head to suckle. Rosalind sobbed in response and thrashed beneath him, her nails curling into his skin.

He lifted his head for a moment to look at her, and in a voice that broke around the edges, said, "Tell me you want me." And she moaned in response. "I want you. Only you. Now . . . please."

That final word broke his resolve. He held her hips, and demanded in a gritty voice, "Open your eyes, darling."

With significant effort, she forced her heavy lids open. And the sight of his face above hers, with the flush of blood standing out across his cheekbones, was the dearest she had ever seen.

"I love you," he said.

And before she could properly absorb the enormity of that, he entered her. Involuntarily her neck arched at the good solid feel of him, and her legs lifted to cling to the small of his back. He moved in her at just the right pace, his hands cupping her behind and lifting her to meet him.

Rosalind closed her eyes and surrendered herself to the moment. She matched him, thrust for thrust, her fingers urging him on. And with every stroke, he moaned her name, and she clung to him with only one thought. *It's never been like this. Not like this. Never. Ever. This is more than just the joining of the flesh. Of two bodies. There's something deeper happening here. Something spiritual. Something miraculous.*

Her fingers flexed rhythmically about the swell of a

bicep, and then slid down to twine about the fingers of his right hand. And he held her tightly with each trembling breath that escaped them both, taking her higher, higher, until she felt that she would surely die. She called his name in a thin thready voice, and said wild, passionate things that caused him to grunt in satisfaction against the column of her neck.

"Oh, God."

His husky moan pushed her over the edge, and she clung to him shuddering, sobbing, not caring about anything, anything at all. His body went rigid as her shudders seeped into him, and the entire world seemed to pause for an instant as he gave himself up to the wonder.

And the last coherent thought that whispered through Rosalind was *Being together with him in this way feels right. So very right that it is almost as though this sweet perfection has been happening between us both since the beginning of time. . . .*

Twenty-two

Later, much later they slept. But not before he had loved her again. This time with a sweet tenderness that brought warm salty tears to her eyes.

Morning broke with stealthy quiet, and Rosalind surfaced slowly, her eyes blinking open in the pale gold morning sunlight. It was a wondrous day. Soft. Quiet. Full of peace and contentment. Her head rested on the flat of Sam's chest, and he slept with both arms wrapped about her, his face relaxed, satiated.

She stretched carefully so that she wouldn't disturb him, and allowed herself the luxury of unhurried thought. He had told her last night that he loved her. She was certain she hadn't misheard him. But people often said things they didn't mean, in the heat of passion. Did he mean it? And what did she feel for him now? She had said nothing in return. The truth be known, she had been too far beyond words at the time. . . .

She brushed the heavy fall of hair away from her face and a shy smile curved the corners of her lips.

"Good morning." She'd been so deep in thought that she hadn't realized that he'd come awake.

He pulled her closer to him with the leg that was still wrapped about hers, and said in a voice that was several measures deeper than normal, "Did you sleep well?"

"Mmm," she said and pressed a little kiss to the side of his mouth. In fact, she had never had such happy sleep. "I don't think I've ever had a better night of sleep."

He smiled at her in a manner that set her heart to pounding in her chest. "We have some things to talk about . . . you and I. But we'll have to save them until later. Sue's coming in today."

"Sue?" And a glimmer of heat entered her eyes. She'd felt sure that she had seen the last of the woman in Las Vegas. Why was Sam bringing her here to New Jersey? Had he really only wanted to get her into bed, and now that he had, he was ready for a fresh replacement?

He rolled away from her, pulling a sheet with him, and completely ignoring her question. "I wish I could spend the entire day in bed with you. But I can't. I've a few things to take care of." He stood. "But if you feel like it, why don't you sleep in?"

She sat up, too, wrapping the sheet about her body. Why was he avoiding her question?

"Why is Sue coming here?"

He climbed into his pants and shrugged on the discarded and very crumpled shirt. "She's working on some stuff for me. She won't be staying here, so don't worry." And he gave her a smile before heading for the door.

She nodded. *Okay.* "I'll take care of ordering the furniture for the house today. And getting a housekeeper."

He turned in the doorway. "If you really want to do that now, go ahead. But don't overtire yourself."

She looked at him with faintly puzzled eyes. He certainly was behaving very differently today. He was not nearly as loving as he had been the night before.

She swung her feet to the thick carpeting. "What about breakfast? Don't you want any?"

"No. I'll have a quick shower and then—" He gave his watch a glance. "I've an appointment at ten. I'll probably grab something to eat while I'm out. I'll see you a little later." And he was through the door without another word.

Rosalind walked across the room to close and lock the door. Well, after a night like the one they had just spent, she would have expected him to be a little warmer. Actually, she had expected him to be all over her just as he had been before. She certainly hadn't thought that his interest in her would begin to wane this quickly.

The ringing of the phone on the bedside table distracted her from her thoughts for a moment, and she went to lift the receiver.

"Hello, Ben," she said after listening for a moment. His voice crackled at her, and she could tell that he was on his cell phone, and was quite probably calling her from a broom closet, or some such thing between rounds.

"Yes, I forgive you," she said in a patient voice. And then, "No, everything's fine. No, I'm not angry with you." And surprisingly she wasn't. There was absolutely no anger in her anymore toward him. If anything, she felt curiously generous now since her emotions were no longer involved.

She forced herself to concentrate on what Ben was saying, and for the first time, she noticed the little elements of weakness in his voice. The absolutely irritating way he had of whining when he wasn't getting his own way. The only reason he wanted her back was probably because he was having trouble doing his laundry and getting regular meals.

"I don't think we should have dinner together, Ben. It would just prolong things. I really meant what I said yesterday. And . . . food and wine won't change my mind. Okay, Ben," she said, relenting just a bit. "I'll meet you for coffee this evening at that little restaurant just opposite the hospital. Yes, six o'clock is fine with me." She would meet him, and explain again, as gently as she could, that they could never get back together. And this time she would give him back his ring.

She hung up and went to take a steaming hot shower. She washed and conditioned her hair and then spent a long while drying and curling the long black tresses into a carefree windblown style. She slid into a pair of faded stone-washed jeans, and a cut-off T-shirt, and then went down to the kitchen to fix herself something to eat.

Over black coffee and toast, she heard the approach of footsteps, and she tried her best to still the almost immediate fluttering of nerves in her stomach. Sam appeared in the doorway, obviously freshly showered, and now dressed as casually as she in a pair of jeans and a matching blue shirt.

Rosalind's eyes flickered over him. He was so handsome. And sexy. He was an extremely sexy man.

"Think I'll have some coffee before I go," he said, and came to sit on the high padded stool directly before her.

She poured him a cup with fingers that had gone suddenly cold. "You should really have something to eat, too."

He accepted the cup, added cream and sugar, and took several sips before saying, "I'm not that hungry today, though God knows I should be." And his eyes glinted at her.

Rosalind sucked in her bottom lip to prevent the smile she was feeling from spreading across her face. She had never been this shy with a man before after spending a passionate night in his arms.

"Well," she said, standing and going across the room to put her dishes in the sink, "I'll try to keep myself busy while you're gone."

He came to stand behind her, parted her hair, and pressed a warm kiss to the bend of her neck. "I'll be back soon."

She turned into his arms. How could she ever have thought that she didn't care for his eyes? They were simply the nicest, kindest pair of eyes she had ever seen.

"Will you be gone all day?" He hadn't told her where it was he was going, and she didn't want him to think that she was beginning to cling to him.

He bent to brush her nose with the tip of his. "I should be back before four. If I'm going to be late, I'll give you a call."

She walked him to the front door and stood in the open doorway watching until he drove away. Then she spent the next several hours calling various housekeeping agencies. With a handful of interviews scheduled for the remainder of the week, she set to work ordering curtains, rugs, paintings, and other knickknacks that would add color and warmth to the house.

The afternoon passed so quickly that at just before four when the phone rang, Rosalind answered it with happy surprise in her voice. "Sam. I had no idea it was this late. . . ."

But the voice on the other end said quite pleasantly, "It's not Sam, Rosalind. It's Sue."

"Oh . . . hello, Sue. Sam's not here." Her voice had

iced over a bit, but the other woman seemed not to notice.

"Yes, I figured as much, since you answered. He's supposed to be picking me up at the airport, but I guess he must be running a little late. Well, don't let me keep you." And she rang off before Rosalind could say anything more.

Rosalind replaced the phone in its cradle and forced herself to return to her work. But try as she might, she couldn't restrain her wayward thoughts. So that was why he hadn't told her where he was going. He had arranged to pick up the Sue Perkins woman. Her brow furrowed. She had told Sue Perkins in Las Vegas that if she really made up her mind to fight for Sam Winter, no one would be able to stand in her way. So far, she had taken Sam's interest in her for granted. She had also been ambivalent about whether or not she wanted him. But she did want him. She was completely clear on that now. And she would fight to keep him.

But how? She would settle things once and for all with Ben, and then put her mind to work on the matter. Maybe Sam didn't fully realize that her feelings for him had changed.

She finished ordering a few other items, and then went up to her room. She wouldn't change. She didn't want Ben to think that she had gone to any particular trouble to look good for him.

She stood for a minute looking out the windows at the rolling green lawns and the deep navy beauty of the glittering pool. It was a spectacular property—that much was certain. With its neat little rose bushes, tall leafy fruit trees and peaceful little windy spots. It was idyllic, really.

Rosalind turned away from the window now and went to run a quick comb through her hair. She spent only a moment over this, and then she sat to write Sam a note. She hadn't told him about meeting Ben for coffee because she had felt sure that he would have been back before she left. But it was almost five-thirty, and he wasn't back yet. He hadn't called her, either.

She finished the note with a flourish, and paused over the signing of it. Should she end with: *"Warmly, Rosalind"*? *"With love, Rosalind"*? Or simply, *"Rosalind"*?

In the end, she just signed it: *"Rosy,"* and went to stick the little slip of paper on the face of the office door. Then she clipped to the front door over the polished tile, wearing spiky black high-heeled slip-ons, let herself out, and walked briskly to her beaten-up little Toyota. She drove down the quiet tree-lined streets at a leisurely pace and pulled up at the Callaloo restaurant a few minutes before six.

Ben was waiting in the parking lot for her, and before she could properly park her car, he was at the driver's door. Rosalind's eyes ran over him quickly as she stepped from the car. He appeared rumpled and haggard, and she experienced a momentary twinge of pity for him.

"Hello, Ben." She didn't say he was looking well, because he certainly wasn't. He had never looked worse.

"Rosalind." He enveloped her in a bear hug. "I'm so glad you actually came. I wasn't sure if you would."

She returned his hug for a brief instant, gave him a pat on the back, and said, "I won't be able to stay very long, Ben. I have to get back."

He took her by the hand. "Let's talk about it inside. I got us a booth in the back, away from the crowds and noise."

She followed him back through the maze of tables and slid into the burnished leather booth. Ben at-

tempted to slide in beside her but thought better of
it after taking a quick look at her face. He went
around to the opposite end and sat. He cracked the
stiffness from his knuckles and said, "Rosalind, I know
none of this would've happened if I had just paid
more attention and—and loaned you that money you
wanted."

She leaned forward and took one of his fidgety
hands, because she really wanted him to understand
her.

"Ben . . . it's not the money. I don't want you to
think it was the money. We've been growing apart for
a long time now. This—this was bound to happen
sooner or later. We're just not right for each other.
We're just too different."

His fingers curled around hers. "Is it Sam Winter?"
And when she didn't answer, he said, "I was a fool. I
should never have let that man get anywhere near you.
I knew the first time I saw him what he was up to . . .
and I wasn't wrong. He manipulated you and Tony
like mindless puppets, throwing his money around, using it to bribe Tony . . . and to influence you."

Rosalind blinked. "Bribe Tony? All Sam did was
help Tony get a job. There's nothing wrong with that."

Ben gave a bark of laughter and the sound seemed
to crack and hang for a moment in the heavy air.

"Is that all you think he did?"

"Look," Rosalind said, and then paused for breath
before going on. She could see he was working himself
up into some sort of temper, and she really didn't feel
up to having another fight with him. He just had to
understand that it was over and done with between
them. It wasn't that she didn't like him as a person.
She did. She just didn't want to marry him. "Whatever
it is you think you know about Sam Winter is not important. I really don't want to hear it."

She removed the little ring box from her handbag and placed it on the table before her. Ben's eyes took on a feral gleam.

"Is that so? Well, I'm sure you'll want to know this. Your irresponsible brother, Tony, was never in any trouble with the Jamaican mob. And not only that, but he thought so very little of you that he was willing to sell you . . . to the highest bidder."

Rosalind's fingers tightened around the velvet box, and her heart thudded heavily in her chest.

"What . . . ?" The very suspicion that had become a niggling doubt in the back of her mind. She had asked Tony about it, and he had assured her that he had not just spent the money. "What do you mean he was never in any trouble?" She couldn't even begin to process the other things Ben had just said.

Ben cracked his knuckles again, a pleased expression on his face. "He was never in any trouble. It was all a lie . . . an elaborate one . . . an expensive one. One that cost Sam Winter two hundred thousand dollars."

Rosalind said nothing at all for a full minute. Ben was lying; that's all there was to it. He was lying to her because he knew that this was the only way he could possibly hurt her now.

"I never thought you would sink this low, Ben," she finally managed. "Why would you say these terrible things? I know you've never liked Tony, but—"

"I'm not trying to hurt you," he said, cutting her off. "I just thought you should know, is all. Sam Winter bought you. Yes, that's right. He bought you, and Tony set the price. Comforting, isn't it, to know that your own brother values you so little that he would actually accept money for you. He delivered you up to Sam Winter like a nice little Thanksgiving turkey. Two hun-

dred thousand for a roll in the sack. You must be one
of the most expensive—"

Rosalind stood, tears sparkling in her eyes. "That's
enough," she said, her voice shaking with a mixture
of rage and fear. "I don't want to hear any more of
your lies. Your insults. I came here today against my
better judgment, but I can see now what a mistake
that was. You're a little man, Ben Mitchell. A little,
little man. And for that I'm sorry. And . . . you'll
never hold on to a woman until you learn how she
should be treated."

She would have said more, but her voice was shaking too much and she didn't want to give him the
satisfaction of seeing her cry. She rushed from the
restaurant in a blind haze, almost mowing down the
waiter who had chosen at that very moment to make
his way over to the table. She had left the ring box
on the table, and as she dashed a hand across her
streaming eyes, she thought, Let him take it or not,
she didn't care.

She threw her car into gear, and roared away from
the parking lot. It was several minutes before she realized that she was heading in the wrong direction.
Automatically she had turned her car toward her
apartment in Madison, and not toward Sam and
Mendham.

She pulled into a vacant parking lot, swung the car
about, and then headed back the way she had come.
She drove through the heavy evening traffic, barely
seeing where she was going, her brain going over and
over Ben's words. *"Your irresponsible brother, Tony, was
never in any trouble with the Jamaican mob. And, not only
that, but he thought so very little of you that he was willing
to sell you . . . to the highest bidder. Sam Winter bought
you . . . paid two hundred thousand for you. . . ."*

She wiped at the tears rolling down the side of her

face with an unsteady hand. How could Tony have done it? This was definitely the worst, the absolute worst thing he had ever done. It couldn't be true. It just couldn't. She would just ask Sam, that was all. She would ask him about everything Ben had said. He would tell her that Ben had told her nothing but lies. He would give her a direct answer. He wouldn't beat about the bush with her.

She pulled into Beaumont Road, and gave the snappy ice-blue BMW Z3 Roadster a cursory glance as she screeched to a halt beside it. No doubt it belonged to Sue Perkins, who was probably even now nicely ensconced in Sam's suite.

She was halfway to the front door when it was thrown open. She took a deep breath. *Sam*. She was so afraid to hear the answers to the questions she had for him.

"Where in the world have you been? I was just about to call the police."

He came toward her, and she met his eyes. There was genuine anxiety in there, she noted absently.

"I left you a note. Taped to the office door. Didn't you see it?" Her voice was soft, scratchy.

"A note? No. It must've fallen—" And he broke off to say with a note of alarm in his voice, "You've been crying. What's the matter? What's happened? Is it Tony?"

He drew her indoors, and then into his arms.

"What's wrong?" he asked again. But she shook her head because a fresh surge of tears was pricking hotly at the backs of her eyes.

"Ben," she managed after a momentary struggle.

"You were with him?" His voice broke on the final word, and she wondered at it. Was he jealous?

"I met him for coffee at the Callaloo restaurant in Morristown."

"And?" She was sure his body tensed with that little word.

She rested her head against him and closed her eyes. And? And her entire little world was about to crumble all around her. And maybe she didn't want to know if Tony had sold her. Didn't want to know if Sam had bought her so that he could turn her into his own personal sex toy.

His hand dipped to her chin, and he turned her face so she was forced to look at him.

"And . . . what? You've decided to go back to him?"

He seemed to be holding his breath, and Rosalind touched the tip of her tongue to her lips before saying, "That's one thing I'll never do."

"Then what?"

She swallowed. "He . . . he told me that you . . ."

He looked down at her with serious eyes. "That I what?"

His voice was suddenly hard, but Rosalind continued, driven now by a fierce need to know. "That you . . . paid Tony for me."

The silence that greeted her remark caused her to step away from him. A mounting feeling of dread rose slowly within her at the lack of expression on his face. It was true. It was true. Ben had not been lying.

"You paid Tony to—to get me here?" It was a question now. And her eyes begged him to deny it. To say that it was all a pack of nonsense. But he didn't. He stood looking at her with eyes that had gone curiously blank.

"It's true," she whispered through dry lips. How had Ben found out about it?

"I didn't intend for you to find out like this. I was going to tell you everything once—"

"Once you'd had your fill of me?" she bit out, her eyes beginning to flash. "I can't believe you did this to me. And to think I was actually beginning to . . . care about you." She had almost used the word *love*. Almost.

His jaw clenched, and his eyes glittered with turbid emotion. "I was willing to take the chance that you might hate me when you found out. It was worth it to me. . . ."

She turned away from him. She didn't know what she was going to do now. He had promised her that he wouldn't hurt her. That she had nothing to be afraid of. She had believed him. Trusted him. But he'd been lying to her all along. Laughing at her naive stupidity behind her back. She couldn't stay with him now. She wouldn't.

She felt his hands close around her shoulders, and she stood as still as a slab of granite as he pulled her back into his arms.

"I had to have you," he said against her ear. "I had to have you." And his lips brushed the soft flesh of her ear. "Forgive me."

A thrill rippled through her at the warm feel of him, but she fought against it, ignored his plea. She didn't want to feel anything for him. He had deceived her. He and Tony had done so. But it had been mostly him. He had been the puppet master behind the entire thing.

"So the whole thing . . . everything was a lie?"

He held her tightly as she tried to squirm out of his grasp. "Would you have come to me . . . if I hadn't done this? You made it abundantly clear to me in L.A. that you wanted nothing whatsoever to do with me."

Well, she had, but he had certainly deserved her treatment of him then.

"I turned down your proposal because it was ridiculous. I hardly knew you. And you definitely didn't know me."

"So I came to New Jersey to know you . . . for you. Did you think it a coincidence that I chose to live just ten or so minutes away from you?"

She had thought about that, but had not wanted to focus on what his presence seemed to imply. She couldn't weaken now, though. His words were sweet, seductive, but probably all lies. . . .

"I—It still doesn't excuse what you did. Do you know how much sleep I lost over the entire thing, thinking that Tony's life was in danger? No wonder you gave me the money so easily, so quickly."

She paused for breath, then went on. "And all that stuff you told me about getting Tony a job . . . and the car and everything. . . . All lies. Right?" The bright anger had faded from her now, and all that was left was a dull, empty feeling.

"Everything else I've ever told you is true. Everything. I would've given you twice the money you asked for—even three times the money—had you needed it. I wasn't buying you in any sense. It was just a means by which to get you close to me."

He released her and took a turn about the room. "Don't hold this against me, Rosy. Don't listen to any twisted explanations of the facts given you by Ben. He doesn't want you to be happy with anyone . . . and definitely not with me. You know in your heart that— that I had no evil intentions when I brought you here."

She wiped a hand across her eyes. It was all too much. Too confusing dealing with everything all at once. She needed time away from everything. Time to think. Time to make sense of what she felt. Time to sort the truth from the fiction.

He took her by the hand and led her into the office,

and as she sat before his desk, she reflected on the irony of it all. This was where everything had started. For her anyway.

She watched him in silence as he sat and pulled open the middle drawer. He rummaged inside for a moment, and then he seemed to find what it was he had been looking for. Rosalind recognized the document right away. The contract. That pseudo legal paper that bound her to him for a year. What was he going to do with that now? Insist that she honor the agreement that they had made? He couldn't possibly. It was all based on nothing. It was surely invalid.

He looked at the folded cream paper in his hand and then handed it to her.

"Here," he said. And his voice was as dull as she herself felt. "Take it. It's yours to do with as you see fit."

She looked across at him, met his eyes. "You mean I'm free to go?"

He spread his fingers on the flat of the desk. "If that's what you choose to do. Then yes. You're free to go. I won't beg you to stay." His voice was cold, his manner almost as remote as it had been on that very first day.

Rosalind fiddled with the paper, bending the edge of one side back and forth so many times that she put a permanent crease in it.

"I need time to think . . . about—about everything," she said finally.

He nodded. "I understand. The blue sports car outside is yours, by the way. So take it with you when you leave."

Her eyes darted to his face. The convertible she had seen outside was hers? And she had thought that the car might belong to Sue Perkins. . . .

"Thank you," she said in a stilted manner. "But I

couldn't accept it. Not now." Her voice shook on the last word, because although he didn't react to her, she sensed the hurt that flashed through him. And it hurt her, too.

He stood with hands shoved deep into his pockets. "It's yours. If you don't want it, then sell it. But I have no use for it."

She stood, too. In the space of only minutes, they had become again like strangers. He no longer made any attempt to embrace her, and it was hard to imagine that they had held each other so intimately, so sweetly, just the night before.

She folded the contract in half and shoved it into the top pocket of her jeans. "I'll go upstairs and pack a bag. Tomorrow I'll cancel the housekeeping appointments I made today."

"Don't bother," he said in a gritty voice. "I'll take care of that. Just leave me a note letting me know everything you've done."

Rosalind felt tears cluster at the backs of her eyes again. *This was it, then.* She willed herself not to cry before him. She had to be strong.

At the door she turned. "I appreciate the car. It was a very . . ." A very what? She was unsure of the right word to use. She had been about to say "a very kind thing to do." But was he being kind, thoughtful, or was it just another manipulation by a man who had more money at his disposal than he knew what to do with?

He held out a hand. "Here're the keys. All the other documents you'll need are in the glove compartment."

She retraced her steps and took the keys from him. Was that what he'd been doing all day long? Buying a car for her? Is that why he hadn't told her where exactly he'd been going?

"Thank you," she said again, and did her best to read his face. But it was completely expressionless, his eyes hard, unloving.

She left the office without another word, and hurried up to her room. She didn't give herself time to think. She simply threw together an assorted jumble of clothes, and with fingers that shook, zipped up her old canvas bag. Then she sat and wrote a quick list of things he needed to be aware of, including all of the items she had ordered for the house.

The entire thing took less than fifteen minutes. And at the end of it all, her eyes were swimming with salty tears, and she had to go to the bathroom to wipe her face with a wet cloth. She spent moments staring at her red eyes in the mirror. She felt such a tearing sense of loss. He obviously didn't care if she stayed or left. He'd said as much. Hadn't he? Or something very close?

She folded the washcloth neatly, resting it on the corner of the sink, gathered up all of her toiletries, and zipped those into a little plastic carry case. In the bedroom again, she hoisted the large bag to her shoulder. She half expected to hear a knock on the door and to see Sam appear in the doorway. But as Rosalind stood there, looking about the room one final time, she knew that there would be no knock at the door. She sensed that his withdrawal from her was almost complete.

Feeling as though she was leaving a home she'd lived in for years, she turned and closed the door quietly, and then almost jumped out of her skin at the voice almost directly behind her.

"Got everything?"

She turned. "Yes. And here's the list you asked for." She willed her fingers not to shake as they brushed against his.

He took the slip of paper and shoved it into his pants pocket without even glancing at it.

"Well," she said in a voice that threatened to tremble, "I guess I'd better get going."

"Yes," he said. "That's what you do, isn't it?"

Her eyes flashed to his face. "What?"

"That's what you do whenever things don't go exactly to your liking. You leave. Run away like a scared little rabbit. Nothing's ever important enough to make you stand and fight. You ran from me six years ago . . . and I came after you. I won't this time."

She stood staring at him, her heart fluttering like a wild bird. He was talking nonsense. She didn't run from things. She had never run from a thing in her entire life. She had left L.A. because . . . because. . . . Well, there had been a good reason at the time.

His eyes bored into hers, and she was reminded again why so many in the business community feared him.

"If you come back to me . . . only do so if you're ready to love me. I won't accept lukewarm affection from you any longer. This time it's up to you. Decide once and for all whether or not you want me. Flaws and all."

And with that, he turned and left her.

Twenty-three

Rosalind was unsure of how exactly it was she got back to her apartment. She hardly noticed the smooth purring of the brand-new convertible. She just followed the road, turning the wheel this way and that, but didn't really notice a thing that she passed. She had a burning feeling somewhere deep inside. His words had pierced the protective shell around her heart. The one she had built so many years before to protect herself from the many assaults of life. But Sam was wrong about her. There were things she was willing to fight for. Lots of things. People. Tony, for instance. Even though he was irresponsible and untrustworthy, and only God knew what else. She still loved him, and would always, always fight for him. She didn't run from important things, things that were real and not part of some grand manipulation scheme. And why did he think her feelings for him were lukewarm? So she had never told him that she loved him. But so what? Surely he could tell that she cared about him? Couldn't he?

She climbed the short flight of stairs, opened the door and collapsed onto a couch. She felt disoriented, as though she was in someone else's home. Nothing felt familiar. It didn't feel like home somehow. And she curled herself into a tight little ball, squeezed her eyes shut, and willed the pain inside to go away. But his words kept coming back to her. Over and over again.

"If you come back to me . . . only do so if you're ready to love me. I won't accept lukewarm affection from you any longer. This time it's up to you. Decide once and for all whether or not you want me. Flaws and all."

But how could she trust him again? He had lied and manipulated events to get his own way. How could she be sure that he wouldn't do the same again? How could she be sure that he wasn't just manipulating her now?

She rubbed tired hands across her eyes, much as a child might. She just couldn't think. Couldn't think straight. The day had taken everything out of her. Her eyes sagged shut.

Tony found her curled up on the lumpy sofa an hour later, her cheeks streaked with dried tears. He stood watching her sleep for long minutes, and then he sat beside her on the sofa.

"Ros. Wake up." He shook her shoulder. "Come on. Wake up now."

Rosalind opened an eye a crack and muttered an irritable "Go away. I'm never speaking to you again."

"Yes, you are. And not only that. You're going to thank me when I'm done." He pulled her into a sitting position, and shook her gently until she was forced to open her eyes and look at him.

"I know all about what you did," she said thickly. "Sam told me the whole thing. Actually Ben told me."

Tony nodded. "Yes, I know. I told Ben. He came around to see me last night . . . begging me to talk to you."

She blinked at him, momentarily robbed of speech. "You—you told him? But you must have known that the first thing he would do is tell me."

"That's exactly why I did tell him. I did it . . . for you. For Sam."

She got off the couch and went to pull open the fridge. There was nothing edible inside, so she went to stand by one of the windows. Tony came to stand beside her.

"I know you're mad at me. But I did it for you. I—"

"Please don't ever do anything else for me," she said, and a tiny sob crept into her voice. "You've completely ruined things between me and Sam. What you did was—"

"The only thing I could do under the circumstances." He held her shoulders and turned her to face him. "Look at me, sis. How many times over the years have you gotten me out of one jam or another?"

A tear rolled down her cheek, and he wiped it away with the flat of a thumb. "Right. Too many times. I know. And what have I ever done for you?"

Another tear made its way down her face, and again he answered for her, "Nothing. Before now, I've always taken. Isn't that right?"

She nodded, and he held her tightly and rocked her like a babe.

"That's why I did what I did. Don't you see?"

Rosalind made a little sound, because she didn't see at all. He had destroyed her life, and he thought he had done her a favor?

"Sam and I were always cool, you know? Even back in L.A. I mean, we were never exactly friends or anything like that, but we were . . ."

She looked up at him, and managed a croaky "You and Sam?" She certainly hadn't noticed that. But maybe she had been too busy hating Sam to notice anything much at all.

He stroked the corners of her eyes. "Yeah," Tony agreed. "So when we left L.A., not right away, of course . . . maybe a year or so after we left, I got back in touch with him. At first I was going to hit him up for a loan, because I knew—had always known that he had a serious thing for you. But . . . I guess beneath it all, I must really be a decent guy. Because after speaking to him, I couldn't do it."

She was really listening to him now. Tony, missing out on a chance at making an easy buck? She didn't believe it.

"Why didn't you ask him for money?"

"Because he was so torn up about you. I—I felt sorry for him." He shrugged. "It's true. I did. So I told him where you were . . . where we were. And everything grew out of that. I came up with the idea of how I would get you two together. I thought he was a much better man than . . . Ben. And no, it wasn't because of the money. Sam was in love with you. I knew that Ben wasn't."

Rosalind's eyes flickered as she registered the words. Sam had been in love with her? Six years ago?

"You mean . . . the whole Jamaican mob thing was your idea? Not Sam's?"

"My idea," he said. "Actually . . . Sam had to be talked into it. He told me that he would have to tell you everything eventually. And he felt sure that when he did, you would hate him, since you were such a straight shooter . . . you wouldn't be able to see beyond the fact that he had misled you. But I told him that once you knew the truth . . . you'd be okay with everything." He pinched her cheek. "Was I wrong?"

Rosalind pushed away from him. She didn't know whether to strangle him or kiss him, so she settled for something somewhere in between the two options, and gave him a solid punch on the arm.

"You'd better not be lying to me again, Anthony Carmichael."

He looked at her with sincere eyes. "I'm not. I promise you. Didn't Sam tell you I was the one behind the whole thing?"

"No. He just—just said that it was true. What Ben had said. And I—"

"You assumed that he had engineered the whole thing." He shook his head. "Rosalind, why are you so blind when it comes to Sam Winter? I have never in my life seen anyone more in love with anyone. Don't you understand how blessed you are? This sort of love . . . it doesn't come around too often. You know?"

She took a deep filling breath. Tony was right. If Sam did love her . . . if he still loved her, she would go to him. He wasn't perfect, but then again, neither was she. There was a lot he could teach her about life, and there was a lot he needed to learn from her.

She blew her nose in a square of cotton. "Thank you, Tony. I mean for everything you've—"

"Don't tell me," he interrupted. "Tell Sam."

"Okay," she said, wiping at the corners of her eyes. "I wonder if he's still at home, though."

"He's not at home. He's downstairs. Waiting."

She was confused. "Downstairs?" He had told her just a few hours before that he would not come for her ever again. That this time, she would have to be the one to go after him. "He's downstairs?"

"Sitting in his car. He called me just after you left. I came here with him."

Rosalind gave her brother a bear hug. "I love you, Tony."

And he smiled at her. "Go," he said. "Thank me later."

She squeezed his hand one final time, and then pelted from the apartment and went skittering down the stairs barefoot. She saw the car before she saw him. And as she rounded the corner, she ran straight into a pair of strong arms. Arms that clutched her, and held on.

"Sammy," she said, her voice thick with emotion. "I'm sorry. I thought the worst. . . . I've been such a—"

"I thought I'd lost you," he said, holding her tightly. "I really thought that this time I'd lost you."

She stared up at him. "God blessed me with you. How could you lose me? I would've come back to you."

He shifted her away from him so he might look at her. "So you forgive me?"

She touched the side of his face with a tender hand. "There's nothing to forgive. I'm the one who should ask your forgiveness."

He kissed her fingers. "There's one more thing I have to tell you."

"Oh, no," Rosalind said softly, but she was smiling.

"Yes. I want you to know everything so that this time . . . there'll be no secrets between us." He paused, then said, "Sue Perkins . . . was part of this entire plan to get you to notice me as a man."

Rosalind's brow furrowed a bit. Now what was this? "She was?"

"She was. She's actually a happily—very happily married woman. Married to a good friend of mine. She agreed to help make you jealous. . . . We were leaving nothing to chance."

So the scene in the bathroom was staged? The whole slapping and falling thing?

"It's true. She felt sure that her little tactics in Las Vegas were working." He touched her cheek with the back of a finger. "I asked her to come to Jersey . . . because I didn't want to continue the charade. Tomorrow she's going to fill you in on all of the details. But tonight—tonight is just for us."

"Sam Winter," Rosalind said, a mock threatening note in her voice, "if you ever try any of those tricks again . . ."

He got down on a knee, and Rosalind's heart thrashed at her ribs. She couldn't be so blessed? Could she?

"I asked you six years ago to be my wife. . . ."

And suddenly she was down, kneeling with him, taking his face in her hands. "I was a fool six years ago. I thought you liked big-boned, horse-faced women." A little smile curled the corners of her mouth. "And even if you do . . . my answer is still yes." She stroked away a little bead of water that welled in the corner of one of his eyes, and then kissed the exact spot. "I—I'm just getting used to it . . . but I care about you, Sam Winter."

He gave a hoarse chuckle. "Care?

She smiled. That's right. He no longer would accept lukewarm emotion from her. And she would not give it, either.

"I love you," she said. "And I promise you that from now on, I will be completely and hopelessly devoted to you, and only you."

Sam settled his lips on hers, and between sweet little kisses he said, "Thank you, God . . . for hearing me again . . . after all of these years."

Dear Readers,

I hope you enjoyed Sam and Rosalind's story, and I hope you find the love that's out there waiting for you!

Until the next time,
Niqui Stanhope

ABOUT THE AUTHOR

Niqui Stanhope was born in Jamaica, West Indies, but grew up in a small bauxite-mining town in Guyana, South America. Because her parents traveled quite a bit and always took the entire family along, the summers of her childhood were spent exploring the rich culture of the Caribbean and South America. In 1984 she emigrated to the United States of America. She admits that novel writing never occurred to her until after she had graduated from the University of Southern California with a degree in chemistry. She now lives in California.

She would love to hear from you. You can write to her at: P.O. Box 6105, Burbank, CA 91510, or e-mail her at Niquij@aol.com. Her Website address is: http://www.niquistanhope.com

BOOK YOUR PLACE ON OUR WEBSITE AND MAKE THE ARABESQUE ROMANCE CONNECTION!

We've created a customized website just for our very special Arabesque readers, where you can get the inside scoop on everything that's going on with Arabesque romance novels.

When you come online, you'll have the exciting opportunity to:

- View covers of upcoming books

- Learn about our future publishing schedule (listed by publication month and author)

- Find out when your favorite authors will be visiting a city near you

- Search for and order backlist books

- Check out author bios and background information

- Send e-mail to your favorite authors

- Join us in weekly chats with authors, readers and other guests

- Get writing guidelines

- AND MUCH MORE!

Visit our website at
http://www.arabesquebooks.com